The Merry Devils

Also by Edward Marston

The Queen's Head

The Merry Devils

Edward Marston

Poisoned Pen Press

First US Trade Paperback Edition 2001

10 9 8 7 6 5 4 3 2 1

Library of Congress Catalog Card Number: 00-109747

ISBN: 1-890208-55-8

Poisoned Pen Press
6962 E. First Ave. Ste 103
Scottsdale, AZ 85251
www.poisonedpenpress.com
info@poisonedpenpress.com

Printed in the United States of America

Matre pulchra filia pulchrior
Helena
rosa formosa
orbis et cordis

'This I bar, that none of you stroke your beards to make action, play with your codpiece points, or stand fumbling on your buttons when you know not how to bestow your fingers. Serve God and act clearly.'

Thomas Nashe

Chapter One

London was the capital city of noise, a vibrant, volatile place, surging with life and clamorous with purpose. Whips cracked, horses neighed, harness jingled, carts rattled, coaches thundered, pots clinked, canvas flapped, hammers pounded, lathes sang, bells tolled, dogs yelped, poultry clucked, cows lowed, pigs squealed and thousands of urgent voices swelled the tumult of the working day. The whole community was in a state of happy uproar. It was morning.

Nicholas Bracewell shouldered his way through the crowd in Gracechurch Street, ducking beneath frequent obstacles and moving past haphazard ranks of market stalls that were bold, colourful and aromatic, competing loudly with each other for the attention of the swirling mass. Tall, well-groomed and dressed in buff jerkin and hose, Nicholas was at once imposing and nondescript, a striking figure who courted the anonymity of the throng. The weathered face was framed by long fair hair and a beard. The clear blue eyes missed nothing. He combined the physique of a wrestler with the bearing of a gentleman.

As a stout housewife waddled out of a shop and bumped straight into him, he doffed his cap and gave her a polite smile of apology, making light of the fact that she had caused the collision.

'By your leave, mistress.'

His soft West Country tones were drowned by the strident Cockney vowels all around him but his courteous manner conveyed his meaning. Unaccustomed to such civility, the woman nodded her gratitude before being jostled by cruder elbows and rougher tongues. Nicholas plunged on and made steady progress through the sea of bodies. Ahead of him was the familiar outline of St Benet Grass Church, which had given the street its name, and his gaze dwelt for a moment on its thrusting spire. Then he passed beneath the sign of the Queen's Head and swung in through its main gates.

Someone was waiting to ambush him in the yard.

'Thank heavens you have come, Master Bracewell!'

'How now, Master Marwood?'

'All may yet be saved!'

'Saved?'

'God willing!'

'What ails you, sir?'

'I am sore afraid, Master Bracewell.'

'Of what, pray?'

'Certain disaster!'

Alexander Marwood had a close acquaintance with certain disaster. In his febrile imagination, it lurked everywhere and his assiduous pessimism obliged him to rush towards it in willing surrender. Short, thin and balding, the landlord of the Queen's Head was a haunted man with a nervous twitch that animated his gloomy features. It was a face more fit for a charnel house than a taproom and he had none of the geniality associated with his calling.

Nicholas sighed inwardly. He knew what was coming.

'We are in great danger!' wailed the landlord.

'From what source, Master Marwood?'

'Your play, sir.'

'*The Merry Devils*?'

'It is an abomination.'

'You do the piece a wrong.'

'An act of blasphemy.'

'It is wholly free from such a taint.'

'The play will offend the City authorities.'

'*All* plays offend them, Master Marwood,' said Nicholas. 'We have learned to live and work in the shadow of their displeasure.'

'Your devilry will provoke the church.'

'I think not, sir.'

'You will bring the wrath of God down upon us!'

Nicholas put a soothing hand on his shoulder. He found himself in a situation that was all too common. Marwood's capacity for sudden panic was boundless and it created stern problems for those who relied on the goodwill of mine host. Nicholas was the book holder with Lord Westfield's Men, one of the leading dramatic companies, and his primary function was to stage manage their performances. Another crucial task which had fallen to him was that of mollifying the landlord during his periodic fits of terror. Westfield's Men used the yard of the Queen's Head as their regular venue so Alexander Marwood had perforce to be humoured.

'*The Merry Devils* is a harmless comedy,' Nicholas told him. 'It is written by two God-fearing gentlemen and will not raise the slightest blush on the cheeks of Christianity.' He patted the other's back. 'Take heart, Master Marwood. There is no danger here.'

'I have to look to my livelihood, sir.'

'We respect that.'

'I would not fall foul of the authorities.'

'Nor shall you, believe me.'

'Your play will put the Queen's Head in jeopardy.'

'That would hardly serve our turn.'

'I have heard,' said Marwood, eyes bulging and twitch working away, 'the most dread reports.'

'Idle rumours, sir. Ignore them.'

'They say that you bring Satan himself upon the stage.'

'Then they mislead you cruelly.'

'They say you show all manner of Vice.'

'Virtue is our constant theme.'

'They say...' The landlord's voice became an outraged hiss to accommodate the full horror of his final charge. 'They say that you—raise up devils!'

'Indeed, we do not,' said Nicholas reassuringly. 'We merely summon George Dart and Roper Blundell.'

'Who, sir?'

'Two poor, innocent wights who could not frighten a fly between them. These are no real devils, Master Marwood. They are hirelings with the company. Two small lads who are fitted for the parts by their very smallness. Hugh Wegges, our tireman, has costumed them in red with pointed tails and tiny horns, but it is all in jest.' He gave a wry chuckle. 'Our merry devils will cause more merriment than devilry. And, as they hope to go to heaven, George Dart and Roper Blundell will tell you the same.'

Marwood was not appeased. When he sniffed catastrophe—and it was brought in on every wind that blew—he was not easily put off the scent. To assuage him further, Nicholas patiently explained the whole plot then ushered him across to the rectangle of trestles which jutted out into the yard from one wall and which formed the stage on which Westfield's Men would perform their new piece. He indicated the two trap-doors through which the devils would make their appearance and even divulged the secret of how each of them would make such an explosive entry. The landlord was given fresh matter for alarm.

'Gunpowder, sir! Look to my thatch!'

'Everything needful will be done.'

'Fire could destroy me!'

'That is why we will take the utmost care.'

'I am deeply troubled, Master Bracewell,' whined the other. 'My feeling is that you should cancel the play.'

'At this late hour?'

'It bodes ill, sir. It bodes ill.'

The twitch went on a lightning tour of his face and his eyes enlarged to the size and colour of ripe plums. Nicholas wooed him again, reminding him of the long and fruitful relationship that existed between Westfield's Men and the Queen's Head and pointing out that *The Merry Devils*—like every other new play—had had to be submitted to the Master of the Revels before it was granted a licence. Sir Edmund Tilney had given his approval without censoring a single line. Evidently, he did not consider the piece to be in any way blasphemous. When the morose landlord still protested, Nicholas invited him to watch the morning's rehearsal so that he could judge for himself but Marwood declined the offer. He preferred to feed off rumour and instinct, both of which advised him to stop the performance.

'And offer such an insult to Lord Westfield?' said Nicholas.

'Lord Westfield?'

'Our patron will grace your inn with his presence today.'

'Ah…'

'Bringing with him, in his entourage, several other members of the nobility. Can the Queen's Head afford to turn away such custom, sir? Am I to tell Lord Westfield that you refuse him hospitality?'

'Well, no...that is to say...'

'His lordship might instruct us to withdraw altogether.'

'But we have a contract.'

'Then you must honour it this afternoon.'

Marwood was thrown into a quandary. It was not his intention to terminate an arrangement which, with all its pitfalls, was a lucrative one for his inn. He now spied danger both in a performance of the new play and in its summary cancellation. Either way he was doomed. He risked arousing the ire of the City authorities or the displeasure of important members of the nobility. It all served to plunge him into a pool of deep melancholy.

Nicholas Bracewell threw him a rope of salvation.

'Lord Westfield is not without influence.'

'What's that, sir?'

'Were the authorities to object, he would no doubt deal with their objections. They would not proceed against the Queen's Head with his lordship standing guard over it.'

'Would he so protect us?' asked the plaintive landlord.

'He has powerful friends at Court.'

It was a telling argument and it tipped the balance. According to the regulations, the staging of plays within the boundaries of the city was forbidden and theatres had therefore been built in places like Shoreditch and Southwark which were outside the city walls and thus beyond its jurisdiction. Like other establishments with suitable inn yards, the Queen's Head was breaking a law that was never enforced with any vigour or consistency, in spite of a steady stream of complaints from the Puritan faction. Marwood had always escaped before. Under the pressure of circumstance, he elected to take the chance once again.'

'Very well, Master Bracewell. Perform your play.'

'It will put money in your purse, sir.'

'I pray that they do not take it from me in fines.'

'Have faith, Master Marwood.'

'I fear the worst.'

'Nothing will go amiss.'

'Then why do I sense disaster?'

Turning on his heel, the landlord scurried across the yard and took his determined misery towards the taproom. Resolved on calamity, he would admit no other possibility. Nicholas had done well to stave off the threatened cancellation of the play but then he had had plenty of practice with such crises. It seemed to him that he spent as much time subduing Marwood's outbursts as he did in stage managing the company.

As mine host vanished through a door, Nicholas marvelled yet again at the man's perverse choice of profession. He was not schooled for a life of riot and revelry. Death and despair were his companions. Perhaps, mused Nicholas, he was waiting to be called to a higher duty and a truer vocation. When God wished to announce the end of the world, he would surely choose no other messenger than Alexander Marwood.

It was the one job to which he could bring some relish.

Rehearsals for *The Merry Devils* had been dogged by setbacks from the start but those earlier upsets faded into oblivion beside the events of the next two hours. Everything went wrong. Lines were forgotten, entrances were missed, curtains were torn, costumes were damaged, trap-doors refused to open, gunpowder would not explode and the tiring-house was a seething morass of acrimony. Nicholas Bracewell imposed what calm and order he could but his control could not extend to the stage itself where mishap followed mishap with ascending speed. The play was buried beneath a farrago of incompetence, frayed tempers and brutal misfortune.

The diminutive George Dart was less than merry as a devil. Covered in confusion and dripping with perspiration, he came lurching into the tiring-house after another bungled exit. His red costume was far too tight for his body and far too warm for the hot weather. He tugged and pulled at it as he went across to the book holder.

'I am sorry, Master Bracewell.'

'Do your best, George. Nobody can demand more.'

'I mislaid my part.'

'Think harder, lad.'

'I tried, master, but all thought went out of my head when I bumped into that post and saw stars. How did that come about?'

'You were on the wrong side of the stage.'

'Was I?'

'Follow Roper next time.'

'But he has no more idea than me.' He shrugged his shoulders in hopeless resignation. 'We are not actors, Master Bracewell. We are mere stagekeepers. You do wrong to thrust us out upon the stage.'

'Stand by, George! Your entrance is almost due.'

'*Again*?'

'The banquet scene.'

'Lord help me!'

Cued by the book holder, the merry devils made another startling entrance but dissipated its effect by colliding with each other. George Dart dropped the goblets he was carrying and Roper Blundell trod so heavily on his own tail that it parted company with his breeches. Mistakes now multiplied at a bewildering rate. The rehearsal was speeding towards complete chaos.

It was rescued by the efforts of one man. Lawrence Firethorn was the leading actor and the guiding light of Westfield's Men, a creature of colossal talent and breathtaking audacity whose very presence in the cast of a play enhanced its quality. Single-handed, he pulled *The Merry Devils* back from the brink of sheer pandemonium. While everything else was falling to pieces around him, he remained quite imperturbable and soared above it all on wings of histrionic genius.

When accidents happened, he softened their impact by cleverly diverting attention from them. When moves were forgotten, he eased his colleagues into their correct positions in the most unobtrusive way. When huge gaps appeared in the text, he filled them with such loquacious zest that only those familiar with the piece would have realised that memories had faltered. The more desperate the situation, the more immediate was his response. At one point, when someone missed an entrance for a vital scene, Firethorn covered his absence by delivering a soliloquy of such soulful magnificence that it wrung the withers of all who heard it, even though it was culled on the instant from three totally different plays and stitched together for extempore use.

Lawrence Firethorn was superb in a role that fitted him like a glove. Though he was renowned for his portrayal of wise emperors and warrior kings, and for his incomparable gallery of classical heroes, he could turn his hand to low comedy with devastating brilliance. He was now the gross figure of Justice Wildboare, who, thwarted in love, attempts to get his revenge on his young rival by setting a couple of devils on him. Once raised, however, the devils prove unready to obey their new master and it is Wildboare who becomes the victim of their merriment.

The central role enabled Firethorn to dominate the stage and wrest some meaning out of the shambles. He was a rock amid shifting sands, an oasis in a desert, a true professional among rank amateurs. His example fired others and they slowly rallied. Nerves steadied, memories improved, confidence oozed back. With Firethorn leading the way on stage, and with Nicholas Bracewell exerting his usual calming influence in the tiring-house, the play actually began to resemble the text in the prompt book. By the end of Act Five, the saviour of the hour had achieved the superhuman task of pointing the drama in the right direction once more and it was fitting that he should conclude it with a rhyming couplet.

> Henceforth this Wildboare will renounce all evils
> And ne'er again seek pacts with merry devils.

The rest of the company were so relieved to have come safely through the ordeal that they gave their actor-manager a spontaneous round of applause. Relief swiftly turned to apprehension as Firethorn rounded on them with blazing eyes. George Dart quailed, Roper Blundell sobbed, Ned Rankin gulped, Caleb Smythe shivered, Richard Honeydew blushed, Martin Yeo backed away, Edmund Hoode sought invisibility and the other players braced themselves. Even the arrogant Barnaby Gill was fearful.

The comic bleating of Wildboare became the roar of a tiger.

'That, gentlemen,' said Firethorn, 'was a descent into Hell. I have known villainy before but not of such magnitude. I have tasted dregs before but not of such bitterness. Misery I have seen before but never in such hideous degree. Truly, I am ashamed to call you fellows in this enterprise. Were it not for my honesty and self-respect, I would turn my back on the whole pack of you and seek a place with Banbury's Men, vile and untutored though they be.'

The company winced beneath the insult. The Earl of Banbury's Men were their deadly rivals and Firethorn had nothing but contempt for them. It was a mark of his disillusion with his own players that he should even consider turning to the despised company of another patron. Before he could speak further, the noonday bell passed on its sonorous message. In two bare hours, *The Merry Devils* had to be fit for presentation before a paying audience. Practicalities intruded. Firethorn sheathed the sword of his anger and issued a peremptory command.

'Gentlemen, we have work to do. About it straight.'

There was a flurry of grateful activity.

Hunched over a cup of sack, Edmund Hoode stared balefully into the liquid as if it contained the dead bodies of his dearest hopes. He was sitting at a table in the taproom of the Queen's Head and seemed unaware of the presence of his companion. Ralph Willoughby gave his friend an indulgent smile and emptied a pot of ale. The two men were the co-authors of *The Merry Devils* and they had burned a deal of midnight oil in the course of its composition. Both had invested heavily in its success. Hoode was mortified by the awesome failure of the rehearsal but Willoughby took a more sanguine view.

'The piece will redeem itself, Edmund,' he said blithely. 'Even in this morning's travesty, there was promise.'

'Of what?' returned Hoode sourly. 'Of complete disgrace?'

'Rehearsals often mislead.'

'We face ignominy, Ralph.'

'It will not come to that.'

'Our work will be jeered off the stage.'

'Away with such thoughts!'

'Truly, I tell you, this life will be the death of me!'

It was strange to hear such a forlorn cry on the lips of Edmund Hoode. He loved the theatre. Tall, thin and clean-shaven, he had been with the company for some years now as its resident poet and a number of plays—thanks to the hectoring of Lawrence Firethorn—had flowed from his fertile pen. As an actor-sharer with Westfield's Men, he always took care to create a role for himself; ideally, something with a romantic strain though a wide range of character parts was within his compass. When *The Merry Devils* first began to take shape, he decided to appear as the hapless

Droopwell, a lack-lustre wooer whose impotence was exploited for comic effect. Long before the play had been completed, however, and for a reason that was never explained, Hoode insisted on a change of role and now took the stage as Youngthrust, an ardent suitor whose virility was not in doubt. Armed with a codpiece the size of a flying buttress, he whisked away the heroine from beneath the nose of Justice Wildboare.

There was no Youngthrust about him now. Slouched over the table, he reverted to Droopwell once more. He gazed into his sack as yet another corpse floated past and he heaved a sigh of dismay that was almost Marwoodian in its hopelessness.

Willoughby clapped him on the shoulder and grinned.

'Be of good cheer, Edmund!'

'To what end?' groaned the other.

'Heavens, man, our new piece is about to strut upon the stage. Is that not cause for joy and celebration?'

'Not if it be howled down by the rougher sort.'

'Throw aside such imaginings,' said Willoughby. 'The whole company is pledged to make amends for this morning. It will be a very different dish that is set before the audience. Nick Bracewell will marshal you behind the scenes and Lawrence will take you into battle at his accustomed gallop. All things proceed to consummation. Why this blackness?'

'It is my play, Ralph.'

'It is my play, too, friend, yet I am not so discomfited.'

'You are not trapped like a rat in the *dramatis personae*.'

'Indeed, no,' said Willoughby. 'My case is far worse.'

'How so?'

'Since I am to be a spectator of the action, I must endure every separate misadventure whereas you only see those in which Youngthrust is involved.'

'There!' said Hoode mournfully. 'You are resolved on humiliation.'

'I expect a triumph.'

'After that rehearsal?'

'*Because* of it, Edmund. Westfield's Men explored every last avenue of error. There are no mistakes left to be made.' His carefree laugh rang through the taproom. 'This afternoon will put our merry devils in the ascendant. It can be no other way.'

Ralph Willoughby was shorter, darker and slightly younger than Hoode, with an air of educated decadence about him and a weakness for the gaudy apparel of a City gallant. His good humour was unwavering but his relentless optimism was only a mask for darker feelings that he kept to himself. Having abandoned his theological studies at Cambridge, he hurled himself into the whirlpool of London theatre and established a reputation as a gifted, albeit erratic, dramatist. *The Merry Devils* marked his first collaboration with Hoode and his debut with Westfield's Men. His jaunty confidence was gradually reviving his colleague.

'Dare we hope for success?' said Hoode tentatively.

'It is assured.'

'And my portrayal as Youngthrust?'

'It will carry all before it.'

'Truly? This weighs heavily with me.'

'As actor and poet, your reputation will be advanced. I would wager fifty crowns on it—if someone would loan me the money, for I have none to call my own.'

'This lifts my spirits, Ralph.'

'Be ruled by me.'

'Much depends upon today.'

'All is well, Edmund. All is well.'

Hoode actually managed a pallid smile before downing the last of his drink. It was time to think and behave like a professional man of the theatre and surmount any difficulties. He no longer contemplated the prospect of execution. With luck and effort, he might not die on a scaffold of his own creation after all.

Playbills were on display in prominent places all over the city and they brought a large, eager audience flocking to the Queen's Head. Gatherers were kept busy collecting admission money and preventing anyone from sneaking in without paying. A penny bought standing room around the stage itself. Those who parted with an extra penny or two gained access to the galleries which ran around the yard and which offered seating, a clearer view and shelter from any inclement weather. Not that rain or wind threatened *The Merry Devils*. Its premiere was attended by the blazing sunshine of an English summer, warming the mood of the spectators even more than the drink that was on sale.

New plays were always in demand and Westfield's Men adopted the policy of trying to present more of them each year. By dint of their high standards, they built up a loyal following and rarely disappointed them. Lawrence Firethorn was the talk of the town. Barnaby Gill, the company's principal comedian, was an evergreen favourite. Supporting players were always more than competent and the name of Edmund Hoode on any drama was a guarantee of worth and craftsmanship. The hundreds of people who were packing the inn yard to capacity had every right to expect something rather special by way of entertainment, but none of them could even guess at the sensation that lay ahead.

Through the window of the taproom, Alexander Marwood watched the hordes arrive and bit his lip in apprehension. Other landlords might drool at the thought of the profits they would make from the sale of wine, beer, bread, fruit and nuts, supplemented as that income would be with the substantial rent for the use of the yard and money from the hiring of rooms where copulation could thrive throughout the afternoon in brief intervals of privacy. Marwood drew no solace from this. To his jaundiced eye, the standees were made up of pickpockets, cutpurses or drunken apprentices spoiling for a fight, the gorgeous ladies who brightened the galleries were all disease-ridden punks plying their trade, and the flamboyant gallants who puffed at their pipes had come for the express purpose of setting fire to the overhanging thatch.

Then there was the play itself, an instrument of wickedness in five acts. When the landlord glanced upwards at the blue sky, he was surprised to see no thunderbolt waiting to be hurled down.

Almost everyone, of whatever degree or disposition, was in a state of high excitement, savouring the occasion and talking happily about it. The buoyant, boisterous atmosphere was infectious. Yet there was one man who shared Marwood's disapproval. Big, solid, impassive and dressed in sober garb, he paid his money to gain entry, recoiled from the stinking breaths of the groundlings and made his way disconsolately to one of the upper galleries. His grim face was carved from teak, its most startling feature being a long, single eyebrow that undulated with such bristling effect that it seemed as if a giant furry caterpillar was slowly making its way across his lower forehead. Cold, grey, judgmental eyes peered out from beneath their hirsute covering. The mouth was closed tight like a steel trap.

Whatever else had brought Isaac Pollard to the Queen's Head, it was not the pursuit of pleasure.

Wedging himself into a narrow space on a bench, he took stock of the audience and found it severely wanting. Lewd behaviour offended him on every side. Bold glances from powdered whores warmed his cheeks. Profanities assaulted his ears. Foul-smelling tobacco smoke invaded his nostrils. Extra bodies forcing their way on to his bench increased his discomfort. When he gazed down at the baying crowd below, he sensed incipient riot.

Isaac Pollard fumed with righteous indignation then found a new target for his hostility. It was Lord Westfield himself. Flanked by his glittering hangers-on, the company's illustrious patron emerged from a private room to take up a prime position in the lower gallery. A red velvet cushion welcomed his portly frame as he lowered it into his ornate chair. Wearing dresses in the Spanish fashion, two Court beauties sat either side of him and flirted outrageously with the guest of honour from behind their masks. Lord Westfield was in his element. He was a tireless epicurean with a fondness for excess and he outshone his entourage with a doublet of peach-coloured satin trimmed with gold lace, and silver hose with satin and silver panels. An elaborate hat, festooned with jewels and feathers, completed a stunning costume.

The whole assembly turned to admire a noble lord whose love of the drama had provided countless hours of delight for the playgoer. All that Isaac Pollard could see, however, was a symbol of corruption. Lord Westfield was a merry devil.

Separated from their audience by the traverse at the rear of the stage, Westfield's Men were all too aware of them. It set their nerves on edge. An untried play was always a hazardous undertaking but they had additional cause for alarm after the rehearsal. Failure on stage would be punished unmercifully. Even the most tolerant spectators could turn on a piece that failed to please them and they would hurl far more than harsh words at the players. It was no wonder the tiring-house was so full of foreboding. Lawrence Firethorn took his usual positive attitude and Barnaby Gill affected a cheerful nonchalance but the rest of the company were visibly shaking in their shoes.

Nicholas Bracewell moved quietly among them to give advice, to soothe troubled minds and to instil a sense of purpose. He expected apprentices like Richard Honeydew and Martin Yeo to be on edge but he had never seen Edmund Hoode so keyed up before one of his own plays. Tucked in a corner, he was nervously thumbing through the sides on which his part had been written out by the scrivener. It seemed odd that someone whose memory was so reliable should be so concerned about his lines at the eleventh hour.

Inevitably, the major panic was to be found among those who took the title-roles. George Dart and Roper Blundell were convulsed with fear. Their costumes had been let out slightly so that they could breathe more easily but they were not happy in their work.

Nicholas attempted to boost their sagging morale.

'Courage, lads. That is all you need.'

'We have none between us,' confessed George Dart timorously.

'No, master,' said Roper Blundell. 'We are arrant cowards.'

'You will carry your parts well,' Nicholas assured them.

'Not I,' said the first devil.

'Nor I,' said his colleague.

'You will feel much better when the play actually begins.'

'Heaven forbid!' said George Dart.

'I don't know which is more fearsome,' observed Roper Blundell. 'Facing an audience or being called to account by Master Firethorn.'

'We must suffer both!' wailed his fellow.

They were sorry figures. Two small, bruised, dejected human beings, cowering before the heavy responsibility that was laid upon them. George Dart was young and cherubic, Roper Blundell was old and wizened, but they looked identical in their flame-red costumes, timeless images of torment in the after-life.

'My trap-door would not open,' said Dart.

'Nor mine close,' added Blundell.

'I checked the counter-weights myself,' said Nicholas.

The book holder gave a signal that imposed a hushed silence on the tiring-house. Doubts and anxieties had to be put aside now. It was time to begin. When the trumpet sounded to announce the start of the play, a cheer went up in the inn yard. The Prologue entered in a black cloak and spoke in lofty verse.

Next to appear was Lawrence Firethorn, bursting on to the stage in judicial robes with a clerk trotting at his heels. Applause greeted the leading actor. Waving a letter in the air, he vented his spleen with comic intensity.

> Why, sir, what a damnable state of affairs is this! Am I not Justice Wildboare, a man of three thousand pounds a year and a sweetness of disposition to match such a fortune? I am minded to wed Mistress Lucy Hembrow but her father, the scurvy rogue, the bald-pated rascal, the treacherous knave, writes to tell me of two further suitors for her hand. One is Droopwell and t'other is Youngthrust. Am I have to have rivals at the altar? Is the name of Wildboare not sufficient in itself for this fair maid? By Jove, she will have justice! When the boar is put to this pretty little sow, I'll prove wild enough for her purposes, I warrant you. But rivals? I know this Droopwell by his hanging look. He will not stand to much in her account. But I like not the sound of this Youngthrust. I must take him down if I am to inherit this angel as my wife, or she will measure his inches. I must be devilish cunning!

Firethorn mesmerised them. Gesture, movement and facial expression were so apt that he reaped a laugh on almost every line. By the end of his first speech, the spectators had not only been introduced to the latest in his long line of brilliant stage portraits, they had also been given the entire plot. When the scene came to a close, their applause was long and enthusiastic. It invigorated the whole company.

The musicians played with more zest, the backstage minions ran to their tasks with more willingness, and the players themselves shook off their despondence and addressed their work with renewed interest. As a result, *The Merry Devils* blossomed as never before and revealed itself to be as fine a drama as any that Westfield's Men had presented. The miraculous overall improvement was nowhere more clearly reflected than in Edmund Hoode's performance. Shedding ten or more years, he put his whole self into Youngthrust and declaimed his lines with such a compound of passion and pathos that the heart of every woman melted towards him. Richard Honeydew, who played the beauteous Lucy Hembrow, found himself weeping genuine tears of joy at the urgency of the wooing.

Ralph Willoughby watched it all from the middle gallery with a burgeoning satisfaction. Though written by two men, the play spoke with one authentic voice. Hoode had provided the plot and the poetry while Willoughby had contributed the wit and the witchcraft. The blend was perfect. Lord Westfield led the laughter at another comic outburst by the thwarted Justice. Hands clapped loudly as another scene ended.

Only Isaac Pollard smouldered with discontent.

Then came the moment that everyone awaited. It occurred at the start of Act Three when expectation had been built to a peak. Unable to best Youngthrust in any way, Justice Wildboare resorted to a more sinister device. He employed Doctor Castrato to summon up devils who would do their master's bidding. Ripples of delight went through the audience when they saw that Castrato was played by their beloved Barnaby Gill. Speaking in a high-pitched, eunuchoid voice that sorted well with his name, Castrato went through all the preliminaries of sorcery. Weird music played, mystic objects were placed in a circle and strange incantations were uttered. Barnaby Gill invested it all with an amalgam of humour and horror that was spell-binding. He stretched both arms wide to display the magical symbols painted on his huge cloak then he gave a stern command.

'Come forth!'

Gunpowder exploded, red smoke went up, trap-doors opened and two merry devils leapt out. It all happened with such speed and precision that George Dart and Roper Blundell really did seem to have materialised out of thin air. Their trap-doors closed soundlessly behind them and they executed a little dance to music. Justice Wildboare beamed and Doctor Castrato bowed obsequiously. When they finished their sprightly capering, the two devils came to kneel before their new master. Complete silence now fell on the makeshift playhouse.

It was broken with heart-rending suddenness. To the sound of another, much louder, explosion and through a larger effusion of smoke, a third devil shot up on to the stage. There was a surface similarity to the others but there were also marked differences. The third devil was smaller, quicker, more compact. He had longer horns, a shorter tail and a deeper, blood-red hue. Slit-like eyes had a malevolence that glowed. The grotesque face was twisted into a sadistic grin.

Here was no assistant stagekeeper pressed into service.

This merry devil looked like the real thing.

Chapter Two

Not a murmur was heard, not a movement was made. Everyone was hypnotised. The newcomer had taken instantaneous command. Actors were rooted to the spot. Groundlings became standing statues. Galleries were frankly agog. They were not quite sure what they were witnessing but they did not dare to turn away. Revelling in his power, the third devil held them in thrall and gazed menacingly around the massed gathering. With a wild cry and a crude gesture of threat, the creature suddenly jumped to the very edge of the stage and made the audience shrink back in fear. But it was only in jest. After letting out a low cackle of derision, the devil did a series of backsomersaults in the direction of the players.

George Dart and Roper Blundell fled at once to the tiring-house and Barnaby Gill flinched but Lawrence Firethorn stood his ground manfully. It was his stage when he was upon it and he would defy Satan himself to rob him of his authority. The devil landed on his feet in front of him, spun round and regarded him with malicious glee. Showing great dexterity and speed, he then knocked Firethorn's hat off, pulled the cloak up over Gill's head, pushed over a table, kicked aside two stools then hurled the circle of mystic objects into the crowd. After cartwheeling around the stage in a red blur, the interloper vanished down the trap-down that had been left open and pulled it shut behind him.

A buzz ran through the audience. They did not know whether to be afraid or amused but they were all astonished. Some laughed to break the tension, others put hands to pounding hearts, others again shuffled towards the exits. Firethorn moved quickly to re-establish his control and to smooth any ruffled feathers. Pretending that the intrusion was all part of the play, he strode down to the trap-door and banged his foot on it, collecting yells of admiration at his bravery.

The voice of Justice Wildboare rang out with conviction.

> This was the merriest devil of them all. Come forth again, sir, and know thy master. Show that impish face. I would have you before me that I may judge your case and pass sentence. An' you knock off my hat again, you saucy varlet, I'll fetch you a box o' the ears that shall make your head ring all the way back to Hell. Stand forth once more, thou restless spirit. If you can do such tricks as these to order, I'll have you play them on the lusty Youngthrust to still the throbbing codpiece of his ambition. Return, I command.

Firethorn pounded on the timber with his foot but there was no answering flash of devilry. The creature had gone back to the place from which he came. Given time to recover his wits, Barnaby Gill came across to support his fellow in an extempore duologue, in the course of which it was decided to summon the devils again. Music played and Doctor Castrato went into his macabre ritual, dispensing with the circle of mystic objects which had been scattered far and wide. The audience watched with bated breath.

High drama was taking place in the tiring-house where the merry devils were refusing to go back on stage again. George Dart was still shuddering and Roper Blundell speechless with agitation. Gentle persuasion from the book holder was having no effect and so he adopted a more forthright method. As the incantations reached their height and the devils were called forth, they were more or less propelled out from behind the curtains by the strong hands of Nicholas Bracewell. No sprightly jig this time, only abject fear as they fell to their knees and prayed that their devilish companion would not return again.

Stepping between them, Firethorn gave each a squeeze of encouragement on the shoulder, then fed them lines as solicitously as a mother spooning medicine into the mouth of a sick child. Very slowly, they were coaxed back into their roles and the play resumed its former course. Other players ventured out with trepidation but Edmund Hoode came on with uncharacteristic assertiveness and threw himself into the fight to salvage his work. He would not let a supernatural accident—if that was what it was—come between him and his dearest hope. Too much was at stake.

The Merry Devils gradually revived. Wit sparkled, skul-duggery thickened, drama heightened. By the end of the last act, the spectators were so absorbed in the action once more that they heaved a collective sigh of disappointment when it was all over. A sustained ovation was accorded to Westfield's Men. Standing before his company to give a series of elaborate bows, Lawrence Firethorn kept a wary eye on the fatal trap-door. He was not ready to relinquish one second of his precious applause to another eruption from the nether-world.

Ralph Willoughby joined in the acclamation but his mind was in a turmoil. He had written the scene in which the devils were raised up and had discussed with Nicholas Bracewell the special effects required. They had devised everything around two devils. If a third came uninvited, then it was a dire warning, a punishment inflicted on them for dabbling in the black arts. It was highly disturbing. Still outwardly debonair, Willoughby was plunged into profound spiritual torment.

As he made his way towards the exit, the playwright walked straight into the bustling figure of Isaac Pollard who was pushing his way down the stairs. Two worlds came face to face.

'Out of my way, sir!' said Pollard.

'By your leave.'

'I must quit this house of idolatry!'

'You did not like the comedy, sir?'

'It was a profanation of the worst kind.'

'Why, then, this rapturous applause?' said Willoughby.

'An audience of heathens!'

'I think you do not love the playhouse.'

'It is the creation of the Devil!' affirmed Pollard. 'I will not rest until every such place in London is burned to the ground!'

With a final snarl of disgust, he unfurled his bristling eyebrow and took his Christian conscience hurriedly down the stairs.

He was a man with a mission.

Hysteria enveloped the whole company. The effort of getting through the performance had concentrated their minds but there was a general collapse now that it was all over. Fear held sway over the tiring-house. Almost everyone was convinced that a real devil had been summoned up, and those who had not actually witnessed the creature now claimed to have been party to other manifestations.

'I felt a fierce heat shoot up through my body.'

'And I an icy cold that froze my entrails.'

'The ground did shake wondrously beneath my feet.'

'I heard the strangest cry.'

'My eyes were dazzled by a blinding light.'

'I saw a vision of damnation.'

'The devil called me privily by my name.'

It all served to stoke up the communal delirium.

George Dart and Roper Blundell could not tear off their costumes fast enough, Richard Honeydew wept copiously for his mother, Barnaby Gill needed a restorative cup of brandy, Caleb Smythe pulled out a dagger to protect himself, Martin Yeo hid in a basket, Ned Rankin beat himself on the chest with clenched fists and Thomas Skillen, the ancient stagekeeper, who had long since strayed from the straight and narrow, and who had not entered a church for over a decade, now fell meekly to his knees and gabbled his way through the only psalm that he could remember.

Nicholas Bracewell stood apart and viewed it all with calm objectivity. He had caught only the merest glimpse of the third devil and it was a startling experience, but he was still keeping an open mind. Actors were superstitious by nature and the incident touched off their primal anxieties, convincing them that they were marked by Satan for an early demise. The book holder knew that he had to keep a cool head so that he could search for an explanation of the phenomenon.

Lawrence Firethorn came over to lean on him for support.

'May I never see such a horrid sight again!' he said.

'You were equal to it, master.'

'Someone had to confront the creature, Nick. The foulest fiend will not fright me from my calling. A true actor never deserts his place upon the stage.'

'You were at the height of your powers.'

'I surpassed myself,' said Firethorn bluntly then he slipped a conspiratorial arm around the other's shoulder. 'There is much matter here, Nick, and we must debate it to the full at another time. For the nonce, duty beckons.'

'I know,' said Nicholas with a rueful smile.

'Master Marwood must be answered.'

'It will be a labour of Hercules.'

'That's why I assign it to you, dear heart,' said the actor with evident affection. 'Your silver tongue and my golden talent hold Westfield's Men together. We are the prop and mainstay of this company.'

'Shall you speak with mine host as well?'

'Heaven forbid! I could knock the wretch to the ground as soon as look at him. Keep that mouldy visage away from me! But he must be satisfied. This over-merry devil will drive us from the Queen's Head else.'

'What will I say to Master Marwood?'

'That which will keep our contract alive.'

'He will tax me about this afternoon's business.'

'Tell him it was all part of the play,' suggested Firethorn. 'And if that tale falls on stony ground, swear that it was a jest played on us by Banbury's Men, who furnished us with one more devil than our drama required.'

'That may yet turn out to be the truth,' said Nicholas.

'Villainy from our rivals?'

'It must be considered.'

'No,' growled the other into his beard. 'I looked that creature full in the face. Those eyes of his were aflame with evil. That was no human being come to scare us. It was a fiend of Hell.' He eased the book holder towards the door. 'Now go and lie to Marwood for all our sakes. And keep him ignorant of what I have just told you.'

Nicholas nodded and was about to leave.

'One thing more, Nick.'

'Master?'

'I blame Ralph Willoughby for this.'

'Ralph? On what grounds?'

'Ill omens!'

Without pausing to enlarge upon his accusation, Firethorn swept across the tiring-house towards the other door. Nicholas was disturbed. He had grown fond of Willoughby during their work together on the play and instinctively defended him against the criticism which the latter excited in the company. It would be both sad and unfair if the playwright were made the scapegoat for what had happened. Nicholas made a mental note to forewarn the man so that he might be forearmed against Firethorn.

Alexander Marwood was the immediate problem. Fortunately, he was not in the habit of watching performances in his yard but he would certainly have heard the reports of this one. Nicholas could picture him all too clearly, wringing his skeletal hands, working himself up into a lather of misery, prophesying death and destruction for all concerned. Facing such a man in such a situation was not an enticing prospect but it had to be done. Relations between landlord and tenants were already fragile. Unless swift action was taken, they would worsen drastically. Rehearsing his lines, Nicholas went off to his forbidding task.

Something diverted him. As he sought to explain away the arrival of the third devil, he asked himself a question that had never occurred to him before. How did the creature vanish from the stage? If, as both Gill and Firethorn vouched, the intruder disappeared through the trap-door, then a further question arose: why was it open? It had been designed to close as soon as George Dart or Roper Blundell shot up through it, and Nicholas had checked the mechanism himself. It would be wise to do so again.

Crawling beneath the trestles, he made his way to the first of the trap-doors and found it intact. To ensure a self-closing door, he had designed a counter-weight that ran on pulleys. At his instigation, the carpenter had lined the edge of the trap with a thick strip of cloth to deaden the sound when the door slammed shut. Nicholas tested the simple device and it worked perfectly. Bending low, he moved across to the other trap-door and lifted it. There was no resistance. Once it was flipped up into a vertical position, it stayed there, resting against its own hinges. The piece of metal used as a counter-weight had been rendered useless. Nicholas noted with interest that the twine had been cut through.

Two more questions now presented themselves for answer.

Why did the creature need to have a prepared exit?

More to the point, was the trap-door in a makeshift stage set up in a London inn yard the legitimate route to the domain of Hell?

Nicholas brightened. When he went off to find the landlord, he did so with a new spring in his step. The case was altered somewhat. Marwood might yet be pacified.

Lord Westfield was surrounded, as was customary, by an adoring coterie of friends. Seated in a high-backed oak chair in a private room at the Queen's Head, he sipped his Canary wine and basked in the glow of admiration as his companions scattered their superlatives.

'Your lordship has the finest company in London.'

'In England, I vow! In the whole of Europe.'

'And this was their greatest triumph.'

'Was ever a piece so full of mirth as *The Merry Devils*?'

'Could anything so fright a man out of his skin?'

'Can any actor i' the world challenge this Firethorn?'

'He's a crown prince among players.'

'The jewel of his profession.'

'Your lordship made an exquisite choice in this fellow.'

Among those showering the patron with this praise was a tall, thin, complacent individual in his twenties. Attired in a black satin doublet trimmed with black and gold lace, he sported a plumed hat that was almost as ostentatious as that of Lord Westfield himself. His name was Francis Jordan, as smooth, plausible and ready with a quip as any in the group, a man well-versed in the social graces. As the favourite nephew of Lord Westfield, he enjoyed a position that he had learned to exploit in all manner of subtle ways. Francis Jordan had style.

'What think you, nephew, of Castrato?' asked Lord Westfield.

'He will cause no offence to the ladies.'

'Did not this fellow carry his part well?'

'Only because he had less weight in his codpiece.'

'Come, sir. This Castrato was no true *castrato*.'

'That Doctor was doctored,' said Jordan with a comic gesture to indicate a pair of shears. 'He is strangely fallen off, uncle.'

'Barnaby Gill is a cut above most players.'

'And a cut below most honest men!'

There was general amusement at this banter and brittle laughter filled the room. It was terminated by the arrival of Lawrence Firethorn, who was ushered in by a liveried servant and who began with a dramatic bow to his patron. Gloved hands clapped him and plaudits came thick and fast. He waved his gratitude. All trace of the hapless Justice Wildboare had left him now and he stood there as a supreme actor, handsome and mesmeric, exuding a confidence that bordered on arrogance and conveying a sense of virility and danger.

Lord Westfield performed the introductions and Firethorn responded with beaming humility, lingering over his contact with the two ladies in the group. Nothing delighted him so much as the approbation of beautiful women and he wooed them with pleasantries as he kissed each of them on the hand. Francis Jordan was the last to meet Firethorn but he proved more effusive than all the rest.

'Your playing was truly magnificent, sir!'

'We strive to do our best,' said the actor.

'Such a work has never been seen on a stage before.'

'That much is certain,' conceded the other with slight unease.

'How came that third devil into the action?'

'Yes,' said Lord Westfield. 'What brought him forth like that? He stirred us all up into such a sudden flood of terror. Who was he?'

'A hireling with the company, my lord.'

'His antics were exceeding merry.'

'The fellow but obeyed direction.'

'By what means did he burst forth in such a fine frenzy?'

'A cunning device, my lord,' said Firethorn, airily gliding over the truth of the matter. 'It was conceived by Nick Bracewell, our book holder, as artful a soul as any in this strange profession of ours. More than that, I cannot tell you lest it discredit his mystery.'

Lord Westfield toyed with his pomander while the two ladies buzzed around him in a flurry of satin. Their whispered entreaties were very much to his taste and helped him to reach a decision.

'I would see this comedy again, sir.'

'*Again*, my lord?' Firethorn concealed his rising disquiet.

'Yes, uncle,' said Jordan with genial enthusiasm. 'I would have it played at Parkbrook House, in the long hall, when my refurbishment is complete. Order shall be given for it. The idea grows on me apace. With your permission, I am resolved on it.'

'Would you have these merry devils in your home, Francis?'

'They will bring a feast of joy to the occasion.'

'Have you no qualms, nephew?'

'None, sir. Parkbrook welcomes such jollity.'

'So be it, then. I'll indulge your whim.'

'Thank you, uncle, with all my heart!'

Francis Jordan had recently taken possession of a property on Lord Westfield's estate in Hertfordshire and he was having alterations made before he moved in. He planned to have a banquet to mark his arrival as the new master of Parkbrook House and that day of celebration would now include *The Merry Devils* as its central feature.

Lord Westfield voiced a slight reservation.

'When will the work be done, Francis?'

'In a month or so.'

'That is too long to wait,' said his uncle impatiently. 'I'll not tarry until Parkbrook be in a fit state to receive my company. In ten days, I return to the country myself. These merry devils will caper for my delight before I leave. See to it, Master Firethorn.'

The actor-manager started and gave an apologetic shrug.

'Your request is not easy to satisfy, my lord.'

'Then my request will become my command.'

'But we already have plans for our next performances.'

'Change them, sir.'

'*The Merry Devils* does not figure in our list.'

'Insert it.'

Firethorn gritted his teeth. Having survived one ordeal with the play, he did not wish to be confronted with another quite so soon. Nor did he relish the idea of forcing a reluctant company to present a work which had such unfortunate associations for them.

'Is there no other comedy in our repertoire that would please you, my lord?' he said. 'You have only to choose.'

'That is what I have done, sir.'

'*The Merry Devils* will be very difficult to mount again.'

'No more evasion,' said his patron with a dismissive sweep of his hand. 'We would have this play again and we would have it with that fiery creature in his flash of red smoke. We shall know when to expect him next time and he will not make our hearts leap so readily into our mouths.' He drained his wine. 'Make arrangements, sir.'

'And do not forget the visit to Parkbrook House,' said Jordan seriously. 'That still stands, Master Firethorn. I would have devilry in my own home, so I would. You will be recompensed.'

Lawrence Firethorn capitulated with a deep bow.

'We are, as always, my lord, your most obedient servants.'

A submissive smile covered his face but his mind was wrestling with practical problems. If they risked staging the play again, how could they guarantee the requisite number of devils? Would the intruder deign to return on cue? Could they, indeed, prevent him from doing so?

St Benet Grass Church had served its parishioners with unwavering devotion for over four long centuries and in that time it had witnessed all manner of worship, but it had never before encountered anything quite so incongruous as the sight which now presented itself in the chancel. Kneeling at the altar rail was a figure of such showy elegance that he seemed more fitted for a gaming den than for a house of prayer. It was as if he had wandered into the church by mistake and been vanquished by the power of God. A shudder went through his body then he prostrated himself on the cold stone steps, assuming an attitude of extreme penitence so that he could have conference with his Maker.

A mitred bishop in the meanest brothel could not have looked more out of place. The man remained prone for several minutes, a colourful guest in the consecrated shadows, a living embodiment of the sacred and the profane. When he raised his eyes to the crucifix, they were awash with tears of contrition. Racked with guilt and speared with pain, he muttered a stream of prayers under his breath then slowly dragged himself to his feet. He backed down the aisle and genuflected when he reached the door.

Ralph Willoughby went out into bustling Gracechurch Street.

His affability returned at once. In his cheerful progress through the crowd, there was no hint of the malaise which took him to St Benet's, still less of the turbulence he experienced while he was there. His innermost feelings were cloaked once more. Willoughby now gave the impression that he did not have a care in the world.

When he reached the Queen's Head, he went straight to the yard where the stage was being dismantled. Westfield's Men were not due to perform there until the following week and so their temporary playhouse could make way for the ordinary business of the inn. Everybody worked with unwonted alacrity, eager to clear away all trace of *The Merry Devils* so that they could put behind them the memory of what had happened that afternoon. There was none of the usual idle chat. They went about their task in grim silence.

Nicholas Bracewell came out of a door and crossed the yard. He had laboured long and hard with Marwood and the effort had taken its toll, but it had brought a modicum of success. The landlord had been sufficiently quelled by the book holder's reasoning to hold back from tearing up the contract with Westfield's Men. The players were neither welcome nor expelled from the Queen's Head. Nicholas had won them a period of grace.

Pleased to see Willoughby, he bore down on him.

'A word in your ear, Ralph,' he said.

'As many as you choose, dear fellow.'

'Master Firethorn was roused by that third devil of ours.'

'So we were all!'

'His anger glows. Avoid him until it has cooled.'

'Why so, Nick?'

'Be warned. He lays the blame on you.'

'Ah!' sighed the other softly.

'Away, sir!' urged Nicholas. 'He'll be here anon. He stays but for brief converse with Lord Westfield.'

'This is kind advice but I'll stand my ground in spite of it.'

'Fly the place now, Ralph.'

'I'll not turn tail for any man.'

'Master Firethorn will rant and rave unjustly at you.'

'He has good cause.'

'What's that?'

'It *was* my fault.' Willoughby shook his head and smiled wryly. 'Lay it at my door, Nick. I penned that scene and I summoned that furious devil from Hell.'

'No, not from Hell. His journey was of much shorter length.'

'How say you?'

'It was a creature of flesh and blood, Ralph.'

'But I saw the fiend with my own eyes.'

'Only in a twinkling.' Nicholas pointed to the trestles that were being taken down. 'If that was one of Satan's brood, why did he leave by an open trap whose device had been cut for the purpose?'

'A devil may do as he wishes,' argued Willoughby. 'He could have disappeared down the trap or up the nearest chimney, if fancy had seized him that way. This was no illusion, Nick. It was real and authenticate.'

'I cannot believe that.'

'What other explanation suits the case?'

'The creature was placed there for our discomfort.'

'By whom, sir?'

'We have rivals, we have enemies.'

'But how came they to have intelligence of our play? This was no random fiend, breaking forth wildly to mar all our doings. This merry devil knew exactly when to appear. No rival could have prompted him.'

It was a valid point and it halted Nicholas in his tracks. Plays were the exclusive property of the companies who staged them and they were jealously guarded during the rehearsal period. Plagiarism was rife and Westfield's Men—it was an article of faith with Firethorn—took especial care to protect their interests while, at the same time, keeping a close eye on the work of their rivals to see if they themselves might filch an occasional idea or steal some occasional thunder. Only one complete copy of *The Merry Devils* existed and it had been entrusted to the capable hands of Nicholas Bracewell, who kept it under lock and key when not using it as a prompt book.

Nobody outside the company had had a sight of the full text of the play. It was impossible for someone to introduce a third merry devil into the action without prior knowledge of the time, place and manner in which George Dart and Roper Blundell emerged on to the stage.

Ralph Willoughby jabbed a finger to reinforce his argument.

'The devil came forth in answer to my call.'

'If devil it was,' said Nicholas sceptically.

'Of that there can be no doubt.'

'I am not persuaded, Ralph.'

'Then I must unfold something to you,' said the other, peering around to make sure that they were not overheard. 'The speeches of Doctor Castrato were not invention. Those incantations were not the product of my wayward brain. I took counsel.'

'From whom?'

'A man well-versed in such matters.'

'A sorcerer?'

'An astrologer of some renown, practised in all the arts of medicine, alchemy and necromancy. Every aspect of demonology is known to him and he instructed me patiently in the subject.'

Nicholas did not need to be told the name. The description could only apply to one person in London, an astrologer of such eminence that his services had been retained by Queen Elizabeth herself and by various members of the royal household. An educated man like Ralph Willoughby would have no dealings with mountebanks who performed their wizardry in back alleys. He would search out the best advice and that would surely come from the celebrated Doctor John Mordrake of Knightrider Street.

'He showed me the charms to use,' said Willoughby. 'He taught me the correct form of words.'

'Did Edmund know of all this?'

'I had no reason to tell him, Nick. It fell to me to write that fatal scene and I wanted a ring of truth in it. I had no notion that I would raise a devil in broad daylight.'

'Were you not warned against it?'

'My mentor assured me that the summons would only work in private, in some cloistered place where darkness was softened by candlelight. Yet here was this fiend of Hell for all to see.'

Ralph Willoughby was no credulous fool who could be tricked by a flash of gunpowder and a flame-red costume. Watching intently from the gallery, he was convinced that he had seen a real devil materialise upon the stage. Nicholas still had vestigial doubts.

'The cord was cut, the trap was up.'

'A devil could have done that.'

'But why?'

'To spread more confusion, Nick. To mislead us afresh.'

'My instinct takes me to another explanation.'

'It was a devil,' insisted Willoughby. 'I was the one who called him and I was the one who was punished. Master Firethorn is right to put the blame on me. I raised up this spirit.'

Further dispute with him was useless. He would never be shifted from his belief and Nicholas was forced to admit that his friend did actually witness the supernatural event. So did the four actors on stage at the time and they were of the same mind as Ralph Willoughby. Panic scattered the entire company with the honourable exceptions of Lawrence Firethorn and Edmund Hoode. It was the latter who now excited curiosity.

'Why was Edmund not unnerved?' said Willoughby.

'He is a brave man in his own way.'

'His performance went beyond bravery, Nick.'

'He was driven forward.'

'It was Youngthrust to the life.'

'That was his fervent hope.'

'In his place, I would have been trembling with fear.'

'Edmund was armoured against it. There is something that is even stronger than fear, Ralph.'

'Is there?'

'Love.'

'*That* is the cause?'

'Why do you think he chose to play Youngthrust?' asked Nicholas with a kind smile. 'Edmund Hoode is in love.'

Grace Napier was not an overwhelming vision of loveliness. Men beholding her for the first time would notice her pleasant features and her trim figure, her seemly attire and her modest demeanour. They were impressed but never smitten. Hers was a stealthy beauty that crept up on its prey and pounced when least expected. She could reveal a vivacity that was usually banked down, a hidden radiance that came through to suffuse her whole personality. Those who stayed long enough to become fully acquainted with Grace Napier found that she was a remarkable young woman. Behind her many accomplishments lay a strong will and a questing intelligence, neither of which involved the slightest sacrifice of her femininity.

'You deserve congratulation, Master Hoode,' she said.

'Thank you, thank you!'

'Your portrayal was sublime.'

'I dedicate it to you, mistress.'

'It is the finest I have seen of your performances.'

'The role was created with my humble talents in mind.'

'There is nothing humble about your talent, sir,' she said firmly. 'As a poet and as a player, you are supremely gifted.'

'Your praise redeems everything.'

Edmund Hoode was in a private room at the Queen's Head, enjoying a rare meeting with Grace Napier. The presence of her companion, the pert Isobel Drewry, imposed a restraint as well as a propriety on the occasion but Hoode was not deterred by it. In the few short weeks that he had known her, he had fallen deeply in love with Grace Napier and would have shared the room with a hundred female companions if it gave him the opportunity to speak with his beloved.

Isobel Drewry giggled as she offered her critique.

'It was such a happy comedy,' she said, tapping the ends of her fingers together. 'I laughed so much at Droopwell and Justice Wildboare. And as for Doctor...' Another giggle surfaced. 'There! I cannot bring myself to say his name but he gave us much mirth.'

'Barnaby Gill is one of our most experienced players,' said Hoode. 'No matter what lines are written for him, he will find the humour in them. He has no equal as a comedian.'

'Unless it be that third merry devil,' observed Grace.

'Indeed, sir,' agreed Isobel. 'He gave us all a wondrous shock.'

'That was our intent,' said Hoode dismissively, anxious to keep off the topic of the uninvited devil. 'Tell me, Mistress Napier, for which of his several good parts did you admire Youngthrust the most?'

Isobel suppressed a giggle but Grace gave a serious answer.

'I was touched by his sighing,' she said.

'Were you?' he sighed.

'He suffered so much from the pangs of love.'

'Oh, he did, he did!'

Hoode was thrilled by this new evidence of her sensitivity. With so many other things to choose from, Grace Napier singled out the quality he had tried above all else to project. The sighing and suffering that was provoked by Lucy Hembrow in the play was really aimed at Grace herself and she seemed almost to acknowledge the fact. In every conceivable way, she was a rare creature. Unlike most young ladies, Grace came to the playhouse to see rather than to be seen, and her knowledge of drama was wide. She watched most of the London companies but her favourite—Hoode gave silent thanks for it—was Westfield's Men.

Isobel Drewry might be thought by some to be the more attractive of the two. Her features were prettier, her eye bolder, her lips fuller and her manner less guarded. Again, Isobel's dress was more arresting in its cut and colours. Her combination of worldliness and innocence was very appealing but Hoode did not even notice it. All his attention was devoted to Grace Napier. This was the first time she had come to the Queen's Head without bringing her brother as a chaperone and Hoode saw this as an important sign. She consented to a brief meeting with him after the play and she confessed that she had been touched by the pathos of his performance. That was progress enough for one afternoon.

'We must bid you adieu, sir,' she said.

'A thousand thanks for your indulgence!'

'It was a pleasure, Master Hoode.'

'You do me a great honour.'

'I would see you play again,' said Isobel brightly. 'When will Westfield's Men take the stage again?'

'On Friday next at The Curtain.'

'Let's attend, Grace. We'll watch the company in another piece.'

'I am as eager as you, Isobel. We'll visit The Curtain.'

'That might not be altogether wise,' said Hoode quickly. 'If it is comedy that delights your senses, pray avoid us on Friday at all costs. We play *Vincentio's Revenge*, as dark and bloody a tragedy as any in our repertoire. I fear it may give offence.'

'Darkness and blood will not offend us, sir,' said Isobel easily. 'Tragedy can work potently on the mind. I like the sound of this play, Grace, and I would fain see it.'

'So would I,' returned her friend.

'Consider well, ladies,' he said. 'It may not be to your taste.'

Grace smiled. 'How can we judge until we have seen it?'

'Be ruled by me.'

But they declined. No matter how hard he tried to persuade them against it, they stood by their decision to watch *Vincentio's Revenge*. Hoode was unsettled. He wanted Grace Napier to see him at his best and the tragedy gave him no opportunity to shine.

He was cast as a lecherous old Duke who was impaled on the hero's sword in the second act. There was no way that he could speak to his beloved through the character of the Black Duke. She would despise him as the degenerate he played.

Grace read his mind and tried to soothe it.

'We do not expect a Youngthrust in every play, sir,' she said.

'I am not well-favoured in Friday's offering,' he admitted.

'We will make allowances for that. I'll not condemn you because you appear as a villain. I hope I've learned to separate the player from the play.' She touched his arm lightly. 'My brother and I saw you as the Archbishop of Canterbury in *The History of King John* but I did not then imagine Edmund Hoode to be weighed down with holiness. Whatever you play, I take pleasure from your performance.'

'This kindness robs me of all speech,' he murmured.

Grace Napier crossed to the door and Isobel followed her. Hoode moved swiftly to lift the latch for them. Isobel bestowed a broad smile of gratitude on him but he was not even aware of her presence. Grace leaned in closer for a final word.

'I would see Youngthrust on the stage again,' she confided.

'*The Merry Devils?*'

'Your part in your play. A double triumph.'

'I am overcome.'

'But next time, sir, let him sigh and suffer even more.'

'Youngthrust?'

'He should not have his love requited too soon,' she said. 'The longer an ardent wooer waits, the more he comes to prize his fair maid. It can only increase their happiness in the end.'

She touched his arm again then went out with Isobel, their dresses swishing down the corridor and their heels clacking on the paving slabs. Edmund Hoode was tingling with joy. He had clear direction from her at last. Grace Napier welcomed his love and urged him to be steadfast. In time, when he had endured the pangs of loneliness and the twinges of despair, she might one day be his. She had transformed his life in a few sentences.

From the depths of Hell, he now ascended to the highest Heaven.

Chapter Three

St Paul's Cathedral was the true heart of the city. It dominated the skyline with its sheer bulk and Gothic magnificence. Within its walls could be found the teeming life of London in microcosm. Paul's Walk, the middle aisle with its soaring pillars and vaulted roof, was a major thoroughfare where gallants strutted in their finery, soldiers escorted their ladies, friends met to exchange gossip, masters hired servants, jobless men searched the advertisements on display, lawyers gave advice, usurers loaned money, country people gaped, and where all the beggars and rogues of the neighbourhood congregated in the hope of rich pickings.

Crime flourished in a place of divine worship and yet the sacred glow was somehow preserved. St Paul's was not simply an imposing structure of stone and high moral purpose, it was a daily experience of everything that was best and worst in the nation's capital.

The cathedral stood at the western end of Cheapside. Its churchyard covered twelve and a half acres with houses and shops crowding around the precinct walls. At the centre of the churchyard was Paul's Cross, a wooden, lead-covered pulpit from which political orations were made on occasion and from which sermons were regularly preached.

'There indeed a man may behold hideous devils run raging over the stage with squibs in their mouths, while the drummer makes thunder in the tiring house and the hirelings make lightning in the Heavens.'

The sermon which was being delivered there on that sun-dappled morning was fiery enough to draw a large audience and to capture the interest of those who were browsing in the bookshops or loitering by the tobacco stalls. Standing in the pulpit, high above contradiction, was a big, brawny man with a powerful voice and a powerful message. He waved a bunched fist to emphasise his point.

'Look but upon the common plays of London and see the multitude that flocks to them and follows them. View the sumptuous playhouses, a continual monument to the city's prodigality and folly. Do not these vile places maintain bawdry, insinuate knavery and renew the remembrance of heathen idolatry? They are dens of iniquity!'

There was a ground swell of agreement among the listening throng. Isaac Pollard developed his argument with righteous zeal.

'Nay!' he said. 'Are not these playhouses the devourers of maidenly virginity and chastity? For proof whereof, mark the running to The Theatre and The Curtain and other like houses of sin, to see plays and interludes, where such wanton gestures, such foul speeches, such laughing and leering, such winking and glancing of wanton eyes is used, as is shameful to behold. The playhouse is a threat to Virtue and a celebration of Vice!'

Pollard was really into his stride now, his single eyebrow rising and falling like a creature in torment. He pointed to the heavens, he pummelled the pulpit, he smashed one fist into the palm of his other hand. In launching his attack on the theatre, he was not averse to using a few theatrical tricks.

'But yesterday,' he continued, 'but yesterday, good sirs, I went to view this profanity for myself. Not up in Shoreditch, I say, not yet down in Bankside but within our own city boundaries, at the sign of the Queen's Head in Gracechurch Street. There I beheld such idleness, such wickedness and such blasphemy that I might have been a visitor to Babylon. Men and women buy this depravity for the price of one penny and our city authorities do nought to stop them. Yet upon that stage—I call it a scaffold of Hell, rather—I saw the visible apparition of devils as they capered for amusement. That is no playhouse, sirs, it is the high road to perpetual damnation!'

The more vociferous elements gave him a rousing cheer.

'The theatres of London,' said Pollard with booming certainty, 'are the disgrace and downfall of the city. Among their many sinful acts, there be three chief abominations. First, plays are a special cause of corrupting our youth, containing nothing but unchaste matters, lascivious devices, shifts of cozenage and other ungodly practices.'

Support was even more audible now. A woman in the crowd clutched her two children to her bosom, as if fearing that they would go straight off to the nearest playhouse to lose their innocence.

'Second, theatres are the ordinary places for vagrant persons, thieves, beggars, horse-stealers, whoremongers, coney-catchers and other dangerous fellows to meet together and make their matches to the great displeasure of God Almighty.'

Pollard drew himself up to his full height and his shadow fell across those who listened down below. Both arms were outstretched for effect as he came to his final indictment.

'Third, plays draw apprentices and other servants from their work, they pluck all sorts of people from resort unto sermons and Christian practices, and they bind them to the worship of the Devil. Playhouses mock our religion. Destroy this canker in our midst, say I. Perish all plays and players!'

There was a deathly hush as his imprecations hung upon the wind, then a derisive laugh was heard from the rear of the congregation. Isaac Pollard turned eyes of hatred upon a personable figure in doublet, hose and feathered hat. The man had the look of a gallant but the air of a scholar.

It was Ralph Willoughby.

The house in Shoreditch was not large and yet it served Lawrence Firethorn and his wife, their children, their servants, the four young apprentices with Westfield's Men and sundry other members of the company who needed shelter from time to time. It fell to Margery Firethorn to make sure that people did not keep bumping into each other in the limited space and she presided over her duties with a ruthless vigilance. A handsome woman of ample proportions, she had an independent mind and an aggressive charm. Firethorn could be fearsome when roused but he had married his match in her. Pound for pound, Margery was redder meat and she was the only person alive who could rout him in argument. He might be the captain of the domestic ship but it was his wife's hot breath which filled the sails.

'The room is ready, Lawrence,' she said.

'Thank you, my dove.'

'Refreshment has been set out.'

'Good. We deal with weighty matters.'

'Nobody will dare to interrupt!'

Her raised voice was a threat which could be heard in every corner of the house. She glided off to the kitchen and Firethorn was left to conduct his two visitors into the main room. Barnaby Gill puffed at his pipe and took a seat at the table while Edmund Hoode curled up on the settle in a corner. Firethorn remained on his feet so that he could the more easily assert his ascendancy.

It was a business meeting. All three of them were sharers with Westfield's Men, ranked players whose names were listed in the royal patent for the company. They took the leading parts in the plays and had a share in any profits that were made. There were four other sharers but most of the decisions were made by Firethorn, Gill and Hoode, a trio who combined wisdom with experience and who represented a balance of opinion. That, at least, was the theory. In practice, their discussions often degenerated into acrimonious bickering.

Barnaby Gill elected to strike the first blow this time.

'I oppose the notion with every sinew of my being!'

'No less was expected of you,' said Firethorn.

'The idea beggars belief.'

'Remember who suggested it, Barnaby.'

'Tell Lord Westfield that it is out of the question.'

'I have told him that we accede to his request.'

'*You* might, Lawrence,' said the other testily, 'but I will never do so, and I speak for the whole company.'

Barnaby Gill was a short, plump, round-faced man who tried to hold middle age at bay by the judicious use of cosmetics. Disaffected and irascible offstage, he became the soul of wit the moment he stepped upon it and his comic routines were legendary. Tobacco and boys were his only sources of private pleasure and he usually required both before he would shed his surliness.

Lawrence Firethorn grasped the nettle of resistance.

'What is the nature of your objection, Barnaby?'

'Fear, sir. Naked, unashamed fear.'

'Of another apparition?'

'Of what else! I am an actor, not a sorcerer. I'll not meddle with the supernatural again. It puts me quite out of countenance.'

'But we survived,' said Firethorn reasonably. 'The devil came and went but we live to boast of our ordeal.'

'It might not be so again, Lawrence.'

'Indeed not. The creature might decline to visit us next time.'

'He'll get no invitation from me, that I vow!'

Firethorn reached for the flagon on the table and poured three cups of ale, handing one each to the two men. He quaffed his own drink ruminatively then turned to Edmund Hoode.

'You have heard both sides, sir. Which do you choose?'

'Something of each, Lawrence,' said the playwright.

'You talk in riddles.'

'I think that *The Merry Devils* should be seen again.'

'Excellent wretch!'

'An act of madness!' protested Gill.

'Hold still, Barnaby,' said Hoode. 'I agree with you that we must not run the risk of bringing back that real devil.'

Firethorn was perplexed. 'How can you satisfy us both?'

'By amending the play. Here's the manner of it.'

Edmund Hoode had given it considerable thought. Instinct urged him to refuse to be involved again in a work that had taken them so close to catastrophe, but the words of Grace Napier echoed in his ears. His performance as Youngthrust had started to win her over. If he were allowed to give it again—replete with all the sighing and suffering that his beloved could wish for—then he would move nearer to the supreme moment of conquest. To make the play safe, he proposed a number of alterations, principally in the scene where Doctor Castrato summoned the merry devils.

'Ralph's magic was too potent,' he said. 'I will get him to cast some new spells that are too blunt to raise anything more than George Dart and Roper Blundell. It is a simple undertaking for Ralph.'

'Not so,' said Firethorn sternly. 'Do it yourself, Edmund.'

'But that scene came from his hand.'

'Which is exactly why it caused so much trouble. Ralph Willoughby has been the bane of this company for long enough.

Ever since he worked with us, we have been plagued by setback. Misfortune attends the fellow. I spoke with him yesterday and severed the connection. We paid him for his share of the play and he has gone. It is up to you now, Edmund.'

'But we were friends and co-authors,' said Hoode defensively.

'That time is past.'

'I never liked him,' admitted Gill sourly, tapping out his pipe on the edge of the table. 'Willoughby was the strangest soul. There was a darkness behind that bright smile of his that I could not abide.'

'Ralph is the finest dramatist in London,' insisted Hoode.

'That is open to dispute,' said Firethorn.

'He has worked with all the best companies, Lawrence.'

'Then why have they not retained his services?'

'Well...'

'Everyone seeks a resident poet, Edmund, which is why you are the envy of our rivals. But none of them has pressed Master Willoughby to stay. He writes well, I grant you, but he brings bad luck—and that is too heavy a burden to bear in the theatre.'

Hoode withdrew into his settle and brooded over his ale. Gill pondered. Firethorn let out a wheeze of satisfaction, feeling that he had carried the day with far less aggravation than he anticipated.

'Thus it stands, then,' he said. 'Lord Westfield will have his entertainment to order. Are we agreed?' He took their silence for consent. 'It is but a case of striking out one play and inserting *The Merry Devils*. We'll give it on Tuesday of next week at The Rose.'

'That we will not!' said Gill, exploding into life.

'I have made the decision, Barnaby.'

'Well, I resist it with all my might and main. *Cupid's Folly* was destined for The Rose. Strike out another play, if you must, but do not tamper with *Cupid's Folly*.'

'The Rose is most suited to our purposes, Barnaby.'

'You'll not find me there as Doctor Castrato.'

'Put the needs of the company above selfish desire.'

'I mean this, Lawrence. I'll leave Westfield's Men before I'll submit to this. That is no idle threat, sir, be assured.'

Barnaby Gill's tantrums were a regular feature of any business meeting and his fellow-sharers learned to humour him. Once he had flared up, he soon burned himself out. This time it was different. He was in earnest. *Cupid's Folly* was his favourite comedy, the one play in their repertoire that offered him total domination of the stage. His performance in the leading role had been honed to such perfection that he could orchestrate the laughter from start to finish. He was not going to be robbed of his hour of triumph. Folding his arms and pouting his lips, he turned an aggrieved face to the window.

Firethorn glanced over at Hoode and attempted a compromise.

'I have the answer,' he said guilefully. 'Edmund, did you not say that Doctor Castrato might have a dance or two more?'

'No, Lawrence.'

'Come, sir. You did.'

'I have no knowledge of the matter.'

'Then your memory is leaking. You urged it only yesterday.'

Unseen by Gill, he gestured wildly to Hoode for his support. The latter gave a resigned nod and went along with the lie, but his voice lacked any conviction.

'Now I bethink me, you are right. Another jig, I said.'

'Two, Edmund.'

'Oh, at least.'

'And a new song for the Doctor. His role must be extended.'

'At the expense of Justice Wildboare?'

'We need not go to that length,' said Firethorn hastily.

'Dances and a song, then. I will see to it.'

'Not on my account,' said Gill. 'I want *Cupid's Folly*.'

'But your new Castrato will dazzle the galleries at The Rose,' urged Firethorn. 'This is fair recompense for the change of play.'

'No, Lawrence. I am immoveable.'

And he turned his back on them in a spectacular sulk.

Firethorn exploded. He bullied, he badgered, he threatened, he aimed a torrent of abuse at his colleague. His voice was so loud and his language so florid that he made the whole room shake and dislodged four spiders from the beams above his head. It was the towering rage of a great actor in full flight and it would have brought a lesser man to his knees but Barnaby Gill was proof against the tirade. He simply refused to be a one-man audience to the extraordinary performance.

Impasse was reached. In the bruised silence that followed, Gill held his pose and Firethorn glared vengefully across at him. There seemed to be no way around the problem until Edmund Hoode intervened.

'We do not have to cancel *Cupid's Folly*,' he said.

'Indeed, we do, sir!' snarled Firethorn. '*The Merry Devils* must be our offering at The Rose.'

'And so it shall be.'

'Have you lost your wits, Edmund? We cannot stage both plays in the same afternoon. One must give way to the other.'

'That was not my meaning,' said Hoode quietly. '*The Merry Devils* will be presented at The Rose and *Cupid's Folly* will take its turn on Friday at The Curtain.'

Firethorn was momentarily dumbfounded but Gill bubbled with joy.

'There you have it, Edmund!'

'The play we strike out is *Vincentio's Revenge*.'

'Have a care what you suggest, sir!' growled Firethorn.

'*Vincentio's Revenge* is a tedious piece,' said Gill airily. 'It will not be missed. Oh, we know that you touch the heights in the title role, Lawrence, and it is one of your most assured successes, but is it not time to ask—I put this to you in the spirit of friendship—if you are not a trifle long in the tooth to be a young Italian hero?'

Firethorn bared his teeth for Gill to assess their length.

'Is not this the best answer?' asked Hoode cheerily.

'Yes, sir!' said Gill.

'No, sir!' countered Firethorn.

'Edmund shows the wisdom of Solomon.'

'Then why does he talk like the village idiot?' The actor-manager stalked the room. 'I have fifteen special moments in *Vincentio's Revenge* and I'll not be denied one of them. It stays.'

'And so does *Cupid's Folly*,' said Gill petulantly.

It was stalemate again. While the two of them withdrew once more into a hurt silence, Edmund Hoode tried to sound impartial as he proffered his advice. But the removal of *Vincentio's Revenge* suited his purposes very well. Losing the part of a decrepit old lecher, he instead became a lovelorn shepherd in the pastoral comedy of *Cupid's Folly*. It would give him the chance to impress Grace Napier with his readiness to bear the cross of unrequited passion. Hoode worked hard to soothe Firethorn, telling him how incomparable his performance as Vincentio was, yet reminding him of his dazzling role as a prince in the other play. Siding imperceptibly with Gill, he slowly brought Firethorn to the realisation that there was no alternative. Without *Cupid's Folly*, they would have no Doctor Castrato. Vincentio would have to forgo his revenge.

'Put the company before yourself for once,' said Gill spitefully.

'Lawrence always does that,' said Hoode. 'And I am sure that he will make this supreme sacrifice for the sake of Westfield's Men and our esteemed patron.'

Firethorn showed one last flash of surging arrogance.

'But for *me*, there would be no company. I *am* Westfield's Men.'

'Right, sir,' sniped Gill. 'Play Doctor Castrato yourself, then.'

'Gentlemen, gentlemen…' calmed Hoode.

'Play Droopwell. Play Youngthrust. Play the merry devils themselves.' Gill's tone was cruelly sarcastic. 'Since you have such an appetite for solo performance, carry a fan to hide your beard and play Lucy Hembrow into the bargain.'

'Enough, sir!'

Firethorn's exclamation was like the roar of a cannon. Circling the room in a frenzy, he kicked a chair, pounded the table, spat into the empty fireplace and sent a warming pan clattering from its nail on the wall. He came to rest before a window and stared out unseeing at the small but well-tended garden.

Hoode waited a full minute before he dared to speak.

'Is it agreed, Lawrence?'

There was an even longer pause before the hissed reply came.

'Castrato is to have *no* new songs or dances!'

'It's agreed!' shouted Gill in exultation, then he expressed his gratitude to Hoode by kissing him on the lips. 'God bless all poets!'

Yet another meeting thus reached its amicable conclusion.

Anne Hendrik was not a typical resident of Bankside. In an area that was notorious for its brothels, bear gardens and bull rings, for its cockpits, carousing and cutpurses, she was a symbol of respectability. She was the widow of Jacob Hendrik, who had fled from his native Holland and settled in Southwark because the City Guilds did not welcome immigrants into their exclusive fraternities. Overcoming initial problems, Jacob slowly prospered. By the time he married a buxom English girl of nineteen, he could offer her the comfort of a neat house in one of the twisting lanes. Though childless, it was a happy marriage and it left Anne Hendrik with many fond memories. It also gave her a liking for male company.

'Ralph Willoughby has gone?'

'Banished from the company.'

'What does Master Firethorn have against him?'

'Everything, Anne.'

'It seems so unfair.'

'Unfair, unwarranted and unnecessary.'

'Can Edmund Hoode revise the play on his own?'

'I have my doubts.'

They were sitting over the remains of supper at the Bankside house. The mood was relaxed and informal. Nicholas Bracewell had lodged there for some time now and had come to appreciate all of his landlady's finer qualities. Anne Hendrik was a tall, graceful woman in her thirties with attractive features of the kind that improved with the passage of time. She was a widow who never settled back into widowhood, and there was nothing homely or complacent about her. Intelligent and perceptive, she had a fund of compassion for people in distress and a practical streak that urged her to help them. Her apparel was always immaculate, her manner pleasant and her interest genuine.

'What will Master Willoughby do?' she asked.

'I have no idea.'

'Poor man! To be hounded out like that.'

'Master Firethorn can be brutal at times.'

'Yet he wants the play staged again?'

'Lord Westfield's command.'

Anne had liked him from the start. He was solid, reliable and undemanding in a way that reminded her of her husband. Nicholas was also a very private man with an air of mystery about him and she loved that most of all because it was something that Jacob Hendrik did not possess. In place of a dear but predictable partner, she had taken on a deep and thoughtful individual who could always surprise her. Their friendship soon matured and they now enjoyed a closeness that was untrammelled by any need for a formal commitment on either side. They could trust and confide in each other.

'Give me your true opinion, Nicholas,' she said.

'Of what?'

'The apparition.'

'I hardly saw it, Anne.'

'But those on stage who did took it for a devil.'

'Each one of them. As did Ralph Willoughby.'

'Yet you are not convinced.'

'I am trying to be.'

'What holds you back?'

'A vague feeling, no more.'

'Do you not *believe* in devils?'

He looked at her shrewdly for a moment then chuckled softly, reaching across to pat her arm with an affectionate hand. The concern on her face changed to puzzlement.

'Answer my question,' she pressed.

'It was answered the day I was baptised,' he said evasively. 'A man who bears the Devil's name must perforce believe in Hell. I am Old Nick. The Prince of Darkness. His Satanic Majesty. Lucifer.'

'You have still not given me a fit reply.'

'Very well.' He sat back and became serious. 'I will tell you the truth, Anne. I do not know. I do not know if devils exist and if I believe in them. I've lived long enough and travelled far enough to see some strange sights, but none of them came straight from Hell. Ralph Willoughby and the others saw a real devil but I did not. If I had done so, I would have believed in it. That is my honest reply.'

And what of God?' she said.

'No doubts there, Anne,' he affirmed. 'I have seen God's hand at work many times. You cannot go to sea without entrusting yourself to His special providence. When I sailed around the world, I witnessed more than enough miracles to strengthen my faith. I *know* that there is a God in Heaven.' He smiled pensively. 'What I cannot yet accept is that there was a devil in Gracechurch Street.'

There was a tap on the door and the maid came in to clear the table. Anne studied her lodger. After all their time together, there were still many things she did not know about him. The son of a

West Country merchant, Nicholas voyaged with Drake on the *Golden Hind* and survived the onerous circumnavigation of the globe. Those three years spent beneath the billowing canvas of an English ship had made a lasting impression on him yet he never talked about them. Nor would he ever explain how and why he chose to move into the choppy waters of the London theatre. Nicholas Bracewell felt the need to be secretive in such matters and she had come to respect that.

When the maid left the room, he looked across at Anne once more.

'I have a favour to ask.'

'Do but ask it and it will be granted.'

'Your hospitality is without fault.' They traded a short laugh. 'I would like you to visit The Rose next week.'

'*The Merry Devils?*'

'Yes, Anne. I need a pair of eyes in the gallery.'

'Do you expect this devil to appear again?'

'We should be prepared for that eventuality,' he said. 'I will tell you exactly what to look out for and when it may happen. In the meantime, I hope you will also enjoy the play.'

'That I shall, Nicholas.'

They got up from the table and crossed to the door. Something made her stop suddenly and turn back to him with a furrowed brow.

'When they saw that devil on the stage…'

'When they *thought* they saw it,' he corrected.

'Were they not alarmed?'

'Demented with fear. All except Master Firethorn, who carried on as if nothing untoward had happened.'

'He must have nerves of steel.'

'Only one thing can frighten him.'

'What's that?'

'His wife, Margery, when she is on the rampage. Hell may open its gates to send up its merriest devils but they will have to take second place to that good lady.'

'And what of Master Willoughby?'

'Oh, he was afraid,' recalled Nicholas. 'Deep down, I think that he was more shaken by the experience than any of them. He took the full blame upon himself. For a reason that I cannot comprehend, Ralph Willoughby is quite terrified.'

He slept for no more than ten minutes but lost all awareness of his surroundings. When his eyelids flickered, he could feel the darkness pressing in upon them and he had to make a conscious effort to shrug off his drowsiness. He was unwell. His head was pounding, his mouth nauseous, his stomach churning and his whole body lathered with perspiration. He groaned involuntarily. Then something moved beneath him and he realised with horror that he was lying naked in the arms of a young woman. By the uncertain light of the candle, he could see the powdered face that was now split by a jagged smile of ingratiation.

'Did I please you, sir?' she said hopefully.

Revulsion set in at once and he rolled over on to the bare floor, groping around in the gloom for his clothing. The girl sat up on the mattress to watch him, her long, matted hair hanging down around her bony shoulders. She was painfully thin and her breasts were scarcely fully formed. Sixteen was the oldest she could be. In the lustful warmth of the taproom downstairs, she seemed quite entrancing and he had brought her drunkenly up to her squalid chamber. Deprived of her flame-coloured taffeta, she looked plain, angular and distinctly unwholesome. Yet it was into this frail body that he had plunged so earnestly in search of refuge.

'Must you leave, sir?' she whispered.

His embarrassment grew. Grabbing his purse, he fumbled inside it then tossed some coins at her. She scooped them greedily up and held them tight in her little fist. Half-dressed and still only half-awake, he grunted a farewell then lurched out into the passageway.

Ralph Willoughby was overcome by the familiar sense of shame.

As he rested against her door and hooked up his doublet, he tried to work out exactly where he was. Somewhere in Eastcheap, but which tavern? Could it be the Red Lion? No, that was the previous night. The Lamb and Flag? No, that was the previous week. Was it the Jolly Miller? Unlikely. That particular haunt of his had a musty smell that he could not detect here. In that case, it had to be the Brazen Serpent, an appropriate venue for his latest disgrace. Fornication with some nameless girl in her wretched lodging at the Brazen Serpent in Eastcheap. Guilt burned inside him and the pain in his head became almost unbearable.

Willoughby put his hands together in prayer and recited quickly in Latin. Perspiration still ran from every pore. Consumed by an inner grief, he began to sway gently to and fro. Approaching footsteps jerked him out of his confession. Three people were coming noisily up the stairs, laughing and joking as they banged against the walls. Willoughby stood motionless and waited in the dark. The newcomers soon staggered along the passageway towards him.

The man had an arm around each of the two women so that he could both fondle and lean on them. His voice suggested that he was young, educated, flushed with wine and very accustomed to the situation in which he found himself. There was also a lordly note that showed he was used to giving orders and being obeyed. The moon shone in through the window to guide their footsteps along the undulating oak floorboards over which so many men had walked to perdition.

Willoughby shrank back but they were far too absorbed in their own drama to notice his presence. When they were still a couple of yards away from him, they went into a room and closed the door behind them. He waited no longer. Scurrying along the passageway, he hurled himself down the stairs as if the tavern were on fire. Seconds later, he was outside in the road but his headlong flight was delayed. As his stomach turned afresh, he felt a rising tide of vomit and bent double in humiliation.

Up in the chamber, the other man was ready to savour his pleasures. Flopping on to the bed, he stretched both arms wide and invited his two companions to practise their witchcraft.

'Come, ladies. Unbutton me now.'

Francis Jordan was clearly there for the whole night.

Isaac Pollard was formidable enough when delivering a sermon from a pulpit. He had a way of subduing his congregation with a glare and of browbeating them with his rectitude. But it was his voice that was his chief weapon, a strong, insistent, deafening sound that could reach a thousand pairs of ears without the least sign of strain. When it was heard at Paul's Cross, it was a powerful instrument of earthly salvation. Encountered in a domestic setting, however, it was frankly overwhelming.

'It outrages every tenet of public decency!'

'Do not shout so, Isaac.'

'The very fabric of our daily lives is at risk!'

'I hear you, sir. I hear you.'

'We demand stern action from our elected guardians!'

'Leave off, man. My head is a very belfry.'

Henry Drewry was a short, rotund, red-faced man in his fifties with an ineradicable whiff of salt about him. He was the pompous Alderman for Bishopsgate, one of the twenty-six wards of the City which chose a civic-minded worthy to represent them. A freeman of London, Drewry was also of necessity a member of one of the great Livery Companies. The Salters were vital contributors to the diet of the capital since their ware was used as a condiment at table and as a preservative for meat and fish. First licensed in 1467, the Salters' Company received its royal charter in 1559. In his portly frame and proud manner, Henry Drewry was a living monument to a flourishing trade which helped to control the taste of the citizenry.

Isaac Pollard returned to the attack with unabated volume.

'We seek support and satisfaction from you, Henry!'

'Seek it more mildly,' implored the other.

'The authorities must act to stop this corruption now!'

'What do you advocate, Isaac?'

'First, that the Queen's Head be closed forthwith!'

'Ah!' said Drewry gratefully. 'That lies not within my ward. If a tavern in Gracechurch Street exercises your displeasure, you must speak with Rowland Ashway. He is Alderman for Bridge Ward Within.'

'Master Ashway will not hear me.'

'Then he must be deaf indeed, sir.'

'When I talk of morality,' said Pollard solemnly, 'he thinks only of profit. Master Ashway, as you well know, is a member of the Brewers' Company. He sells his devilish ale to the Queen's Head and to the other taverns in Gracechurch Street. Sordid gain is all to him. The Alderman would not see the premises of a customer closed down, however sinful its workings.' The eyebrow crawled vigorously. 'I tell you, Henry, if it lay within my jurisdiction, I would shut down every brewery and tavern in the city!'

'Oh, I would not go to *that* extreme,' said Drewry, thinking of the dozen barrels of Ashway Beer that he kept in his own cellars. 'The people of London must be allowed some pleasure.'

'*Pleasure!*'

The word sent Pollard back up into the pulpit at Paul's Cross and he delivered a virulent homily against the sins of the flesh. Henry Drewry could do nothing to stem the flow. They were in the salter's house in Bishopsgate and the host was wishing that he had not agreed to meet the fiery Puritan. Isaac Pollard was a friend of his because he found it politic to gain the acquaintance of any person of influence in the community. That friendship was now being put under intense strain.

Pollard moved back to the issue which had brought him there, ranting about plays in general and *The Merry Devils* in particular. He described the lewd behaviour of the audience and then the appalling spectacle on the stage. Drewry was so buffeted that he could not take it all in but he did hear the questions that were hurled straight at him.

'Do you frequent the playhouse?'

'My duties and my trade forbid it,' said Drewry virtuously.

'Will you not condemn this filth?'

'With all my heart.'

'Unless it be checked, this corruption will spread until nothing is safe,' warned Pollard. 'How would you like *your* daughter to view such profanity?'

'I would not, sir. I hope I am a sensible parent.'

But even as he spoke, Henry Drewry felt an odd twinge of alarm. Something which his wife had told him now flitted across his mind. Their daughter, Isobel, returned from some outing in a state of excitement. For the first time in years, Drewry wished that he had listened to his wife properly. Isobel was a headstrong girl at the best of times and it was not impossible that she had attended a play.

The anxious father now sought more details.

'When was this offending performance?'

'But two days since.'

'At the Queen's Head, you say?'

'A stage was set up in the yard by Westfield's Men. All manner of people flocked to the place. Women, too, which shocked me most.'

The time was correct. Isobel Drewry could indeed have been one of the females whose presence had so disturbed Pollard. But why was the girl there and what in fact had she seen?

'And a *devil* appeared upon the stage?'

'Three, sir. There was no end to their blasphemy.'

'What followed?'

'Bedlam. The whole inn yard became Bedlam.'

The hospital of St Mary of Bethlehem was housed in the buildings of an old priory outside Bishopsgate. Founded over three centuries earlier, it had now acquired notoriety as an asylum for the insane. The unfortunate souls who were confined there were not shown the compassion that they deserved. Bethlehem Hospital—or Bedlam, as it was known—was famed for its brutal regime. Instead of caring for its inmates within the privacy of its walls, it punished them unmercifully and put them on display. Watching the lunatics was a regular pastime, as much a normal part of recreation as bear-baiting or playgoing. The weird antics of the mentally disturbed were a form of entertainment.

'We have all kinds here,' said Rooksley. 'Those that bay at the moon like wild dogs and those that speak not a word from one year's end to the next. Those that fight each other and those that do harm only to themselves. Those that laugh the whole day and those that weep without ceasing. Those that are tame and those that need a whip to teach them tameness. Bedlam contains a whole world of lunacy.'

'How came they here?' asked Kirk.

'Some twenty or so are supported by their parishes. The others are all private patients maintained at regular charges. Families pay between sixteen and sixty pence a week to keep their imbecile members locked away here.'

'That is a high price, Master Rooksley.'

'We earn it, sir. We earn it.'

It was Kirk's first day there. A muscular young man of medium height, he had a faintly ascetic air about him. Rooksley, the head keeper, was older, bigger and much more cynical. A livid scar down one cheek suggested that the job was not without its physical dangers. Rooksley was conducting his new colleague around the dank corridors and explaining his duties to him.

'We rule by force at Bedlam,' he said. 'It is the only way.'

'Beating will not cure the mind.'

'It will subdue the body, sir.'

'Is that the sole treatment for these poor wretches?'

'Most of them.'

As they turned a corner, a maniacal laugh came from a room ahead of them. It set off a series of other inmates and the whole corridor echoed with the strange cachinnation. Kirk was rather startled but the head keeper was unperturbed. The sound of whips confirmed that the staff were busy. Laughter changed to howls of pain.

Rooksley stopped outside a door with a small grille in it. He invited Kirk to peer into the gloom within. A young man in white shirt and dark breeches was sitting on the floor and gazing up at a fixed spot on the ceiling. He seemed to be deep in meditation.

'This one's a true gentleman,' said the head keeper. 'The chamber is bare, as you see, with no pictures on the walls or painted cloths about the bed, nor any light except what creeps in through that tiny casement. We give him warm meat three times a day and feed him *cassia fistula* for the good of his bowels.'

'Does he never leave this chamber?'

'Never, sir. We have orders for it. He is restrained here.'

Hearing their voices, the man turned his dull gaze upon them and smiled with childlike innocence. Then, without warning, he suddenly fell to the floor and threshed about in a convulsive fit that was frightening in its violence. When it finally subsided, Kirk turned to his companion.

'What ails the man?'

'The Devil,' said Rooksley. 'He is possessed by the Devil.'

Chapter Four

The announcement that Westfield's Men were to stage *The Merry Devils* for a second time caused great consternation. Memories of the first performance were still fresh enough to haunt and harrow. Thomas Skillen was not the only member of the company forced to rediscover his Christian faith that afternoon and the few who had actually been able to sleep since had been prey to recurring nightmares. What they all desired was the much safer material of *Vincentio's Revenge* and *Cupid's Folly*. Seven gruesome deaths in the former and eight broken hearts in the latter were infinitely preferable to the risk of raising a devil. Protest was intense but Lawrence Firethorn overruled it with imperious authority.

Nicholas Bracewell came behind him to pick up the pieces.

'Be not downhearted, lads!'

'I quake,' said George Dart.

'I quail,' said Roper Blundell.

'There is no just cause.'

'I cannot do it, Master Bracewell,' gibbered Dart. 'I will not, I must not, I *dare* not.'

'Nor I,' said his fellow. 'This is work for a younger man.'

'For no man at all,' returned Dart. 'I am young enough but I'll not venture upon it. I hope to be as old as you one day, Roper, and I would not be dragged off to Hell before my time.'

'That will not happen,' promised Nicholas.

'The play is cursed!' said Blundell.

'We are fools to touch it again,' added Dart.

'Lord Westfield has spoken,' reminded the book holder.

Blundell wheezed, 'Then let his lordship face that foul fiend!'

They were chatting during a break in rehearsal at The Curtain. Neither of the assistant stagekeepers was cast in *Cupid's Folly* and they were pathetically grateful. Any acting ambitions they might have nursed were dashed to pieces at the Queen's Head and all they sought now was backstage anonymity. They made a curious pair. George Dart, with his face of crumpled hope, was dog-loyal to a company whose reward was to treat him like a dog. The most menial and degrading jobs were always assigned to him and he was a convenient whipping-boy if anything went wrong. Roper Blundell had such a gnarled visage that it looked as if it had been carved inexpertly from a giant turnip. Hair sprouted all over it. His body was small, wiry and surprisingly nimble for his age but he was often short of breath.

'I understand your feelings in the matter,' said Nicholas.

'Then do not press us,' said Roper Blundell.

'Someone must persuade you.'

'We are beyond persuasion,' asserted George Dart. 'Nothing would drive us back into those red costumes.'

'You must speak with Edmund Hoode.'

'He will have no influence over us,' said Blundell.

'Hear him out,' advised Nicholas. 'He will tell you how he has altered the play to render it harmless. There is no chance of summoning up another devil. Were he to explain that, might you not both think again?'

'No!' they said in unison.

'Would you let Westfield's Men down in their hour of need?'

'We must put our lives first,' said Dart.

'What life would you have *without* this company?' asked Nicholas.

His voice was gentle but it did not muffle the blow. The two small figures were shaken. George Dart suddenly looked very young and vulnerable, Roper Blundell, very old and desperate. In the hazardous world of the theatre, jobs were scarce and companies in a position to choose. If they were cut adrift from Westfield's Men, neither of them would find it easy to secure employment elsewhere.

Nicholas Bracewell was highly sympathetic to their plight. He liked them both and would not willingly part with either, but the decision did not rest with him. He thought it only fair to warn them of what might lie ahead.

'Master Firethorn is adamant.'

George Dart was distraught. 'Would he turn us out?'

'We must have merry devils at The Rose.'

'Help us,' begged Roper Blundell. 'You have been our good friend this long time, Master Bracewell. We would not go through that torture again and yet we would not leave the company either. It is our home. We have no other. Help us, sir.'

Nicholas nodded and put a consoling arm around each of them. 'I will bethink me.'

Henry Drewry waddled around the room to build up his moral indignation.

'Why did you not tell me of this dreadful visit beforehand?'

'You did not ask, Father,' said Isobel.

'I have a right to be consulted about your movements.'

'You were not here. Had you been so, you would not have listened.'

'Do not be insolent, girl!'

'I am being truthful,' she replied levelly. 'Mother will say it as well as I. You are deaf to any words that we speak.'

'I am still the master of this house!' he blustered.

'That is why I do not bother you with trifling matters.'

'This is no trifling matter, Isobel!'

'I went to a play, that is all. Wherein lies my crime?'

'In *that*, young lady!'

Henry Drewry stopped in the middle of the room to confront his daughter. Everything about her irritated him, not least the fact that she was a few inches taller. Isobel had her mother's looks, her father's ebullience and a stubbornness that was all her own. Her serene smile enraged him.

'Do not smile at me so!'

'How, then, should I smile at you, Father?'

'I will not endure this impudence!'

'But I am not trying to upset you, sir.'

'You study it,' he accused. 'Why did you visit the Queen's Head?'

'To see a comedy.'

'Is there laughter in blasphemy?'

'I shared in the laughter but saw no blasphemy.'

'Who enticed you to that evil place?'

'Grace Napier,' she said. 'But it was not evil.'

He blenched. 'The two of you? Unchaperoned?'

'Her brother escorted us there,' she lied.

'So the Napier family is to blame for leading you astray.'

'No, Father. I went of my own free will.'

'That is even worse,' he said, stamping a foot. 'Can you not see the peril you courted? Plays are a source of corruption!'

'Have *you* never been to a playhouse?' she asked with a giggle. 'Come, I know you have. Mother has told me. There was a time when you organised an interlude at the Salters' Company. And you often went to see a comedy at the Bel Savage in Ludgate. You liked plays then, Father, and they did not corrupt you.'

'Leave off these jests!'

'Grace and I watched three merry devils in a dance.'

'It was an act of profanity!'

'It was the funniest sight that ever I saw but it did me no harm, except to make my ribs ache from laughing.'

'I will not bear this!' he howled.

Drewry took a deep breath and tried to regain his composure. Why was it that other fathers had so little trouble with their daughters when he had so much? What fatal errors had he made in rearing the girl? Had he been too soft, too indulgent, too preoccupied with his civic duties and his business affairs? By now, Isobel should be married and ready to present him with his first grandchild, but she had rejected every husband that he chose for her and done so in round terms. It was time she learned that she could not flout his authority.

'You should not have gone to the Queen's Head,' he said.

'Why not, Father?'

'Because of my position as an Alderman. My dignity must be upheld at all costs. I would not have my daughter seen at a common playhouse.'

'But I was not seen—I wore a veil.'

'You are forbidden to go near a theatre!'

'That is unfair,' she protested.

'It is my decree. Obey it to the letter.'

'But I have agreed to go to The Curtain with Grace this very afternoon. Do not make me disappoint her.'

'Tell Mistress Napier you are unable to go. And urge her, on a point of moral principle, not to attend the theatre herself.'

'Father, we both *want* to go there.'

'Playgoing is banned forthwith.'

'Why?'

'Because I would have it so,' he declared.

Before she could argue any further, he waddled out of the room and closed the door behind him. Isobel seethed with annoyance. Her father seemed to prohibit all the things in life that were really pleasurable. The need to maintain his dignity in the eyes of his peers was a burden on the whole family but especially on her. It imposed quite intolerable restraints on a young woman who craved interest and excitement. Isobel Drewry was trapped. She was still in a mood of angry dejection when a servant showed in Grace Napier.

The newcomer was attired with discreet elegance and brought a delicate fragrance into the room. Something had put a bloom in her cheeks. Grace Napier was positively glowing.

'Master Hoode has sent a poem to me, Isobel.'

'Written by himself?'

'No question but that it is. A love sonnet.'

'You have made a conquest, Grace!'

'I own that I am flattered.'

'It is no more than you deserve,' said Isobel with a giggle. 'But show it me, please. I must see these fourteen lines of passion.'

'It is beautifully penned,' said Grace, handing over a scroll.

'The work of some scrivener, I vow.'

'No, Isobel. It is Master Hoode's own hand.'

Shrugging off her own problems, Isobel shared in her friend's delight. She read the poem with growing admiration. It was written by a careful craftsman and infused with the spirit of true love. Isobel was puzzled by the rhyming couplet which concluded the sonnet.

> 'To hear the warbling poet sing his fill,
> Observe the curtained shepherd on the hill.'

'It is a reference to *Cupid's Folly*,' explained Grace. 'He takes the part of a shepherd at The Curtain this afternoon.'

'A pretty conceit and worthy of a kiss.'

'See how he plays with both our names in the first line.'

'"My hooded eyes will never fall from grace",' quoted Isobel. 'And watch how he rhymes "Napier" with "rapier". Your swain is fortunate that it was not *I* who bewitched him.'

'You?'

'He could not tinker so easily with "Isobel". And I defy him to find a pleasing rhyme for "Drewry". I will not suffer "jury" or "fury".'

'You forget "brewery".'

They laughed together then Isobel handed the scroll back. She was thrilled on her friend's behalf. It was always exciting to attract the admiration of a gentleman but to enchant a poet gave special satisfaction. Like her, Grace Napier was not yet ready to consign herself to marriage and so was free to amuse herself with happy dalliance.

Envy competed with pleasure in Isobel's fair breast.

'I wish that I could take an equal part in your joy.'

'And so you shall, Isobel. Let us go to The Curtain.'

'It must remain undrawn for me, Grace.'

'Why so?'

'My father keeps me from the theatre.'

'On what compulsion?'

'His stern command.'

'Does he give reason?'

'He would not have me corrupted by knavery or drag his good name down by being seen at the playhouse.'

'These are paltry arguments.'

'Does not your father say the like?'

'Word for word,' replied Grace. 'I nod and curtsey in his presence then follow my inclination when he is gone. Life is too short to have it marred by a foolish parent.'

'You speak true!' said Isobel with spirit.

'I would see my warbling poet this afternoon.'

'Then so will I.'

'And if you cannot disobey your father?'

'What must I do?'

'Mask your true intention.'

Grace Napier lifted up the feathered mask that hung from a ribbon at her wrist. Placing it over her own face, Isobel Drewry giggled in triumph. It was a most effective disguise and would hide her from any Aldermanic wrath. She thanked her friend with a peck on the cheek. Of the two, Isobel was by far the more extrovert and assertive. Not for the first time, however, it was the quiet Grace who turned out to have the stronger sense of purpose.

Cupid's Folly was an ideal choice for The Curtain. On a bright summery afternoon, a pastoral comedy was much more acceptable to an audience that tended to be unruly if it was not sufficiently entertained. Dances and swordplay were the favoured ingredients at The Curtain, and Westfield's Men could offer both in abundance. Barnaby Gill was primed to do no less than four of his jigs and there were several comic duels to punctuate the action. Still jangled by their experience at the Queen's Head, the company could relax slightly now. *Cupid's Folly* was harmless froth.

'Is my cap straight, Nick?' asked Edmund Hoode.

'Too straight for any shepherd.'

'And now?' said the other, adjusting its angle.

'It is perfect. But do not shake so or the cap will fall off.'

'There is no help for it.'

'What frights you, Edmund?'

'It is not fear.'

Nicholas understood and left the matter tactfully alone. He had seen the subtle changes that Hoode's role underwent during the rehearsal. Flowery verse had been introduced into his speeches. Deep sighs were now everywhere. The lovelorn shepherd explored the outer limits of sorrow. The part had been cleverly reworked. It was Youngthrust in a sheepskin costume.

'Let's you and I speak together,' said Hoode.

'At your leisure, Edmund.'

'When the play is done?'

'And I am finished here.'

The book holder moved off to make a final round of the tiring-house before calling the actors to order. It was almost time to begin. There was the usual mixture of nervousness and exhilaration.

They had a full audience with high expectations. It would be another day of glory for Westfield's Men—and not a devil in sight!

Barnaby Gill marshalled the womenfolk in the play.

'Kiss me on the forehead in the first scene, Martin.'

'Yes, master,' said Martin Yeo.

'And do not fiddle with my beard this time. Dick?'

'Master Gill?'

'Be more sprightly in our dance. Toss your hands thus.'

Richard Honeydew nodded as the actor demonstrated what he meant.

'As for you, Stephen, do sweeten your song.'

'Am I too low, master?' asked Stephen Judd.

'Indeed, yes. You are a shepherdess, sir, and not a bear in torment. Do not bellow so. Sing softly. Please the ear.'

'I will try, Master Gill.'

The three apprentices made very convincing females in their skirts, bodices, and bonnets. Young, slender and well-trained in all the arts of impersonation, they were skilful performers who added to the lustre of the company's work. *Cupid's Folly* made no real demands on them. All three took the roles of country wenches who were pursued in vain by the diseased and doddering Rigormortis. Pierced by Cupid's arrow in the opening scene, the old man fell in love with every woman he saw and yet, ironically, spurned the one female who loved him. This was Ursula, a rural termagant, fat, ugly and slothful but relentless in her wooing. She chased the object of her desire throughout the play and finally bore off the reluctant groom across her shoulders.

Barnaby Gill luxuriated in the part of Rigormortis. Apart from giving him the chance to display his full comic repertoire, it allowed him a fair amount of licensed groping on stage, particularly of Richard Honeydew, the youngest, prettiest and most tempting of the apprentices. Gill's proclivities were no secret to Westfield's Men and they were tolerated because of his talent, but there was a tacit agreement that he would not seduce any of the boys into his strange ways. He had to look outside the company for such sport. *Cupid's Folly* did not abrogate that rule but it gave his fantasies some scope.

'How do I look, Master Gill?'

'God's blood!'

'Am I ill-favoured enough, sir?'

'You would frighten the eye of a tiger!'

'When shall I kiss you on stage?'

'As little as possible.'

The lantern-jawed John Tallis had been padded out as Ursula and fitted with a long, bedraggled wig of straw-coloured hue. Cosmetics had turned an already unappealing face into a grotesque one. The thought of being embraced by such a hideous creature made Gill shiver.

'Oh, the sacrifices that I make for my art!'

'Shall I practise carrying you?' said Tallis helpfully.

'Forbear!'

'I only strive to please, master.'

'Then keep your distance.'

The voice of Nicholas Bracewell now stilled the hubbub.

'Stand by, sirs!'

The play was about to start. During its performance, Nicholas ruled the tiring-house. In spite of his leading role, Barnaby Gill was subservient to him. Even Lawrence Firethorn, cast as a frolicsome lord of the manor, acknowledged his primacy. Actors had their hour upon the stage. Behind it—where so much frenetic activity took place—the book holder held sway. The audience would see *Cupid's Folly* as a riotous comedy that bowled along at high speed but it was also a complicated technical exercise with countless scene changes, costume changes, entrances and exits. It needed the controlling hand of a Nicholas Bracewell.

The trumpet sounded above and they were away.

After the shortcomings of the Queen's Head, playing at The Curtain was a pure delight. Located in Shoreditch, it was a tall, purpose-built, circular structure of stout timber. Three storeys of seating galleries jutted out into a circle and this perimeter area was roofed with thatch. Open to the sky, the central space was dominated by an apron stage that thrust out into the pit. High, handsome and rectangular, it commanded the attention of the whole playhouse. At the rear of the acting area was a large canopy supported on heavy pillars that came up through the stage. The smooth inner curve of the arena was broken by a flat wall, at each end of which was a door. Directly behind the wall was the tiring-house.

The place was a superb amphitheatre with attributes that the Queen's Head could never offer. There was an additional bonus. It had no Alexander Marwood. There was no prevailing atmosphere of gloom, no long-faced landlord to depress and inhibit them. The Curtain was a theatre designed expressly for the presentation of plays. It conferred status on the actors and their craft.

> Come, friends, and let us leave the city's noise
> To seek the quieter paths of country joys.
> For verdant pastures more delight the eye
> With cows and sheep and fallow deer hereby,
> With horse and hound, pursuing to their lair
> The cunning fox or nimble-footed hare,
> With merry maids and lusty lads most jolly
> Who find their foolish run in Cupid's folly.

The opening words of the Prologue set the tone admirably. When Barnaby Gill danced on stage to music, he was given a warm welcome. The audience knew where they were and liked what they saw. Rigormortis was quite irresistible. It was a performance of verbal dexterity, visual brilliance and superb comic timing. As the play progressed, it grew in stature. Each new love affair brought further complications and Gill milked the laughter with practiced assiduity.

Firethorn shone, too, as the lively Lord Hayfever but it was only a supporting role for once. The three apprentices made wonderful, nubile shepherdesses and John Tallis was an immediate success as the daunting Ursula. Nor was the romantic theme neglected. Edmund Hoode wallowed in a pit of poetic anguish and the female section of the audience was visibly touched. Watching from her cushioned seat in the gallery, Isobel Drewry was almost in tears as the lovesick shepherd bewailed his plight. Many of his lines seemed to be directed straight at Grace Napier and she herself was moved by the ardour of his appeal. The more she got to know of Hoode, the more fond of him she became but it was an affection that was tinged with sadness. He was so ready to commit himself wholeheartedly while Grace felt something holding her back.

Lord Westfield and his cronies preened themselves in their privileged seating and led the laughter at the wit and wordplay.

They were particularly diverted by a special effect that had been suggested by Nicholas Bracewell. It came in a scene that was set in the garden of Lord Hayfever's house and which featured a large conical beehive. The amorous Rigormortis was paying his unwanted attentions to Dorinda, the winsome shepherdess. Refusing to be deflected by her protestations, he pursued her with such vigour around the beehive that his elbow knocked it over. A swarm of bees burst forth—a handful of black powder tossed covertly in the air by Gill himself—and angry buzzing sounds were made by members of the company secreted beneath the stage. Stung in a dozen tender places, Rigormortis ran and jumped his way off-stage with a series of yelps and cries that made the audience rock with mirth.

Lord Westfield turned to his nephew to share a joke.

'Where the bee stings, there sting I!'

'The fellow will not sit for a week,' said Francis Jordan.

'He should not have courted the queen of the hive.'

'Queen, uncle?'

'That shepherdess is young *Honey*dew!'

'Well-buzzed, I say!'

They watched the stage as fresh merriment arrived.

Cupid's Folly was always popular with the company but they found another reason to like it that afternoon. It healed their wounds. It blotted out the dark memory of *The Merry Devils*. It restored their shattered morale and put new zest into their playing. A glorious romp and an appreciative audience. Westfield's Men were wholly revived. Fear no longer lapped at the back of their minds. They were almost home and dry. Then came the final scene.

To end on a note of rural festivity, the playwright had contrived a dance around a huge maypole. Slotted into a hole in the middle of the stage, it looked as solid and upright as the mainmast of a ship. The countryfolk held a ribbon apiece and tripped around the pole to weave intricate patterns. Music drifted down from the gabled attic room where Peter Digby and his musicians were stationed. It was an engaging sight. Colour and movement entranced the spectators.

At the height of the dance, there was a sudden intrusion.

Rigormortis had been rejected by the three shepherdesses and driven away from the area. He now came sprinting back on to the village green with the panting Ursula on his tail. Fresh gales of laughter were produced by the elaborate chase sequence. Unable to outrun his pursuer, Rigormortis took refuge in the one place where she could not follow him—at the top of the pole. With great nimbleness, he shinned up the maypole and clung to it for dear life. Ursula pawed the ground below and yelled at him to come down.

Her command was obeyed instantly.

There was a loud crack and the pole split in two at a point only a few feet below the old man. Barnaby Gill lost his high eminence and dropped like a stone, landing heavily but rolling over immediately to get back to his feet. John Tallis gaped.

'Carry me out!' hissed Gill.

'What, master?'

'Over your shoulder, boy!'

Ursula did as she was told and bore Rigormortis offstage to a resounding cheer. The action had been so swift and continuous that it seemed like a rehearsed part of the play. When Barnaby Gill reappeared to take his bow with the company, he was given an ovation. His fall from the maypole had been as dramatic as it had been comic.

He bowed graciously and smiled expansively but Nicholas Bracewell was not deceived. Blood was seeping through the sleeve of Gill's costume and the man was clearly in pain. The maypole was hewn from old English oak and would never snap of its own accord. Nicholas decided that it had been sawn almost through by someone who concealed his handiwork beneath the coloured ribboning that swathed the pole. Rigormortis was meant to fall from the top. He could have been seriously injured.

Westfield's Men evidently had a dangerous enemy.

Margery Firethorn clucked solicitously over the patient like a mother hen.

'Dear, dear! There, there! How now, sir?'

'I believe I will recover,' said Gill wearily.

'Would you care for some wine?' she asked.

'No, thank you.'

'Some ale, then? Some other beverage of your choice?'

'I could touch nothing in my present state, Margery.'

'You suffer much in the cause of your profession, sir.'

'It is needful.'

'Is there pain still?'

'Sufficient.'

He winced and set off another round of maternal clucking.

Barnaby Gill was making the most of it. A surgeon had been called to dress the wound in his arm then he had been brought back to Firethorn's house because of its proximity to the theatre. Apart from the small gash which had produced the blood, he had sustained only a few bruises and abrasions. Reclining in a chair, he had now got over the accident but he did not tell that to Margery Firethorn. He was enjoying far too much the chance to exploit her gushing sympathy.

'Did the surgeon give you physic, Barnaby?' she said.

'He prescribed rest, that is all.'

'Call on us, sir. Your needs will be provided.'

'I value that kindness.'

'Do not fear to ask for anything.'

'I will not, Margery.'

'If you wish to stay here, a bed can be found.'

'That will not be necessary, my angel,' said Firethorn, butting in on the conversation because he was no longer the centre of attention in his own house. 'It is only Barnaby's arm that is grazed, my dove. His legs are still sturdy enough to carry him back to his lodging. Besides, he has too much pride to impose on us.'

Gill shot him a hurt look. He was not so enamoured of Margery as to seek her hospitality for a few days but he relished the idea of sleeping under the same roof as the four apprentices and having the opportunity to play on their sympathies. His invitation had now been summarily cancelled by his host.

Margery Firethorn shifted her interest to the accident.

'How came that maypole to break in such a manner?'

'Act of God,' said Gill ruefully.

'Of the devil, you mean,' corrected Firethorn. 'Someone had cut through the oak to weaken it. Nick Bracewell showed me how it was done.'

'Master Bracewell must bear some of the blame,' said Gill sourly. 'It is his job to check that all our properties and stage furniture are safe. There has been laxity.'

'He saw the maypole do its duty during the rehearsal,' said Firethorn. 'Nick found it secure enough then. He did not realise that it was later tampered with by some villain.'

'My life was put at risk, Lawrence. He should be upbraided.'

'He has already upbraided himself.'

'This calls for a stern warning from you.'

'I'll be the judge of that, Barnaby.'

'If it was left to me, I'd dismiss the fellow.'

'Oh, no!' exclaimed Margery.

'I would sooner dismiss myself,' said Firethorn. 'Nick has no peer among book holders and I have known dozens. Westfield's Men owe him an enormous debt.'

'I do not share that sense of obligation, Lawrence.'

Barnaby Gill had always disliked the book holder, resenting the way that he took on more and more responsibility in the company. He could not bear to see Nicholas being treated like a sharer when the latter was only a hired man.

'You involve him too much in our councils.'

'Thank goodness I do. He has saved us many a time.'

'He did not save me up that maypole.'

'Nor was he the cause of your fall,' said Firethorn testily. 'Someone plotted your accident and only Nick Bracewell will be able to find out who it is. We need him more than ever.'

'Besides,' said Margery fondly, 'he is a true gentleman.'

Gill snorted. Abandoning all hope of persuading them, he announced that he felt well enough to return to his own lodging. He pretended that he was still in intense pain but said he would endure it with Stoic demeanour rather than be a nuisance to them. Margery pressed him to stay but her husband countermanded the offer.

'Go early to your bed, Barnaby.'

'I may not leave it for days.'

'We have another performance tomorrow. Be mindful.'

'Today's play still weighs upon me, sir.'

'We'll find the culprit,' said Firethorn confidently.

'Some minion employed by Banbury's Men no doubt.'

'Or some viper within our own circle.'

'What's that?'

'He has been the villain all along.'

'Who, Lawrence?'

'He hacked through that maypole by way of farewell.'

'Tell us his name,' said Margery.

'Willoughby.'

'Ralph Willoughby?'

'I can think of no man more likely,' he said gravely. 'Damn the fellow! He knew the action of the play and at what point in it he could most damage us. Yes, I see the humour of it now. Willoughby was mortally wounded when I dismissed him from the company. We saw the extent of his anger this afternoon in that foul crime. It was his revenge.'

Life as the book holder of Westfield's Men was highly exacting at all times. Nicholas Bracewell was always the first to arrive and the last to leave. Having set everything up for the morning's rehearsal, he now supervised the withdrawal from the theatre. They would not be playing at The Curtain again for a couple of weeks and all their scenery, costumes and properties had to be safely transported back to the room at the Queen's Head where it was kept. As well as co-ordinating the efforts of his men, Nicholas had yet again to find some means to lift their spirits. The accident with the maypole had plunged them back into despair. First with *The Merry Devils* and now *Cupid's Folly*, they had suffered a disaster that was not of their own making. It was unnerving.

'Shall we ever be free of these uncanny happenings?'

'No question but that we shall.'

'I am anxious, Master Bracewell.'

'Overcome your anxiety.'

'It is too great, sir.'

'Fight it, George. Strive to better it.'

'Roper thinks that Satan has set his cloven hoof upon us.'

'Roper Blundell has a wild imagination.'

'He was sober when he spoke.'

'Sober or drunk, he is not to be heeded.'

'Then who *did* attack us today, master?'

'I have no answer to that,' admitted Nicholas, 'but this I do know. There was sawdust in the tiring-house where the maypole was kept before it was used. Some person cut through that solid oak when the place was unattended. Satan would have no need of such careful carpentry. He could have split the pole at his will.'

'And may yet do that!'

George Dart was desolate. Spared the ordeal of an acting role in *Cupid's Folly*, he and Roper Blundell did make an appearance on stage when they set up the maypole. In carrying it on, they unwittingly assisted in the downfall of Barnaby Gill and it preyed on them. Nicholas tried to reassure the assistant stagekeeper but Dart was inconsolable. There had been two calamities on stage already.

'When will the third strike us, Master Bracewell?'

'We must ensure that it does not.'

George Dart shrugged helplessly and trudged off. He and Roper Blundell left the theatre together, companions in misery. Their lowly position in the company made their jobs thankless enough at the best of times. Now they were being put on the rack as well. Neither would survive another devil or a second broken maypole.

After a final tour to check that all was in order, Nicholas came out of the playhouse himself. He was just in time to witness a brief but affectionate leavetaking. Two young ladies, dressed in their finery, were parting company with Edmund Hoode. Both were attractive but one had the more startling beauty. Yet he ignored her completely. Transfixed by the quieter charms of the other, he took her proffered hand and laid a tender kiss upon it, blushing in the ecstasy of the moment. The women raised their masks to their faces then sailed gracefully off to the carriage that was waiting for them. Hoode watched until the vehicle rattled away down Holywell Lane.

Nicholas strolled across to his still-beaming friend.

'You wanted to speak with me, Edmund.'

'Did I?'

'We arranged to meet when my work was done.'

'Ah, yes,' said Hoode, clutching at a vague memory. 'Forgive me, Nicholas. My mind is on other matters.'

'Let us turn our feet homeward.'

They walked in silence for a long while. Suppressing his natural curiosity, Nicholas made no mention of what he had just witnessed. If his companion wished to discuss the subject, he would raise it. For his part, Hoode was torn between the need for discretion and the urge to confide. He wanted both to keep and share his secret. Nicholas was a close friend who always showed tact and understanding. It was this consideration which finally made Hoode blurt out his confession.

'I am in love!'

'The possibility occurred to me,' said Nicholas wryly.

'Yes, I wear my heart on my sleeve. It was ever thus.'

'Who is the young lady?'

'The loveliest creature in the world!'

It was a description that Edmund Hoode used rather often. Drawn into a series of unsuitable and largely unproductive love affairs, he had the capacity to put each failure behind him and view his latest choice with undiminished wonder. It was the triumph of hope over cynicism. Hoode was indeed a true romantic.

'Her name is Grace Napier,' he said proudly.

'It becomes her well.'

'Did you not see that eye, that lip, that cheek?'

'I was struck at once by her qualities.'

'Grace is without compare.'

'Of good family, too, I would judge.'

'Her father is a mercer in the City.'

Nicholas was duly impressed. The Mercers' Company included some of the wealthiest men in London. Merchants who dealt in fine textiles, they gained their royal charter as early as 1394 and were now so well-established and respected that they came first in order of precedence at the annual Lord Mayor's Banquet. If Grace Napier were the daughter of a mercer, she would want for nothing.

'How did you meet her?' asked Nicholas.

'She is bedazzled by the theatre and never tires of watching plays. Westfield's Men have impressed her most.'

'And you have been the most impressive of Westfield's Men.'

'Yes!' said Hoode with delight. 'She singled me out during *Double Deceit*. Is that not a miracle?'

'*Double Deceit* is one of your best plays, Edmund.'

'Grace admired my performance in it as well.'

'You always excel in parts you tailor for yourself.'

'Her brother approached me,' continued Hoode, 'and told me how much they had enjoyed my work. I was then introduced to Grace herself. Her enthusiasm touched me to the core, Nick. We authors have poor reward for our pains but she made all my efforts worthwhile. I loved her for her interest and our friendship has grown from that time on.'

Nicholas was touched as he listened to the full story and could not have been more pleased on the other's behalf. Hoode had a fatal tendency to fall for women who—for some reason or another—were quite unattainable and his ardour was wasted in a fruitless chase. Grace Napier was of a different order. Young, unmarried and zealous in her playgoing, she was learning to welcome his attentions and thanked him warmly for the sonnet she inspired. The luck which eluded the playwright for so long had at last come his way.

'And who was that other young lady, Edmund?'

'*What* other young lady?'

The point was taken. Nicholas withdrew his enquiry. After letting his friend unpack his heart about Grace, he tried to guide him back to the reason that had brought them together on their walk. Shoreditch had now become Bishopsgate Street. Through a gap between two houses, they could see cows grazing in the distance.

'Why did you seek me out?' said Nicholas.

'Why else but to talk of Grace?'

'You had some other purpose, I fancy.'

'Oh.' Hoode's face clouded. 'I had forgot.'

As the conversation took on a more serious tone, they stopped in their tracks. Neither of them noticed that they were standing outside Bedlam. Nor did they guess that something which might have an important bearing on their own lives was going on behind its locked doors. The hospital was simply a backdrop to their exchange.

'It is Ralph Willoughby,' said Hoode.

'What of him?'

'I need his help with *The Merry Devils*.'

'But he has been outlawed by Master Firethorn.'

'That will not deter me.'

There was a defiant note in his voice but a question in his raised eyebrow. He was ready, of course, to disregard a major decision taken by Lawrence Firethorn. What he needed to know was whether or not Nicholas would support him in his action.

'I'll not betray you, Edmund.'

'Thank you.'

'Ralph was not well-treated by us,' said Nicholas. 'I've no quarrel with him and would be glad of his advice about the play.'

'He wrote that scene and only he should alter its course.'

'I accept that.'

'It would be wrong to proceed without him.'

'Work together in private and nobody will be the wiser.'

'I am vexed by a problem, Nick.'

'Of what nature?'

'There is no sign of Ralph.'

'You have been to his lodging?'

'He has not slept there for nights,' said Hoode. 'I can gain no clue as to his whereabouts. That is why I came to you for some counsel. Ralph Willoughby has vanished from London.'

The house in Knightrider Street was a large, lackadaisical structure whose half-timbered frontage sagged amiably forwards. Through the open window on the first floor came the rich aroma of a herbal compound, only to lose its independence as it merged with the darker pungencies of the street. A face appeared briefly at the window and a small quantity of liquid was dispatched from a bowl. It fell to the cobbled surface below and sizzled for a few seconds before spending itself in a mass of bubbles. The face took itself back into the chamber.

Evening shadows obliged Doctor John Mordrake to work by candlelight. Up in the cluttered laboratory with its array of weird charts and bizarre equipment, its learned tomes and its herbal remedies, he crouched low over a table and used a pestle and mortar to pound a reddish substance into a fine powder. There was an intensity about him which suggested remarkable concentration and he was not deflected in the least by any of the harsh sounds that bombarded him through the window. He had created his own peculiar world around him and it was complete in itself.

Mordrake was a big man who had been made smaller by age and by inclination. His shoulders were round, his spine curved, his legs unequal to the weight placed upon them. Time had cruelly redrawn the lines on his visage to make it seem smaller and less open than it was. Long, lank, sliver-grey hair further reduced the size of his face, which terminated in a straggly beard. He wore a black gown and black buckled shoes. A chain of almost mayoral pretension hung around his neck and gold rings enclosed several of his skinny fingers.

Old, tired, even ravaged, Doctor John Mordrake yet conveyed a sense of power. There was an inner strength that came from the possession of arcane knowledge, a glow of confidence that came from a surging intellect. Here was an ordinary man in touch with the extraordinary, an astrologer who could foretell the future, an alchemist who could manipulate the laws of nature, a cunning wizard who could speak to the dead in their own language. Mordrake was an intercessory between one life and the next. It gave him a luminescent quality.

Footsteps creaked on the oak stairs outside and there was a knock on the door. The servant showed in a visitor, bowed humbly and shuffled out. Mordrake did not even look up at the satin-clad gallant who had called on him and who now stood tentatively near the door. The old man worked patiently away and a thin smile flitted across his lips.

'Good evening, sir. I thought you would come again.'

'Did you so?' said the visitor.

'I have been expecting you for days.'

'Have you?'

'We both know what brings you to Knightrider Street.'

'I am afraid, sir.'

Ralph Willoughby had come to talk about devils.

Chapter Five

Bankside was anathema to the Puritans. It was the home of all that was lewd and licentious and most of them sedulously avoided its fetid streets and lanes. Isaac Pollard was a rare exception. Instead of shunning the area, he frequently sought it out on the grounds that it was best to measure the strength of an enemy whom you wished to destroy. He hated his journeys through the narrow passages of Bankside but they always yielded some recompense. New outrages were found on each visit. They served to consolidate his faith and to make him continue his mission with increased vigour. If London were to be purged of sin, this was the place to start.

Pollard belonged to the hard core of activists in the Puritan fold. Although there were no more than a few hundred of them, they were powerful, well-organised and fearless in the pursuit of their cause. With influential backing in high places, they could on occasion exert strong pressure. Their avowed aim was to remodel the Church of England on Calvinist or Presbyterian lines, introducing a greater simplicity and cutting away what they saw as the vestigial remains of Roman Catholicism. But the Puritan zealots did not rest there. They wanted everyone to live the life of a true Christian, observing a strict moral code and abjuring any pleasures.

It was this aspect of their ministry that brought Isaac Pollard for another walk in the region of damnation that evening. In his plain, dark attire with its white ruff, he was an incongruous figure among the gaudy gallants and the swaggering soldiers. From beneath his black hat, he scowled fiercely at all and sundry.

Believing that integrity was its own protection, he nevertheless carried a stout walking stick with him to beat off any rogues or pickpockets. Pollard was more than ready to strike a blow in the name of the Lord.

A group of revellers tumbled noisily out of a tavern ahead of him and leaned against each other for support. Laughing and belching, they made their way slowly towards him and jeered when they recognised what he was. Pollard bravely stood his ground as they brushed past, hurling obscenities at him and his calling. Even in the foul stench of the street, he could smell the ale on their breaths.

It was a brief but distressing incident. When he came to the next corner, however, he saw something much more appalling than a gang of drunken youths. Huddled in the shadow of a doorway down the adjacent lane, a man was molesting a woman. He had lifted her skirts up and held her in a firm embrace. Pollard could not see exactly what was going on but he heard her muffled protests. Raising his stick, he advanced on the wrongdoer and yelled a command.

'Unhand that lady, sir!'

'I fart at thee!' roared the man.

'Leave go of her or I will beat you soundly.'

'Let a poor girl earn her living!' shrieked the woman.

'Can I not help you?' said Pollard.

She answered the question with such a barrage of abuse that he went puce. Now that he was close enough to realise what they were doing, he was mortified. Far from protesting, the woman had been urging her client on to a hotter carnality. The last thing she needed during her transaction was the interference of a Puritan.

'A plague upon you!' she howled.

'Cast out your sins!' he retaliated.

'Will you have me draw my sword?' warned the other man.

As a fresh burst of vituperation came from the woman, Pollard backed away then strode off down the street. Within only a short time of his arrival in Bankside, he had enough material for an entire sermon. There was worse to come. His steps now took him along Rose Alley, past the jostling elbows of the habitués and beneath the dangling temptation of the vivid inn signs. Crude sounds of jollity hammered at his ears then something loomed up to capture all his attention. It was London's newest theatre—the Rose. Built on the site of a former rose garden in the Liberty of the Clink, it was of cylindrical shape, constructed around a timber frame on a brick foundation. To the crowds who flocked there every day, it was a favourite place of recreation.

To Isaac Pollard, it was a symbol of corruption.

As his anger made the single eyebrow rise and fall like rolling waves, he caught sight of a playbill that was stuck on a nearby post. It advertised one of the companies due to perform at The Rose in the near future.

Westfield's Men—in *The Merry Devils*.

Pollard tore down the poster with vicious religiosity.

'What you tell me is most curious and most interesting, Master Willoughby.'

'Yet you do not seem surprised.'

'Nor am I, sir.'

'You *knew* that this would happen?'

'I entertained the possibility.'

'But you gave me no forewarning.'

'That was not what you paid me to do.'

Doctor John Mordrake was a man of encyclopaedic knowledge and sound commercial sense. Having devoted his life to his studies, he was going to profit from them in order to buy the books or the equipment that would help him to advance the frontiers of his work. He dealt with the highest and the lowest in society, providing an astonishing range of services, but he always set a price on what he did.

Ralph Willoughby was conscious of this fact. He knew that his visit to Knightrider Street would be an expensive one. Mordrake's time could not be bought cheaply and he had already listened for half-an-hour to the outpourings of his caller. Willoughby, however, had reached the point where he was prepared to spend anything to secure help. Doctor John Mordrake was his last hope, the one man who might pull him back from the abyss of despair that confronted him.

They sat face to face on stools. Mordrake watched him with an amused concern throughout. Most people who consulted him came in search of personal gain but Willoughby had wanted an adventure of the mind. That pleased Mordrake who sensed a kindred spirit.

'You were at Cambridge, I believe, Master Willoughby?'

'That is so, sir.'

'Which college?'

'Corpus Christi.'

'At what age did you become a student?'

'Seventeen.'

'That is late. I was barely fourteen when I went to Oxford.' The old man smiled nostalgically. 'It was an ascetic existence and I thrived on it. We rose at four, prayed, listened to lectures, prayed again, then studied by candlelight in our cold rooms. We conversed mostly in Latin.'

'As did we, sir. Latin and Hebrew.'

'Why did you leave the university?'

'Its dictates became irksome to me.'

'And you chose the *theatre* instead?' said Mordrake in surprise. 'You left academe to be among what Horace so rightly calls *mendici, mimi, balatrones, hoc genus omne?*'

'Yes,' said Willoughby with a wistful half-smile. 'I went to be among beggars, actors, buffoons and that class of persons.'

'In what did the attraction lie?'

'The words of Cicero.'

'Cicero?'

'*Poetarum licentiae liberoria.*'

'The freer utterance of the poet's licence.'

'That is what I sought.'

'And did you find it, Master Willoughby?'

'For a time.'

'What else did you find, sir?'

'Pleasure.'

'Cicero has spoken on that subject, too,' noted Mordrake with scholarly glee. '*Voluptas est illecebra turpitudinis.* Pleasure is an incitement to vileness.'

Willoughby fell silent and stared down at the floor. Though he was dressed with his usual ostentatious flair, he did not have the manner that went with the garb. His face was drawn, his jaw slack, his hands clasped tightly together. Mordrake could almost feel the man's anguish.

'How can I help you?' he said.

It was a full minute before the visitor answered. He turned eyes of supplication on the old man. His voice was a solemn whisper.

'Did I see a devil at the Queen's Head?'

'Yes.'

'How came it there?'

'At your own request, Master Willoughby.'

'But you told me it could not happen in daylight.'

'I said that it was *unlikely* but did not rule it out. The devil would not have come simply in answer to the summons in your play.'

'What brought it forth, then?'

'You did, sir.'

'How?'

'You have an affinity with the spirit world.'

Willoughby was rocked. His darkest fear was confirmed. Words that *he* had written raised up a devil. The apparition at the Queen's Head had come in search of him.

'You should have stayed at Cambridge,' said Mordrake sagely. 'You should have taken your degree and entered the Church. It is safer there. The duty of a divine is to justify the ways of God to man. Christianity gives answers. The duty of a poet is to ask questions. That can lead to danger. Religion is there to reassure. Art disturbs.'

'Therein lies its appeal.'

'I will not deny that.'

Mordrake pulled himself to his feet and shuffled across to a long shelf on the other side of the room. It was filled with large, dusty leather-bound volumes and he ran his fingers lightly across them.

'A lifetime of learning,' he said. 'For ten years, I travelled all over Europe. I worked in the service of the Count Palatine of Siradz, King Stephen of Poland, the Emperor Rudolph, and Count Rosenberg of Bohemia. Wherever I went, I searched for books on myth and magic and demonology. In Cologne, I found the most important work of them all.' He took down a massive volume and brought it across. 'Do you know what this is?'

'*Malleus Malleficarum?*'

'Yes,' replied Mordrake, clutching the book to his chest like a mother cradling a child. '*Hexenhammer*, as it is sometimes called. The *Hammer of Witches*. First printed in 1486. Written by two Dominicans from Germany. Jakob Sprenger and Heinrich Kramer, scholars of great worth and reputation.' He sat on the stool again. 'It is a wondrous tome.'

'Can it help me, Doctor Mordrake?'

'It can help any man.'

'Truly, sir?'

'Here is the source of all enlightenment.'

Ralph Willoughby touched the book with a reverential hand before looking up to search his companion's grey eyes. Hope and apprehension mingled in his breathless enquiry.

'Will it save my soul?'

Westfield Hall was a vast, rambling mansion set in the greenest acres of Hertfordshire. From a distance, it looked more like a medieval hamlet than a single house, being a confused mass of walls, roofs and chimneys on differing levels. It presented to the world a black and white face that glowed in the afternoon sun beneath hair of golden thatch. The house was as splendid and dramatic as its owner, with a hint of Lord Westfield's paunch in its sagging eaves and a reflection of his capricious nature in its riotous angles.

Francis Jordan stayed long enough to feel a twinge of envy then he turned his head away. Spurring his horse, he went on past Westfield Hall for half a mile or so and came to a long, wooded slope. His bay mare took him through the trees at a steady canter until they reached a clearing. A sturdy man in rough attire was carrying a wooden pail of water towards a small cottage. Jordan brought his mount to a sudden halt and directed a supercilious stare at the man. Instead of the deferential nod that he expected, he was given a bold glance of hostility. Jordan fumed. His horse felt the spurs once again.

When he emerged from the woods and got to the top of the ridge, he reined in the animal once more. From his vantage point, he gazed down at the dwelling in the middle distance. Parkbrook House was true to its name. Set in rolling parkland, it was almost encircled by a fast-running brook that snaked its way through the grass. The house was built of stone and replete with high casements. With its E-shaped design, it was more austere and symmetrical than Westfield Hall and could lay claim to none of the latter's antiquity, but it still did not suffer by comparison in the mind of Francis Jordan. There was a unique quality about Parkbrook House that lifted it above any other property in the county.

It was his.

As soon as he began to ride down the hill, he was spotted. By the time Jordan arrived, an ostler was waiting to help him dismount and take care of his horse. The steward was standing nearby.

'Welcome, master!' he said with formal enthusiasm.

'Thank you, Glanville,'

'All is ready for your inspection.'

'I should hope so, sir.'

'They have worked well in your absence.'

Joseph Glanville was a tall, impassive, dignified man of forty. As steward of the household, he had power, privilege and control over its large staff of servants. He was dressed with a restrained smartness that was made to look dull beside the colourful apparel of his master. Over his grey satin doublet and breeches, Glanville wore a dark gown that all but trailed on the ground. A small, tricornered hat rested on his head and his chain of office was worn proudly. He had been at Parkbrook House for some years and addressed his duties with the utmost seriousness.

'Take me in at once,' said Jordan peremptorily.

'Follow me, sir.'

The steward conducted him across the gravel forecourt and in through the main door. A group of male servants were standing in a line in the entrance hall and they bowed in unison as their master passed. Jordan was pleased and rewarded them with a condescending nod. He walked behind Glanville across the polished oak floor. When they reached the Great Hall, the steward stood aside to let him go in first.

Francis Jordan viewed the scene with a critical eye.

'I thought the work would be more advanced.'

'Craftsmanship of this order cannot be rushed, sir.'

'There is hardly any progress since my last visit.'

'Do not be misled by appearances.'

'I wanted results, Glanville!'

His barked annoyance caused everyone in the hall to stop what he was doing. The plasterers looked down from their scaffolding. The painters froze on their ladders. Carpenters working on the moulded beams held back their chisels and the masons at the far end of the room put down their hammers. Francis Jordan had wanted to redesign and redecorate the Great Hall so that it could become a focal point of his social life. As he strolled disconsolately over sheets of canvas, it seemed to him that the work was not only behind schedule but contrary to his specification. He swung round to face his steward.

'Glanville!'

'Yes, sir?'

'This is not good. It is less than satisfactory.'

'If I might be permitted to explain…'

'This is explanation enough,' said Jordan, waving an arm around. 'I looked to have the place finished ahead of time.'

'Problems arose, sir. Some materials were difficult to come by.'

'That is no excuse.'

'But the men are working to the very limit of their capacity. I can promise you that everything will be completed in a month.'

'A month! It must be ready in two weeks.'

'That is well-nigh impossible, master.'

'Then *make* it possible, sir!' snarled the other. 'Bring in more craftsmen. Let them work longer hours—through the night, if need be. I must and will have my Great Hall ready for the celebrations. I can wait no longer.'

'As you wish, sir,' said Glanville with a bow.

Jordan sauntered on down to the far end where the major alteration had occurred. A huge bay window had replaced the old wall and it allowed sunlight to flood in from the eastern aspect. As he shot a glance of reproof at them, the masons began to hammer away again in earnest. Jordan examined their work then looked back into the hall as if trying to come to a decision. He pointed a long finger.

'We will need the stage there, Glanville.'

'Stage, master?'

'A play will be performed at the banquet.'

'I understand, sir.'

'Westfield's Men will require a platform for their art.'

'They shall have it.'

Glanville bowed again, anxious not to incur any further displeasure. To be chastised so sharply in front of others was a blow to his self-esteem. He did not want to give his new master another chance to arraign him so openly. Joseph Glanville was a sensitive man.

'One last thing,' said Jordan.

'Yes, master?'

'I rode past a cottage in the woods.'

'Jack Harsnett lives there, sir.'

'Harsnett?'

'Your forester.'

'Dismiss him forthwith. I do not like the fellow.'

'But he has worked on the estate all his life.'

'He goes today.'

'For what offence, sir?'

'Incivility.'

'Jack Harsnett is a good forester,' said Glanville defensively. 'Times are hard for him just now, sir. His wife is grievously ill.'

'Clear the pair of them off my land!'

Francis Jordan brooked no argument. Having issued his command, he marched the full length of the Great Hall and stormed out. Glanville's face was as impassive as ever but his emotions had been stirred.

One of the carpenters came across for a furtive word.

'Here's a change for the worse!'

'We must wait and see,' said the steward tactfully.

'Jack Harsnett turned out. The old master would not have done it.'

'The old master is not here any longer.'

'More's the pity, say I!' The carpenter put the question that was on all their lips. 'Where *is* the old master, sir?'

'He has gone away.'

The hospital of St Mary of Bethlehem worked to an established routine. It could not be changed by one man, however much he might desire it. Kirk had been at Bedlam only a matter of days before he realised this. What he saw as the cruel and inhumane treatment of lunatics could not easily be remedied. Though he tried to show them more compassion himself, it did not always meet with their gratitude and he had been attacked more than once by impulsive patients. What distressed Kirk most was that he had himself reverted to the very behaviour he criticised in the other keepers. Bedlam was slowly brutalising him.

At the end of one week, he was given a new assignment by Rooksley. He was to take over the care of some of the patients who were locked away in private rooms and did not consort with the others. They were sad cases. One emaciated man was convinced that he was on the point of freezing to death. Even on the hottest days, when his face was running with sweat, he would lie in bed and shiver uncontrollably beneath the thick blanket. Kirk fed him on warm soup and tried to talk him out of his delusion.

Another of his charges was a querulous old woman, the wife of a wealthy glover. Her husband committed her because of her obsession. Barren throughout her life and now well past the age of childbirth, she believed that she was pregnant and feared that she was in imminent danger of bringing a black baby into the world. Kirk learned to humour her and promised not to tell her husband about her imagined affair with a handsome Negro.

But it was the young gentleman who most interested the keeper and engaged his sympathy. In the grim surroundings of Bedlam, the patient in the white shirt and the dark breeches still had an air of distinction. To all outward appearances, he was a normal, healthy, educated young person from a good family. Kirk was not told his name. All he knew was that the patient was incarcerated there by someone who paid a weekly rent and who stipulated that he was to come to no harm. He was supposed to be possessed by the Devil but Kirk saw little sign of this during his daily visits.

'Good morning!'

'Ah!' The man looked up with childlike happiness.

'I've brought you some food, my friend.'

'Oo!'

'Shall I sit down here beside you?'

Kirk lowered himself to the floor where the patient was sitting cross-legged. The young man had been humming a song. He could make noises of pleasure and pain but he was unable to form words properly. It did not seem to bother him. He had an amiable disposition.

Kirk lifted the plate from the tray across his lap.

'It's meat,' he said.

'Ah.'

'Warm and tasty to tempt the palate.'

'Ah.'

'Will you feed yourself today, my friend?'

The patient grinned and shook his head violently.

'Would you like me to help you again?'

There was frantic nodding. The young man inhaled the aroma of the meat and his grin broadened. He thrust his head forward.

'Open your mouth,' said Kirk.

The keeper offered him the first spoonful. It was a slow, methodical process. The young man liked to chew his meat for a long time before he swallowed it and the other had to be patient. Eventually, the meal was almost over. Kirk loaded the spoon for the last time and raised it to the young man's lips but the latter had had enough. Shaking his head to indicate this, he caught the spoon with the side of his jaw and knocked the meat down the inside of his shirt. It threw him into a panic.

'Ee! Ah!'

'Calm down, sir. I'll find it for you.'

'Yah! Oh! Nee!'

The patient grabbed his shirt and tore it open down to his navel. Three small pieces of meat were resting on his body and Kirk plucked them off at once. The young man gave a cry of relief.

'Leeches!' he said.

It was the first word that Kirk had ever heard him speak and it was an important one. The patient was afraid of leeches which had obviously been used on him in the course of some blood-letting treatment. Kirk was sorry for the distress that had been caused but grateful to have made a discovery. The young man could talk after all. It was a distinct advance and it was followed by another when the keeper glanced at the bare chest in front of him. Scratched across it in large, fading letters was a name.

David.

'Is that you?' he asked. 'Are you David?'

The young man looked down at his body as if seeing the letters for the first time. Using a finger, he traced each one very carefully and tried to work out what it was. When he finally succeeded, tears of joy rolled down his cheeks.

'David!' he said.

They had given him back his name.

Anne Hendrik could not bear to be idle. Though she had money enough to live a life of relative leisure, she preferred to keep herself busy and took an active part in the running of her husband's business. After initial resistance from her employees, she won them over with her acumen, her commitment and her willingness to learn every last detail about the art of hat-making. Anne Hendrik revealed herself to be a highly competent businesswoman—and she could even speak a fair amount of Dutch. There was another value to her work life. It gave her something to chat about with Nicholas Bracewell.

'And that is how Preben came to design the new style.'

'Has the hat found favour with your customers?' he said.

'We have had a number of orders already.'

They were in the little garden at the rear of the Bankside house. Nicholas was carrying a basket and Anne was cutting flowers to lay in it. Taking care not to prick herself on the thorns, she used her shears to snip through the stem of a red rose.

'But enough of my tittle-tattle,' she said briskly. 'What of Westfield's Men?'

'Happily, there is nothing to report.'

'The performance went off without incident?'

'Yes, Anne. No devil, no falling maypole, no accident of any kind.' Nicholas grimaced. 'With the exception of Master Marwood, that is. The fellow is devil, maypole and accident rolled into one.'

'What did you play this afternoon?'

'*The Knights of Malta*.'

'Did it give your landlord cause for complaint?'

'None at all,' he said. 'But he is yielding to other voices. The Puritans have written to him again and an Alderman called at the

Queen's Head to voice his disapproval. One Henry Drewry. We will weather this storm as we have weathered all the rest.'

'Has Master Gill recovered from his fall?' she asked.

'Completely, Anne, but he will not admit it. He still holds his shoulder at an angle and walks with that limp.'

They laughed at the actor's vanity. When the last of the flowers had been cut, they took them back into the house. Anne searched for a pot in which to stand them and looked forward to the supper she was about to share with him. Nicholas had a disappointment for her.

'I fear that I must soon leave you.'

'Why?'

'I have an appointment to keep in Eastcheap.'

'Eastcheap!' she echoed in mock annoyance. 'You prefer a tavern to my company, Master Bracewell? Things have changed indeed, sir!'

'You mistake my meaning, Anne.'

'What can Eastcheap offer but taverns and trugging-houses?'

'Nothing,' he agreed. 'And I intend to visit both.'

'Has it come to *this* between us?' she said in hurt tones.

'I do not go there on my own account.'

'Then why?'

'To find someone,' he explained. 'A wandering playwright. Ralph Willoughby has disappeared and we have need of him. I have left sundry messages at his lodging but to no avail. If he will not come to us, then I must go to him.'

'This news is softer on my ears.'

He slipped an arm familiarly around her waist and kissed her gently on the lips. Their friendship was very important to Nicholas and he would not trade it in for one wild night in Eastcheap. She saw him off at the door and urged him not to be too late. With quickening footsteps, he went off to begin his search.

A boat took him back across the river and he made his way to Eastcheap with all due haste. Ralph Willoughby was well-known in the area but he had scattered his patronage far and wide. The search could take Nicholas well into the night. Bracing himself, he began his journey at the White Hart and found himself the only sober human being on the premises. Willoughby was not there. Next came the Jolly Miller which also produced no missing playwright. The Royal Oak, the Lamb and Flag, even the Brazen

Serpent were unable to help. In each establishment, the revelry was loud and lascivious and he was pressed to stay by bawds of every kind. It was not difficult to refuse the entreaties.

Six more taverns had to be visited before he picked up a trail. A barmaid at the Bull and Butcher remembered seeing Willoughby earlier in the evening. There was a chance that he might still be there.

'Nell was always his favourite,' she said.

'Nell?'

She narrowed her eyes as she saw the hope of profit.

'How eager are you to find this friend of yours, sir?'

Nicholas gave her some coins. It was eagerness enough.

'Nell has a room upstairs,' she volunteered.

'Which one?'

'The first on the right, sir, and it has no bolt within.'

'Thank you, mistress.'

He pushed his way out of the crowded taproom to get clear of the noise and the stink of tobacco smoke. The staircase wound its way upwards and he followed its crooked steps. When he reached the passageway at the top, he paused at the first door on the right and tapped. There was no reply and so he used his knuckles more firmly.

'Who is it?' asked a crisp female voice.

'Nell?'

'Come in, sir,' she said, sounding a more girlish note.

Nicholas opened the door and stepped into a low, cramped chamber that had room for little more than the bed that stood against the window. Candles threw a begrudging light on the scene. Nell was a big, buxom young woman with a generous smile. Lying half-naked on the bed, she was pinned to it by the prostrate figure of Ralph Willoughby. He was still dressed and wheezing aloud in his sleep.

Nell was completely undaunted by the situation.

'You catch me incommoded, sir,' she said with a laugh. 'The poor fellow had more drink in him than desire. If you could shift his carcass off me, then I would be glad to oblige you in his stead.'

'How long as he been here?'

'An hour at least, sir. I dozed off myself to keep him company.'

'Come, let me relieve you of your burden.'

'I like not dead weight between my legs, sir.'

'Then let me extract him from you.'

He took hold of Willoughby beneath the armpits and lifted him off the bed. Lowering him into a sitting position on the floor, Nicholas shook him vigorously but could not wake him up. The playwright was in a complete stupor.

Nell rearranged herself into a more alluring pose.

'Drag him outside, sir, and return for his reward.'

'Alas, mistress, I am not able to take his place.'

'But you are the properer man of the two, I can tell.'

'I must needs take my friend home.'

'I did not know he *had* a home,' she observed. 'Unless it be up here. He spent last night in my arms and the one before. A stranger bedfellow I could not wish for, sir.'

'In what way?'

'Men love to talk of sin when they sup at my table. Yet when this one tasted my ware, he babbled of nothing but religion.'

'Religion?'

'Haply, I excited his spirit,' said Nell. 'But I did not mind this speech. It is all one to me. His bishop in a purple cap went neatly into my confessional box and stayed till he was excommunicate.'

Nicholas was amused by the metaphor and saw that she was no ordinary whore. Her ample frame and ready turn of phrase made her the particular choice of Ralph Willoughby. Whatever turmoil the playwright had been in, she had clearly helped him through it. Reaching into his purse, Nicholas handed her some money for her pains. Nell beamed her gratitude and leapt up off the bed to embrace him in a sensational bear-hug. He detached himself with difficulty and hauled Willoughby out into the passageway. Nell lolled in the doorway.

'Who is the poor creature?' she said.

'A good man fallen on bad times.'

'I know him only as Ralph who comes to take communion with me.'

'He is not fit for the service tonight, I fear.'

'That disappoints me, sir,' she sighed. 'When he was with me last, he made love as if the Devil was dancing on his buttocks.'

It was an apt image and more accurate than she realised.

Nicholas lifted him on to his feet then bent down to let the body fall across his shoulder. Waving a farewell to the irrepressible Nell he went carefully down the stairs so that he did not bang Willoughby's head against the wall.

Coming out into the street, he began the long, slow walk.

Edmund Hoode always worked best in the hours of darkness. When he was closeted in his lodging with no more than a candle and his writing materials, he could devote his full attention to the project in hand. There were far too many distractions during the day and he was, in any case, usually required for rehearsal or performance by the company. When night drew its black cloak around him, however, he came fully alive and his mind buzzed with creativity. As he sat over his table now, verse of surpassing excellence streamed through his brain but it was not part of some new play that he was writing. The inspiration and the object of his poetic impulse was Grace Napier.

She was perfection. As he reflected upon her virtues, he saw that she was the woman for whom he had been waiting all his life. She gave him purpose. She redeemed him. Compared with her, all the other women who had aroused his interest were nonentities, momentary distractions while he waited for his true love to come along. With those others, the chase had often been an end in itself. Consummation was rare and the certain conclusion of a relationship. Cupid was never kind to him. He had known much sadness between the sheets.

Grace Napier was different. She belonged to another order of being. He did not view her in terms of pursuit and conquest because that would demean her and drag her down from the lofty pedestal on which he had set her. All his thoughts now turned on one objective. Marriage to his beloved. In the headlong rush of his ardour, he did not stop to consider the practicalities of such a wild hope. The fact that he had no house to offer her, still less a high income to serve her demands, did not stay his fantasies. He would make any sacrifice for her even if it meant that he left the theatre. Edmund Hoode wanted nothing more than to devote his energies to the composition of odes to her beauty and sonnets in praise of her sweetness.

> I'll wrap my arms around your slender waist,
> My gracious love, I would not be dis-graced.

The lines sprang new-minted from his pen. He studied them on the vellum then rejected them for their banality. Grace deserved better. He killed the couplet with a slash of ink and turned to his Muse once more. Richer lines began to flow. Deeper resonances were sounded. Whenever he glanced up from his work, he saw Grace Napier on her pedestal, giving him that special smile which was poetry in itself.

Horror suddenly intruded. As he looked up at her once more, there was someone else beside her, an arresting figure with the arrogant grin of a practised voluptuary. Hoode recognised him at once.

It was Lawrence Firethorn.

An anxiety which had been at the back of his mind for days now thrust itself forward. Firethorn was a real threat. Dozens of beautiful young ladies were hypnotised by the tawdry glamour of the playhouse and were ready to surrender themselves to its ambiguous charms. Those who worshipped at the shrine of Westfield's Men inevitably tended to see Firethorn as their god. His bravura performances could not be matched by lesser players in smaller roles. Firethorn had no compunction about exploiting the adulation to the full. Swooning females were simply the spoils of war that fell to the victorious general and not even the vigilant eye of his wife, Margery, could stop him from exercising the age-old rites of soldiery. A few discerning acolytes—as Hoode liked to style them—had chosen him in place of the actor-manager. But he was seldom allowed to take advantage of their interest. Lawrence Firethorn had a distressing habit of stepping in and whisking the admirers—quite literally—out from under him.

That was not going to happen with Grace Napier.

> Stay close, my love, avoid the scorching fire,
> Prick not yourself upon that thorn's desire.

They were not lines to be sent to his loved one. Hoode would engrave them upon his own heart to act as a warning. Whatever else he did, he must not introduce Grace to the insatiable Lawrence Firethorn.

Further meditation was interrupted by a banging on the door. He went over to unbolt it then opened it wide. Nicholas Bracewell stood there with a familiar figure over his shoulder. Hoode was pleased.

'Ralph?'

'The whole weight of him.'

'Where did you find him?'

'I will tell you when I have lightened my load.'

Nicholas stepped into the room and lowered the body to the floor, sitting Willoughby up and resting his back against the wall. The slumbering playwright was still dead to the world.

'He was at the Bull and Butcher,' said Nicholas.

'Drink or fornication?'

'One prevented the other, Edmund.'

'He has burned the candle at both ends.'

'There is neither wax nor flame left.'

'Wake up, sir!' said Hoode, shaking his co-author.

'That will not rouse him,' said Nicholas, reaching for the jug on the table. 'Stand aside, I pray.'

With a swing of his arm, he dashed a few pints of cold water into Willoughby's face. The latter twitched, groaned, then spluttered. As he came out of his sleep, he opened an eye to blink at the world.

'Nell?'

'You are here among friends,' said Hoode.

'Edmund?' A second eye opened. 'Nicholas?'

'I fetched you from your revelry,' explained the book holder.

'We have need of you,' said Hoode. 'Our play is staged again.'

'I am no longer with the company, sir.'

'It requires your subtle hand.'

'Master Firethorn banished me.'

'This will not concern him,' said Hoode dismissively. 'We will work together privily. We are co-mates in this drama, Ralph, and I will not see you ousted. I must have your guidance with *The Merry Devils*.'

'Do not perform it again!'

'Rather let us make it *safe* for performance.'

'That is not within my power.'

'What do you mean?'

'It is not the play that holds the peril,' said Willoughby with quiet dread. 'It is my part in its authorship. *I* am the catalyst here, sirs. Put my work on the stage and you will suffer. The devil will surely come again.'

'There was no devil,' said Nicholas firmly.

'I am not certain either way,' admitted Hoode.

Willoughby was adamant. 'Truly, there *was* a devil. I have it from Doctor John Mordrake himself.'

'Mordrake!' Hoode was impressed.

'He consulted his books, his charts, his crystal and all agreed upon my fate. The life of Ralph Willoughby is forfeit. Save yours, my friends, by turning your backs on *The Merry Devils*.'

'It is too late,' said Nicholas.

'Then must you put the whole company at risk.'

'How?'

'Through me. Mordrake was specific on the matter.'

'A prediction?'

'Yes, Nick. Perform my play again—and disaster will strike!'

The warning could not have been clearer.

Grace Napier sat at the keyboard and filled the room with a wistful melody. When she came to the end of her practice, she was applauded.

'Well done!' said Isobel Drewry.

'I improve slowly.'

'You play sweetly, Grace.'

'The instrument pleases my ear.'

'And mine.' Isobel giggled obscenely. 'I wonder if Master Hoode can finger a virginal so delicately!'

'Do not be so vulgar,' said Grace with a smile.

'He longs to play on your keyboard.'

'Desist!'

Isobel stepped across to the virginal and ran her finger along it to produce a tinkling stream of sound. They were in the parlour at Grace's house. Having demonstrated her skill on the recorder, she had shown equal prowess at the keyboard. It was a pleasant way to pass an hour together on a wet morning. Isobel was duly appreciative.

'I could listen to you all day, Grace!'

'You may have to unless this rain stops.'

'But why did you play such sad songs?'

'No reason.'

'The music was exquisite but full of melancholy strains. Is that your mood today? Is your heart really so heavy?'

Grace smiled pensively then got up to cross over to the window. She watched the rain drumming on the glass and sending tiny rivulets on their brief journeys. Isobel came to stand beside her.

'Grace...'

'Yes.'

'Have you ever been in love?'

'Have you?' said the other, deflecting the question.

'Oh, many times,' replied Isobel with a giggle. 'I fall in and out of love with almost any man—if he be tall enough and handsome into the bargain. That afternoon we spent at The Curtain, I fell madly in love with a young gallant who was seated opposite. We exchanged such hot glances across the pit that I wonder there was not a puff of smoke to signify our dealings. But it was all over when the play was done.' She slipped an arm around Grace. 'And what of you?'

'I have *thought* I was in love.'

'But it was not the thing itself.'

'No.' she brightened. 'One thing is certain, however. When the man *does* come along, I will know him.'

'Not if Isobel Drewry should spy him first!' They traded a laugh. 'Then you do not pine for Master Hoode?'

'He is a dear man and I am very fond of him.'

'But he does not make your heart pound?'

'No, Isobel. I have come to value him as a friend.'

'You are the light of his life,' said the other. 'And when you watch *The Merry Devils* at the Rose tomorrow, Youngthrust will find a way to tell you so. I long to hear the outcome.'

'But you will be there to see it for yourself?'

'Unhappily, I will not. Father has put a stricter watch on me.'

'Why, Isobel?'

'One of the servants saw me leave with you the other day. She told father. He taxed me with disobedience and swore that I went to the playhouse to see *Cupid's Folly*. I lied with all my might but I could not dampen his suspicion.'

'How were you seen? You wore a mask.'

'I was recognised by my dress.'

Grace sighed. 'But I did so want your company tomorrow.'

'Let your brother sit beside you.'

'He is busy.'

Grace came into the middle of the room with her hands clasped. She moved around as she racked her brain for a solution, then stamped her foot with joy when she found it.

'It is but a case of wearing a better disguise, Isobel!'

'Disguise?'

'If the servants know *your* dresses, you must wear one of mine.'

'It is a clever idea, certainly.'

'And a hat with a veil. I'll provide that, too.'

'My own father would not know me, then!' Isobel gave her merriest giggle. 'I'll do it, Grace! I'd not miss that play again for anything.'

'Good! There is no risk of discovery.'

'We will travel in secret like spies.'

'Veiled and hooded against all inquiry.'

'I will be veiled—and you will be Hooded!' She took her friend by the hands. 'Oh, I am so happy in this ruse. Father will be deceived.'

'What does he know of The Rose in Bankside?' said Grace. 'It is not as if he would ever visit such a place himself. Forget your fears, Isobel. You will be as safe there as in a nunnery.'

'But a lot more merry, I hope!'

Henry Drewry was finishing his meal alone when the servant brought in the package. Dismissing the man with a curt nod, the salter first washed down his meal with a swig of ale then belched to show his satisfaction. He examined the package and saw that it was addressed to him in his capacity as an Alderman. He could guess the sender and his supposition was confirmed. When he opened the package, he took out a printed text.

A SERMON PREACHED AT PAWLES CROSS
by Isaac Pollard

Imprinted at London by Toby Vavasour and to be sold at his Shop in the Inner Temple, near the Church.

1589

Drewry glanced at the first page to see that it offered a Discourse on the Subtle Practices of Devils. He heard Pollard's boom in every line and put the pamphlet aside. Then he noticed that something else had fallen out of the package. It was a tattered playbill. Smoothing it out and laying it on the table, he saw that it advertised a performance of *The Merry Devils* by Westfield's Men on the following afternoon. Sent to him to stir up his sense of outrage, it instead began to intrigue him.

Unaccountably, he felt the steady pull of temptation.

Chapter Six

Lawrence Firethorn reserved some of his best performances for private consumption. He had a sublime gift for improvisation and could pluck any emotion out of the air at a second's notice. It was a trick that rarely failed. Even those who had seen him use it a hundred times could still be caught out by it. Suddenness was all.

'Rebellion in the ranks!' he yelled. 'When I lead Westfield's Men forward in the charge, I do not expect to be stabbed in the back from behind. Least of all by two such cowardly, such miserable, such lousy, beggarly, scurvy, unmannerly creatures as those before me now!'

George Dart and Roper Blundell were totally cowed.

'Loyalty is everything to me!' declared Firethorn, striking the pose he had used so effectively as King Richard the Lion-heart. 'I will not stomach traitors at any price! Do you know what I would do with them, sirs? Do you know how I would repay their betrayal of me?'

'No, master,' said George Dart.

'How, sir?' asked Roper Blundell.

'I'd have the wretches hanged, drawn and quartered, so I would! Then I'd have their heads set upon spikes outside the Tower, their livers roasted over a slow fire and their dangling pizzles sent to Banbury's Men by way of mockery!'

Dart and Blundell covered their codpieces with both hands.

They were in the room at the Queen's Head that was used for the storage of their equipment. Nicholas Bracewell stood in the background with Caleb Smythe, one of the actors. Both felt sorry for the assistant stagekeepers who had foolishly expressed their doubts about the performance of *The Merry Devils* on the following afternoon. The sad little figures were being summarily ground into submission.

When the book holder tried to intercede on their behalf, he was waved away with magisterial authority. Lawrence Firethorn would allow no interruption. He continued to pound away at his targets with his verbal siege guns until the two men were nothing more than human debris. Choosing his moment brilliantly, the actor now switched his role and became the indulgent employer who has been wronged by his servants.

'Lads, lads,' he said softly. 'Why have you turned against me like this? Did I not take you in when all other companies closed their doors to you? Have I not paid you, housed you, taught you, fed you and nurtured you? George, my son, and you, good Roper, everything I have is yours to call upon. You are not hired men to me. You are friends, sirs. Honest, decent, upright, God-fearing friends. Or so I thought.' He dredged up a monstrous sigh. 'Whence comes this betrayal? What have I done to deserve such treatment?'

'Nothing, master,' bleated George Dart.

'Nothing at all,' agreed Roper Blundell, starting to cry.

Firethorn slipped an arm apiece around them and hugged them to him like lost sheep that have gone astray and been found. Moved by the sincerity of his own betrayal, he even deposited a small kiss on Dart's forehead while drawing the line at any such intimacy with the turnip-headed Blundell. It was a touching scene and he played it to the hilt.

'I thought my lads would die for me,' he whimpered.

'We would,' said Dart bravely.

'Give us the chance, sir,' asked Blundell.

'I do not ask much of you, my friends. Just two bare hours upon the stage in flame-red costumes. What harm is there in that?'

'None, sir.'

'None, sir.'

'You tell me you are unhappy in the parts and I can understand that but happiness must be sacrificed for the greater good of the company.'

'Yes, master.'

'Indeed, sir.'

'We act for our patron,' said Firethorn in a respectful whisper. 'Lord Westfield himself, who puts food in our mouths and clothes on our back. Am I to tell him his merry devils have run away?'

'We are here, sir.'

'We will stay.'

'I will beg, if that is what you wish.' Firethorn pretended to lower himself to the ground. 'I will go down on my bended knee...'

'No, no,' they chimed, helping him back up again.

'Then let me appeal to your sense of obligation. As hired men, as close friends, as true spirits of the theatre—will you help me, lads?'

'Oh, yes!' Blundell was now weeping convulsively.

'We will not let you down,' added the snivelling Dart.

'That is music to my old ears.'

Firethorn bestowed another kiss on Dart's forehead, approximated his lips to the sprouting turnip, thought better of it and released the two men. He drifted to the nearest door to deliver his exit line.

'My heart is touched, lads,' he said. 'I must be alone for a while. Nick here will explain everything to you. Thank you—and farewell.'

He went out to an imaginary round of applause.

Nicholas Bracewell's sympathies were with the assistant stagekeepers but he had to admire the actor-manager's technique. He had now shackled the men in two ways. Fear and duty. There was no escape for them now. The book holder stepped in to join them.

'I'll be brief, lads,' he began. 'Lord Westfield insisted on a second performance because he liked the merry devils, all three of them who took the stage at the Queen's Head.'

Dart and Blundell reacted with identical horror.

'That foul fiend will come again?'

'Not from Hell,' said Nicholas, 'nor anywhere adjacent to it. He will come from beneath the stage at The Rose, as indeed will you. The third devil will not fright you this time, lads. You know him too well.' He signalled Caleb Smythe in. 'Here he stands.'

Caleb Smythe was a short, slight man in his thirties with a bald head and wispy beard. Though taller than his co-devils, he was lithe enough to bend his body to their shape and his talent as a dancer was second only to that of Barnaby Gill. As the unexpected third devil who put the others to flight, he was the best choice available. Caleb Smythe, however, did not share this view.

'I like not this work,' he said lugubriously.

Nicholas swept his objection aside and told them about the alterations that had been made to the play. Doctor Castrato's magic incantations had been shortened and the circle of mystical objects had been removed. None of the preconditions for raising a real devil now existed. The book holder emphasized this point but his companions were not wholly persuaded.

It was the funereal Caleb Smythe who put the question.

'What if a fourth devil *should* appear, Master Bracewell?'

The answer was quite unequivocal.

'Then I shall be waiting for him!'

Light drizzle was still falling as the last few items were brought out of the cottage. Glanville stood under the shelter of a tree and watched it all with grave misgivings. Jack Harsnett and his wife were being evicted. Their mean furniture and possessions were loaded on to a cart. It was sobering to think that they had both lived so long and yet owned so little. The mangy horse that stood between the shafts now cropped at the grass in the clearing for the last time. Like his owners, he was being moved on to leaner pastures.

Harsnett came over to where the steward was standing.

'Thankee,' he said gruffly.

'I tried, Jack.'

'I know, sir.'

'The new master was deaf to all entreaty.'

'New master!'

Harsnett turned aside and spat excessively to show his disgust. By order of Francis Jordan, he should have been turned out of the cottage on the previous day but Glanville had permitted him to stay the night. It was the only concession he felt able to offer and he was taking a risk with that. Harsnett was a surly and uncommunicative man but the steward respected him. The stocky forester was conscientious in his work and asked only to be left alone to do his job. He never complained about the misery of his lot and he held his chin up with a defiant pride.

'Things'll change,' he grunted.

'I fear they will, Jack.'

'We're but the first of many to go.'

'I will work to get you back.'

'No, sir.'

'But you are a proven man in the forest.'

'I'll not serve *him*!' sneered Harsnett.

There was a loan moan from inside the cottage and they both turned towards it. The forester's wife was evidently in great discomfort.

'Let me help you,' said Glanville kindly.

'I can manage.'

'But if your wife is unwell...'

Harsnett shook his head. 'We come into the place on our own, we'll leave the same way.'

He walked across to the cottage and ducked in through the low doorway. A couple of minutes later, he emerged with his wife, a poor, wasted, grey-haired woman in rough attire with an old shawl around her head. The whiteness of her face and the slowness of her movements told Glanville how ill she was. Harsnett had to lift her bodily on to the cart. He returned quickly to the cottage to bring out his last and most precious possession.

It was his axe. Sharp and glittering, it had seen him through many a year and was the symbol of his craft. He slammed the door behind him then turned back to view the place which had been their home throughout their marriage. The cottage was his no more. It belonged to the new master of Parkbrook House. Hatred and revenge welled up in Harsnett and he saw the building as a version of Francis Jordan himself, as a cold, bitter, cruel, unwelcoming place. He swung the axe with sudden violence and sank the blade deep into the front door.

After this last gesture of defiance, he pulled the axe clear of the timber and hurried across to throw it in the back of the cart. When he climbed up beside his wife, she collapsed against him. He took the reins in one hand and put the other arm around his ailing spouse. In response to a curt command, the horse struggled into life.

'God go with you!' said Glanville.

But they had no time to hear him.

Kirk said nothing to his colleagues about the progress he had made. They would not understand it. The other keepers at Bedlam took the simple view that lunatics should be treated in only two ways. They should either be amused with toys or beaten with whips. Play or punishment. It never occurred to them that their charges might respond to individual care of another kind. Rooksley typified the attitude that was prevalent. The head keeper believed that lunatics could not be cured by anything that he and his staff might do. The salvation of the mentally deranged lay entirely with the Almighty. In support of this credo, Rooksley could recite, word for word, from a document which dated from the first year of Queen Elizabeth's reign and which confirmed the institution's status as an asylum for the insane.

> Be it known to all devout and faithful people that there have been erected in the city of London four hospitals for the people that be stricken by the hand of God. Some be distraught from their wits and these be kept and maintained in the Hospital of our Lady of Bedlam, until God call them to his mercy, or to their wits again.

For the vast majority of inmates, therefore, there was no respite and no hope. Stricken by the hand of God, they were repeatedly stricken by the hand of man as well. It was a savage Christianity.

Kirk sought to keep at least one person clear of it.

'I've brought your meal, David.'

'Ah.'

'You have to do better than that, sir,' coaxed the other. 'I will not feed you else. Come, sir, what is that word we learned this morning?'

David's brow knotted with concentration for a moment.

Kirk prompted. 'If I give you something, what is my reward?'

'Th…ank…'

'Try again, David.'

'Th…ank…you…'

'Well done, sir! That deserves a meal.'

David was sitting on the bed in his featureless cell. The keeper sat down beside him and put the plate into the patient's lap. Taking hold of David's right hand, he fitted the spoon into it then guided him down to his meal. The first mouthful was soon being chewed with slow deliberation. David was being helped to feed himself. He smiled at his minor triumph. It was another small sign of advance.

Kirk knew that nothing could be rushed. David could now say his name and mouth a few words but that was all. He had to be taught again from the beginning and that would require time and patience. When the meal was over, Kirk waited expectantly. David was at first puzzled, then he grinned as he realised what was wanted.

'Th...ank...'

'Speak up, sir.'

'Thank you!'

'Excellent!'

Kirk patted him on the back by the way of congratulation. There was still the vacant look in David's eye but he was not so completely beyond reach as the others believed. It was merely a question of opening up a line of communication with him.

'What's your name, sir?' asked Kirk.

'Da...vid.'

'Again.'

'David.'

'Again!'

'David. David. David.'

'And where do you live, David?'

The patient's face clouded over and his lips quivered.

'Where is your home?' said the keeper.

David glanced around and gestured with both hands.

'No, not here. Not Bedlam. This is where you live *now*, David. But where did you live before?'

The question completely baffled the patient. He looked lost and hurt. Kirk tried to jog his memory with a gentle enquiry.

'Was it in London?'

Unsure at first, David gave a hesitant shake of his head.

'Was it in a city?'

A longer wait then another uncertain shake of the head.

'Then you must have lived in the country, David.'

Bewilderment contorted the other's face. He was lost again.

'Did you live in the country?' prodded Kirk. 'Fields and woods around you? Can you not recall animals and birds?'

A radiant smile lit David's face. He nodded enthusiastically.

'You lived in the country. Was it in a village?'

David was more confident now. He shook his head at once.

'On a farm? In a cottage somewhere?'

The patient was clearly grappling with his past in order to wrest some details out of it. A jumble of memories made his expression change with each second. Kirk nudged his mind again.

'Did you live in a small house, David?'

'N...n...n...'

'No. Good. Was it a large house, then?'

David produced the beaming smile again. He laughed aloud.

'A large house in the country. Is that where you lived?'

'Y...y...ye...ye...' The word finally spurted out. 'Yes!'

Parkbrook was a hive of activity. The presence of its new master had put everyone on their mettle. Francis Jordan was a man who liked to exert his authority and the dismissal of Harsnett was a grim warning to other employees in the house and on the estate. The old order had changed with a vengeance. Those who laboured in the Great Hall hardly dared to look up from their work. Even the serene Joseph Glanville was forced to glance over his shoulder. Unease spread everywhere.

Francis Jordan spent the morning on a tour of inspection around the house, cracking the whip of his bad temper whenever he felt inclined. Having coveted Parkbrook for so long, he knew exactly how he wished to run it. He was particularly interested in the wine cellar and checked the stock which his predecessor had laid in. Several bottles were sent up. Over a leisurely meal that was taken alone in the spacious dining room, Jordan worked his way through some of the premier vintages. It left him in a more expansive mood. He hauled himself up the oak staircase and swayed towards the master bedroom. Intending to flop down and sleep off his over-indulgence, he paused when he saw that the room was occupied.

A young chambermaid was changing the linen on the fourposter.

'Who's here?' he asked with a vinous smirk.

'Oh!' She turned around in alarm.

'Do not be afraid, my dear.'

'I did not expect you to be here, sir.'

'I am very glad that I am.'

'Would you like me to leave?'

'No, mistress. What is your name?'

'Jane Skinner, sir.'

'Well, Jane Skinner, I am your new master.'

'Yes, sir,' she said with a dutiful curtsey.

'Finish what you were doing.'

The chambermaid returned to her task. She was a rather plain, plump girl with a country shine to her cheeks and a mop of brown curls. Francis Jordan, however, was roused by the sight of her generous curves and her bobbing posterior. Her simple apparel seemed somehow to heighten her appeal. Leaning against the doorframe, he watched her flit about her work. The bed was soon made and she turned down the counterpane.

'Help me across,' he said.

'Are you not well, sir?'

'A little tired, Jane. I need but a shoulder to rest on.'

'I have that, sir.'

Jane Skinner tripped over to him with a face of youthful innocence. When Jordan lurched at her, she obligingly took his weight. As she helped him across the room, he kneaded her shoulder and took an inventory of her other charms. They reached the bed and he swung round to fall backwards on to it.

'Lift up my feet, Jane.'

'Yes, sir,' she said, scooping his legs up on to the bed.

'Come closer for I would whisper to you.'

'Yes, sir.'

As she bent over him, he got her wrist in a firm grip and gave her a lecherous grin. He liked Jane Skinner more with each moment.

'Undress me.'

'Master!' she exclaimed.

'Undress me slowly, mistress.'

'I will call a valet presently.'

'This is woman's work, Jane.'

'You are hurting my arm, sir.'

'Then do as you are told.'

'But it is not my place.'

'You are mine to command, girl.'

Hope flickered. 'Haply, you jest with me, sir.'

'This is no jest, I assure you. Come, let me give proof of it.'

Jordan made a concerted effort to sit up so that he could catch hold of her properly. There was a fierce struggle. In those few frantic seconds, Jane Skinner may have lost her innocence but she was determined not to yield her virtue. When he pulled her down on the bed and tried to kiss her, she reacted with such vigour that he was shaken off. Before he could stop her, she raced across the room and went out through the door. Jordan's annoyance was dissipated in a huge yawn. The chambermaid faded from his mind and he lapsed back into deep sleep.

Jane Skinner, meanwhile, was crying into her apron and telling her story to Glanville. He listened with controlled outrage and calmed the girl as best he could. She had been very lucky to make her escape.

But she might not be so fortunate next time.

Thoroughness was the hallmark of Nicholas Bracewell's approach. Since the company were due to appear at The Rose on the morrow, he found time that evening to visit the theatre. There were very few people still there and most of those soon drifted away. The book holder had the place virtually to himself. His first task was to test the trap-doors. The stage was much higher than the makeshift one used at the Queen's Head and he was able to move more freely beneath it. Short steps led up to each trap which was fitted with a spring. As merry devils shot up on to the stage, the doors would snap back into position.

Nicholas next checked the sightlines from his own position at the rear of the stage. Watching the action through a gap in the curtain, he would not be able to see much but both trap-doors were directly in his vision. That was important. The Rose had not long been open to the public and there was a pleasing newness to it. Tall pillars climbed up out of the stage to support a decorated canopy that was surmounted by a small hut. By using elementary winching gear, it was possible to raise and lower items of scenery or furniture. Nicholas planned to use the apparatus to dramatic effect in *The Merry Devils*.

Three years at sea had not been the ideal preparation for a life in the theatre but he had learned much from his voyages that could be adapted to his present purposes. Sailing ships like the *Golden Hind* relied on some very basic mechanical devices and Nicholas never tired of watching the crew hoist the sails to catch the wind or winch up the longboats when they returned from shore. Friendship with the ship's carpenters had been a constant education as they carried out running repairs in all weathers across the oceans of the world.

Being cooped up on a vessel for long periods inevitably led to tension and frustration. Nicholas had seen far more spontaneous violence than he had wished but it made him an expert on stage fights. Firethorn always let his book holder direct such episodes when they occurred. The same went for swordplay. A skilful swordsman himself, Nicholas was always on hand to school the hired men and the apprentices in one of the vital tools of their craft.

His seafaring days had given him something else as well and it came to his aid now. Nicholas had a sixth sense of danger, a tickling sensation that was full of foreboding. Standing in the middle of the stage, he had a strong feeling that someone was watching. He swung round to scan the galleries but they appeared to be empty. The sun was now nuzzling the horizon and dark shadows had invaded the theatre. In the half-light, he searched the place for signs of life but saw none. The manager was still on the premises but he was in his office. Besides, the manager was a business colleague and the presence that Nicholas felt was an alien one.

He was about to dismiss it all as a trick of the imagination when he heard a cackle. Before he could even begin to wonder who made the noise, one of the trap-doors suddenly opened and up popped a flame-red devil. The creature had a malevolent face, a crooked body, twisted limbs, long horns and a pointed tail. It looked like the one who had caused such a fright at the Queen's Head. Moving at speed, the devil executed three somersaults then vanished into the tiring-house. Nicholas ran after him but he did not get very far. He heard the sound of the other trap-door and turned back to see that the devil had reappeared. This time the creature cart wheeled off the edge of the stage and was lost in the shadows around the edge of the pit.

Nicholas was both startled and bewildered. He did not know which way to look or search. Forcing himself to make a decision, he ran to the tiring-house to find it quite empty. A search beneath the stage and around the full circumference of the pit also proved fruitless. He was mystified. Had he seen one apparition or two? Was it some random act of malice that had taken place or had the visit been an omen? Did he now know what to expect during the performance next day?

He walked to the front of the stage and rested his elbows upon it as he weighed his thoughts. A creaking sound came from behind him. He turned to look up and see a tall, elegant silhouette in the topmost gallery. The voice was familiar and its tone was fearful.

'*Now* will you believe that it was a real devil?'

Ralph Willoughby had watched it all.

Margery Firethorn ran her household on firm Christian principles. As a variant on her scolding, she sometimes chastised her servants or her children by making them attend an impromptu prayer meeting. In the rolling cadences of the Book of Common Prayer she found both a fund of reassurance and a useful weapon. For most of the occupants of the house in Shoreditch, the regular visit to the Parish Church of St Leonard's was imposition enough. To have the Church brought into the house was a nightmare.

'Let us pray.'

'That includes you, Martin Yeo.'

'Let us pray.'

'Lower your head, John Tallis.'

'Let us pray.'

'Close your mouth, Stephen Judd.'

'Let us *all* pray!'

The day began with a profound shock. It was Lawrence Firethorn who instigated and led the prayers. Inclined to be lax in his religious observances—especially where the sixth commandment was concerned—he astonished everyone by reaching for the prayer book before breakfast. Margery reverted to the scolding while her husband handled the service. Around the table were their two children, the four apprentices, Caleb Smythe, who had spent the night there, and the two assistant stagekeepers, George Dart and Roger Blundell, who had been summoned from their lodgings to partake in a ceremony that might have a special bearing on their safety and their souls.

They listened in silence as Firethorn intoned the prayers. Even on such a solemn occasion, he had to give a performance. When he reached the end of an interminable recitation, he signalled their release.

'Amen.'

'Amen' came the collective sigh of relief.

'That should stand us in good stead,' said Firethorn breezily.

'I feel better for that, master,' confessed George Dart.

'It gives me new heart,' said Roger Blundell.

'I like not prayers,' muttered Caleb Smythe.

'They were most beautifully read,' said Firethorn pointedly.

'It was not the reading that I mind, sir,' said the other. 'It is the weight they place upon my heart. When I hear prayers, I am undone. They make me think so of death.'

'Oh, heavens!' wailed Dart. 'Death, he cries!'

'What a word to mention on a day like this!' said Blundell.

An argument started but Margery quelled it by serving breakfast. She believed in providing a hearty meal at the start of the day and the others fell ravenously upon it. Eleven heads were soon bent over the table in contentment.

When the meal was over, Firethorn retired to the bedchamber for a few minutes. His wife followed him and accosted him.

'What lies behind this, Lawrence?'

'Behind what, dearest?'

'These unexpected prayers.'

'I was moved by the spirit, Margery.'

'It has never shifted you one inch before, sir.'

'You wrong me, sweeting,' he said in aggrieved tones. 'I heard a voice from above.'

'It sounded like Nicholas Bracewell to me.'

'Ah...'

'Why did he call here so early this morning?' she pressed. 'It is not like him to come all the way from Bankside on a whim. Did he bring bad tidings?'

'Nothing to trouble your pretty little head about, angel.'

'My head is neither pretty nor little. It contains a brain as big as yours and I would have it treated with respect. Speak out, sir. Do not protect me from the truth.'

He was aghast. 'When have I held back the truth from you?'

'It has been your daily habit these fifteen years.'

'Margery!'

'Honesty has never been your strong suit.'

'I am the most veracious fellow in London.'

'Another lie,' she said levelly. 'Come, sir, and tell me what I need to know. Why did Master Bracewell come here today?'

'On a personal matter, my love.'

'There is another woman involved?'

'That is a most ignoble thought, Margery.'

'You put it into my pretty little head.' She folded her arms and came to a decision. 'The tidings concerned the play. I will come to The Rose myself this afternoon.'

'No, no!' he protested. 'That will not do at all!'

'Why do you keep me away, Lawrence?'

'I do not, my pigeon.'

'Is it because of this other woman?'

'*What* other woman?'

'You tell me, sir. Their names change so often.'

Firethorn knew that he would never shake her off when she was in that mood and so he compromised. He gave her a highly edited version of what Nicholas Bracewell had told him and since the book holder's report had itself been softened—no mention of Willoughby—she got only a diluted account. When she heard about the devils shooting up from trap-doors, she crossed herself in fear.

'They may not be *real* fiends, Margery.'

'They sound so to me.'

'Nicholas believes otherwise and he is a shrewd judge.'

'What of you, Lawrence?'

He shrugged. 'I only half-believe they came from Hell.'

'Half a devil is by one half too much. I'll not have my husband acting with an apparition. Cancel the performance.'

'There can be no question of that.'

'I mean it, sir.'

'Lord Westfield overrules you.'

'How much warning do you *need*? Fiends were at The Rose.'

'No, my treasure. Silly pranksters out to give us fright.'

'Then why did you read those prayers?'

'I have been something slack in my devotions of late.'

'You feared for the lives of those lads.'

'The merry devils are sad,' he said. 'I sought to ease their misery with a taste of religion.'

'Your prayers were meant to save them!'

Firethorn conceded there was an element of truth in it. If real devils were going to appear, he wanted God to be at his side. He urged her to say nothing to the others. He and Nicholas had agreed to suppress all mention of the incident at The Rose. It would disrupt an already uneasy company. Their task was to present a play to the public.

'You'll keep them ignorant of their danger?' she said.

'I'll see they come to no harm.'

The day was warm and muggy with a hint of thunder in the bloated clouds. A tawny sun played hide and seek all morning. Isaac Pollard was up early to visit church, breakfast with his wife and children, then sally forth to meet his brethren. Four other members of the Puritan faction consented to go with him. His descriptions of *The Merry Devils* had roused their ire against the piece and they decided to view it in order to know its full horror. They fondly imagined that their fivefold presence at The Rose would spread some much-needed guilt around the galleries and scatter some piety into the pit.

Since they met in St Paul's Churchyard, their easiest route to Bankside lay in making straight for the river to cross in a boat. Isaac Pollard ruled against this. Thames watermen were justly famed for their vulgarity and two or more of them engaged in argument could turn the air blue with their language. The last time that Pollard was rowed across in a wherry, he tried to reprove his boatman for this fault of nature and met with such a volcanic eruption of profanity that he had to close his ears to it and so missed the concluding threat of baptism in the river. Accordingly, he now led his colleagues towards the single bridge that spanned the Thames with its magnificence.

As the leader of the expedition, he passed on sage advice. 'Stay close to me, brethren, and guard your purses.'

'Will there be pickpockets?' said one.

'By the score.'

'But would they dare to touch *us*?' said another.

'They would rob an Archbishop of his mitre.'

'As would we, brother,' observed a theologian among them without any trace of irony. 'We would deprive that reverend gentleman of his mitre, his staff, his sacerdotal robes and anything else with such a Romish tinge to them. But tell us more of these pickpockets.'

'Their fingers are ever busy,' warned Pollard. 'Did I not relate to you my experience at the Queen's Head when a young wife but two rows in front of me was deprived of her purse by some rogue?'

'How was it done?' asked the theologian.

'With such skill that she did not discover it until later. Being so close at hand, I could not but overhear what passed between her and her friend, another married lady who had come to that libidinous place without her spouse. "Oh!" said the young woman. "My purse is taken." Her friend asked where it was kept. "Beneath my skirts," said the young woman. "I had thought it would be safe there." Her friend agreed then asked her if she had not felt a man's hand upon her thigh. "Why, yes," replied the young woman, "but I did not think it came there for that purpose."'

Five married men crossed London Bridge in grim silence.

The reputation of *The Merry Devils* went before it and stirred up great interest and anticipation. Large, boisterous crowds descended on The Rose and it was soon evident that the theatre would not be able to accommodate all the potential spectators. There was much good-humoured pushing and shoving at the entrances and gatherers worked at full stretch. Those who had a special reason to be there made sure of their seats by an early arrival and they felt the atmosphere build steadily as other patrons surged in.

Anne Hendrik was there with Preben van Loew, the most skilful and senior of her hat-makers, a dour man in his fifties with a redeeming glint in his eye. The Dutchman was caught in two minds. His Huguenot conscience baulked at the idea of visiting a playhouse yet he could not allow his respected employer to venture there alone. Besides, he soon began to enjoy the envious glances that he was getting from those who assumed he was more than just the consort of the handsome and well-dressed lady at his side. Moral scruples still flickered but he was ready to ignore them for a couple of hours.

Grace Napier and Isobel Drewry had cushioned seats in the middle gallery and stayed behind their veils. Wearing a gown of blue figured velvet that she had borrowed from her friend, Isobel felt armoured against discovery. Settling down to enjoy the occasion to the full, she giggled inwardly at her own daring. Grace Napier was as poised as ever. That morning she had received another sonnet from Edmund Hoode, declaring his love for her once more and urging her to watch his performance for further proof of his devotion. Her affection for him deepened but it was still edged with regret.

Ralph Willoughby made for the highest gallery. He was dressed in emerald green with a slashed doublet, an orange codpiece and hose that displayed the length and shapeliness of his legs. A small, round, jewelled cap was set at a rakish angle on his head. An opal dangled from one ear. He was a debonair and carefree man about town again. Whatever stirred within him was kept well-hidden.

Isaac Pollard brought in his colleagues and they found places in the lower gallery, a solid phalanx of black disapproval amid a sea of multi-coloured excitement. They glared at the stage as if it were the gates of Hell, ready to disgorge its fiendish contents at any moment. Preoccupied in this way, they did not observe the low, portly figure who was seated opposite. Tricked out in finery that indicated wealth and respectability, he had the look of a man who had come to glower yet might stay to laugh. Henry Drewry was mellowing visibly.

Lord Westfield provoked a cheer of recognition as he took his seat amid his entourage. He wore a high-starched collar, a stiffened doublet which had been neatly tailored to allow for the contours of his paunch, padded and embroidered breeches and blue silk stockings. His gloves were of the finest blue leather. He favoured a large hat with an explosion of feathers and looked like the image of a middle-aged dandy. With their patron at his place, Westfield's Men could begin.

The last few spectators were allowed in to join the crush in the pit or shoulder themselves a space on a bench. One silver-haired old man in a long robe inserted himself into a narrow seat in the bottom gallery and looked around the theatre with calculating wonder. He absorbed every detail of its structure and noted every feature of its occupants. It was as if he was repairing the one tiny gap that existed in his knowledge of the universe. Combining scholarly curiosity with scientific detachment, he got the measure of The Rose and was not displeased. He came on the heels of his own prediction. Something sinister was going to happen that afternoon and he wished to be there to see it.

Doctor John Mordrake had a personal stake in the event.

Superstition was the life-blood of the theatre. Most actors carried lucky charms or recited favourite pieces or went through an established ritual before a performance in the belief that it conferred good fortune. It was standard practice. Among Westfield's Men, it now became something far more. *The Merry Devils* enslaved them to superstition. Hardly a man in the company did not take some precautions. Several of them went to the cunning woman in Vixen Lane to purchase charms that would ward off evil spirits. Two of them spent the night in prayer. Three more had parted with a groat apiece for a phial of liquid that was guaranteed to preserve them from any supernatural manifestation, and they were not in the least put out by its close resemblance to vinegar both in appearance and taste. Other charlatans had made their profits in other ways from the credulous players. Their situation was desperate. They would try anything.

Lawrence Firethorn evinced the confidence of old. He had the seasoned calmness of the veteran before battle. Yet even he had made one concession to the possibility of an unexpected guest. He wore his rapier at his side and kept one hand upon it.

Nicholas Bracewell appraised him in the tiring-house.

'Justice Wildboare has no need of a sword,' he said.

'Lawrence Firethorn might.'

'There is no real devil, master.'

'Then a counterfeit one will feel my blade.'

'None will appear.'

'How can you say that after last night?'

They kept their voices low and both wore smiles to mask their inner doubts. It was their duty to set an example to the others and to instil some confidence.

'Has everything been checked?' asked Firethorn.

'Several times, master.'

'Below stage?'

'I was there myself but two minutes ago. All is in order. The gunpowder is in place and the trap-doors are ready.'

'And if something should go awry?'

'It will not, sir.'

'But if it does...'

'Ned Rankin holds the book for me during that scene,' said Nicholas. 'I'll be free to watch more closely and take action if the need arises. Trust in me.'

'I always do, dear heart!'

Firethorn clapped him on the shoulder then wandered off. Nicholas went across to the three men who suffered the most—the merry devils. Seen from behind, George Dart, Roper Blundell and Caleb Smythe looked identical in their startling costumes. Dart was silent, Blundell was wide-eyed with nervousness, Smythe was reciting a children's rhyme to himself by way of a diversion.

Nicholas gave what reassurance he could but it was wasted on Blundell and Smythe who were far too steeped in misery. Dart, however, responded with an uncharacteristic chuckle. The others stared at him. When the most timorous member of the company could face his ordeal with amusement, there was only one explanation.

'Have you been drinking, George?' said Nicholas sternly.

'Yes, master,' came the happy reply.

'You know where you are?'

'In Bankside at The Rose.'

'You know what you have to do?'

Another chuckle. 'Pop up through a trap-door and cry "Boo!"'

'Are you fit for this work?' said the book holder seriously.

'I'll not let you down, master.'

Nicholas did not have the heart to castigate him. It was a strict rule of the company that nobody went on stage inebriated. Dismissal was a real threat to offenders. George Dart was no drunkard. Apart from anything else, his meagre wage would not sustain such a habit. Only the need to combat a terrible fear could have sent him to a tavern. Nicholas understood and made allowances. Dart was sober enough to play his part and drunk enough not to worry about it.

'We count on you, George. Mark that.'

'I know my role, sir.'

'Then do not play it too close to Master Firethorn. You know his rule about drink. Be merry, George, but not to excess.'

'I'll be a devil to the life!'

When the black cloak of the Prologue swished on to the stage, there was a tumultuous reception. It was surpassed only by the cannonade of sound that greeted the entry of Justice Wildboare. The audience surrendered to Lawrence Firethorn before he even opened his mouth. When he did finally launch into his first long, expository speech, he found humour in every phrase—sometimes, in a single word—and set the whole place at a roar. By the time the other characters joined in the action, the spectators had been thoroughly warmed up.

As the play gathered pace and the laughter intensified, it soon became clear that this performance was vastly better in every way than the earlier one. Some important changes had been made. Edmund Hoode had tightened the construction, introduced a new comic duel, provided some new songs and generally improved the whole texture of the play. The most notable alteration came with his own character. Youngthrust had even more prominence now—his codpiece was stupendous—and he wept buckets of glorious blank verse. Some of the words were written for Grace Napier but the whole theatre appreciated them.

Doctor Castrato had lost lines but gained extra stage business. His mincing steps and piping voice mined new veins of hilarity. When he promised Justice Wildboare that he would raise a devil, the loudest shout of the afternoon went up from the onlookers.

This was the moment which they had come to relish and they tensed themselves in readiness.

As she had been instructed, Anne Hendrik kept her eyes on the trap-doors. Henry Drewry stood up to look over the head of the man in front of him. Doctor John Mordrake felt a tingle of premonition. Isaac Pollard bunched his fists and lifted the single eyebrow. Lord Westfield nudged his companions to watch carefully.

Ralph Willoughby went faint with dread.

Castrato went into his attenuated chanting. Then he did an elaborate mime that culminated in his act of summons when he scattered a magic powder in two different places on the stage. Response was immediate. One trap-door opened and out jumped George Dart to the accompaniment of a blinding flash and a resounding bang. The effect was so well-timed that it completely stunned the audience. Emboldened by drink, the first merry devil scuttled around the stage with gleeful abandon.

Nicholas Bracewell was concealed behind the arras to get a better view. He wondered why the second trap-door did not open. Roger Blundell should have appeared simultaneously with Dart. Had there been a problem with the mechanism. He was given no time to speculate. There was a longer, louder, brighter explosion and Caleb Smythe catapulted up through the first trap-door. He did a wild jig, turned a somersault, then went with his co-devil to kneel before their new master.

Justice Wildboare took over.

Nicholas slipped quietly into the tiring-house and made his way to the steps at the rear. He went down under the stage to find it gloomy and permeated with the smells of the multitude. The play continued above his head. It was quite eerie. As he picked his way along, he could hear the actors strutting about on the boards and feel the roar of the spectators pressing in upon him.

Something sparkled in the half-light. It was the protruding eyes of Roper Blundell. He lay flat on his back in a little red heap, gazing up sightlessly at the drama that he should have joined. Nicholas knelt down beside him and learned the worst. Here was one merry devil who would never go up through a trap-door again.

Roper Blundell was dead.

Chapter Seven

Nicholas Bracewell bent over the body and examined it as best he could in the circumstances. He saw no wound, no blood, no mark of any kind. There was nothing at all to indicate the cause of death. A decision now had to be made. Did he take the corpse away or leave it where it was? Decency suggested the former but practicalities had to be taken into account. Nobody else knew about the death of Roper Blundell. To walk back up to the tiring-house with the little body in his arms would be to disseminate terror. The play itself was still running. That was the main thing. Nicholas could not risk bringing it to a premature halt by revealing that it had somehow brought about the demise of an assistant stagekeeper.

Roper Blundell was to remain where he was, lying in state in his echoing tomb, occupying a rectangle of solitude in the very midst of a huge crowd. He had lost his part as well as his life. Realising that he could not chase two devils off the stage, Caleb Smythe, as the third foul fiend, had moved himself up in the order. He became the second devil and did everything in unison with George Dart. With Lawrence Firethorn and Barnaby Gill adapting instantly to the situation, the absence of Blundell was not noticed by the audience. Nicholas touched the old man beside him in a gesture of respect. The theatre could be a cruel place. It had just excised a human being from a drama as if the fellow had never existed.

A rumble of thunder made Nicholas look upward. Justice Wildboare did not miss the cue to work in some lines from another play.

> God is angry, sirs! Hear how the Heavens rebuke us.
> This thunder will send us all down into Hell!

After one last look at the prostrate form, the book holder went back up to the tiring-house and ran into a flurry of enquiries about Blundell. He announced that the old man was not well enough to take any further part in the play and that he would rest where he was. It was important that nobody disturbed him. To this end, Nicholas stationed the venerable Thomas Skillen at the top of the steps and told him to let no man pass. The stagekeeper was a willing guardian.

Westfield's Men performed *The Merry Devils* with a zest and a commitment they would not have thought possible. Now that the danger zone had been safely passed—as they thought—they could devote themselves to the finer points of their art. Roper Blundell was forgotten. Instead of wondering what lay beneath the stage, the actors were more concerned with what stretched above. The sky was now full of swollen clouds and the thunder rumbled ominously.

Nicholas resumed his post and took the book from Ned Rankin. A scene ended and Justice Wildboare came sweeping into the tiring-house. He made straight for the book holder.

'Where's Blundell?'

'Indisposed.'

'What happened to him?'

'He has retired hurt, master.'

'I'll retire the rogue, so help me! Get him here.'

'He is too unwell to be moved,' said Nicholas, signalling in his glance what lay behind the fiction. 'Press on without him.'

'We have no choice, sir.' Firethorn understood but kept the secret well. More thunder was followed by a distant flash of lightning. 'Hell's teeth! This is all we need! Where's your seamanship now, Nick? What must we do, what must we do?'

'Run before the storm!'

'Clap on full sail?'

'That's my advice, master.'

'Will we do it?'

'We can but try, sir.'

'By Jove! This is good counsel.'

Firethorn made a graphic gesture with his hands and everyone in the vicinity understood. They were to speed things up. Their only hope lay in keeping ahead of the tempest that was bound to come. When Justice Wildboare made his next entrance, he did so with an alacrity that signalled a change of pace. Cues were picked up more quickly, speeches were dispatched more briskly, stage business was reduced to a minimum. Two small scenes were cut completely. The play scudded across the waves at a rate of several knots.

What made it all possible was the tacit bargain that was struck with the audience. They were in the same boat. Eager to watch the play, they did not want to get soaked while doing so. A shorter, sharper version was an acceptable compromise. The danger was that the play would gather so much momentum that it would get out of control but Wildboare made sure that it did not. No matter how fast the playing, he was always in judicious command.

They reached Act Five with no more interruption than a few rumbles of thunder. Their luck then ran out. A deep-throated roar came from directly ahead of them and forked lightning flashed with dazzling force. Within seconds, torrential rain fell and drenched the pit. Those in the galleries were protected by the overhanging eaves and anyone upstage had the shelter of the portico but the rest were pelted without mercy.

The groundlings complained bitterly and some ran for cover but most stuck it out so that they could see the end of the play. Sodden themselves, they gained much amusement from other victims of the downpour. Lucy Hembrow's wig was plastered to her face, the merry devils' tails were limp rags between their legs, Doctor Castrato talked about the scorching heat while splashing around in inches of water, Droopwell slipped and fell into a puddle, and the indomitable Youngthrust, shorn of his sighing by the dictates of speed, had to stand in the middle of the stage while the rain cascaded down from his codpiece as if it were the mouth of a drainpipe.

The miracle occurred at the start of the final scene.

As if a tap had just been turned off, the rain suddenly stopped. Clouds drifted apart and the sun burst through to turn everything into liquid gold. The marriage of Lucy Hembrow and Youngthrust took place in a positive blaze of glory. To the sound of stately music, the interior of a church—superbly made and cleverly painted—was winched down from above to act as a backdrop. It was a fitting climax to a play that had been supremely entertaining and intermittently moving and applause rang out for several minutes.

Roper Blundell was unable to take his bow.

Having bottled up the spectators for two hours, The Rose now squeezed them out in a steady jet. Some dispersed with laughter, others lingered to talk, others again loitered to thieve and cozen. *The Merry Devils* had been exhilarating and more than one man was looking for a way to take the edge off his excitement.

'Good afternoon, ladies!'

Grace Napier and Isobel Drewry curtseyed politely.

'Did you enjoy the play this afternoon?'

They both nodded behind their veils.

'Would not you like the pleasure to continue?' said the man, beaming at them as he tried to work out which was the more attractive. 'I can offer the comfort of my carriage to one or both of you.'

The two of them fought to hide their embarrassment.

'Come, ladies,' said the man persuasively. 'London is full of delights and you shall see them all. Will you not sup with me tonight? I promise you shall not lack for anything.'

He shared a flabby leer between the two of them.

Henry Drewry had forgotten how enjoyable an afternoon at the playhouse could be. Having bought a plentiful supply of ale from the vendors, he was further intoxicated by what happened on stage and came reeling out of the building in a state of euphoria. The urge for female company was powerful and he had spoken to a dozen women before he stopped Grace and Isobel. Rejection did not deflate him. He propositioned each new target with unassailable buoyancy.

'Will you see the sights of Bankside with me, ladies?' he said with pompous lechery. 'Or shall we ride back into the city to find our pleasures there? I can judge your quality and will treat you both accordingly.'

Isobel Drewry was profoundly shocked. It was amazing to find her own father at The Rose but to be accosted by him was mortifying. She had always seen him before as a tiresome, self-important man who lived for his work and his Aldermanic ambition. Since he ignored both her and her mother, she never suspected him of the slightest interest in the opposite sex. But Henry Drewry did have passions. Behind that fat, over-ripe tomato of a face and that round, ridiculous body was a creature of flesh and blood with sensual needs. As she saw him now in his true colours, shock gave way to disgust then was mortified by something else. Sheer amusement. The absurdity of the situation took her close to a giggle.

'What do you say to my kind offer, ladies?' he pressed, quite unaware of their identity. 'I am a man of some estate, I warrant you.'

Grace Napier decided that action spoke louder than words. It would also have the vital advantage of preserving their anonymity. Lifting her chin in disdain, she took Isobel by the arm and led her purposefully away. They were soon swallowed up in the departing crowd. Henry Drewry was unabashed. He looked around for new game to hunt and soon found it.

'Well met, good sir.'

'How now, dear lady?'

'Was not that the most excellent play in Creation?'

'I have never seen the like.'

'It has left me in such a mood for pleasure.'

The courtesan was a shapely young woman of middle height in a tight red bodice with patterning in gold thread, an ornate ruff that was decorated with cut-work embroidery and edged with lace, and a French wheel farthingale with the skirt gathered in folds. She was no punk from the stews of Bankside. She plied her trade in the upper echelons and had picked Drewry out as a man of substance. They were soon standing arm in arm and exchanging banter.

The relationship lasted only a few minutes.

'What brings you to this hideous place, Henry?'

'Oh!'

'I did not expect to find you here, sir.'

Isaac Pollard stood in front of the Alderman and the four supplementary Puritans surrounded him. He was ringed by religion and shook off his new acquaintance as if she were diseased.

'It was your playbill that fetched me here, Isaac,' he said.

'Indeed?'

'That and the holy fire of your sermon.'

'You have read it?'

'Twice,' lied Drewry who had not struggled beyond the first paragraph. 'It is an inspiration to us all. I intend to read it to my wife and daughter this very evening. Isobel is a good girl but a trifle wayward at times. I shudder at the thought of her frequenting such a vile establishment as this.'

'My brethren here were astounded by what they saw.'

'So was I, sir. I came hither to judge for myself and I am now totally of your opinion. The Rose is a flower of indecency.'

'Tear the place down, Henry.'

'Alas, we cannot. It lies outside the city boundary.'

'Then close the Queen's Head,' insisted Pollard. 'Plays demean the human soul and players are men who prostitute their art. Let us begin in Gracechurch Street.'

'I will look diligently into the matter.'

'We shall discuss it on our journey. You have your coach here?'

'It is at hand, Isaac.'

'My brethren and I will gladly accept your transport,' said Pollard. 'We all have views that we would impress upon you.'

Drewry gazed wistfully across at the courtesan who had now transferred her attentions to an elderly nobleman who leaned upon a stick. In place of her charms, the Alderman had to settle for five earnest Puritans. Pollard observed the woman as well and his eyebrow rippled quizzically. Drewry threw in a hasty explanation.

'A widowed lady who dwells in my ward,' he said. 'She seeks advice about her husband's estate. An Alderman must help such stricken wives.'

Flanked by the five, he turned his back on pleasure.

Roper Blundell lay on the table in the private room to which Nicholas Bracewell carried him. The corpse was covered in a piece of hessian, a rough but not inappropriate shroud. Small in life, the body looked even smaller in death, the shrunken relic of a man who had served the theatre in his lowly capacity for many years. Word of Blundell's demise had not been released to the company and there was a whirlwind of panic. Nicholas stood guard over the body to ensure it some privacy. Edmund Hoode and Barnaby Gill were his agitated companions.

'Why was I not *told*?' said Gill angrily. 'I would have not acted with a dead man beneath my very feet.'

'That is why I withheld the intelligence,' said Nicholas.

'You were right,' decided Hoode.

'I am a sharer in this company and should know everything that happens when it happens!' Gill went stamping around the room. 'Lawrence was informed and so should I have been!'

Nicholas glanced meaningfully at the corpse. Gill accepted the reproof and showed his respect by reducing his voice to a hiss. Not surprisingly, he saw the incident entirely from his own point of view.

'This is aimed at me, sirs.'

'How can you think that?' said Hoode.

'It is as plain as a pikestaff.'

'Not to us, master,' said Nicholas quietly.

'At the Queen's Head, I summon up a devil and Hell itself answers my call. During *Cupid's Folly*, I climb up a pole and some fiend contrives my downfall. Here at The Rose, I sprinkle my magic powder and one of my devils is killed. Can you not see the connections? In every case, it is I who stand at the centre of the action.'

'The wish was father to the thought,' observed Hoode.

'Do not mock me, Edmund!'

'Then do not invite mockery.'

'I remind you of my rank in this company!'

'Will you ever let us forget it, sir?'

'Gentlemen, please,' said Nicholas, indicating the shrouded figure. 'Roper had little enough respect from us when he was here. Let us give the poor fellow his due amount now that he has gone.'

They mumbled an apology. Gill drifted over to the window.

'Where is Lawrence?'

'Lord Westfield sent for him,' said Nicholas.

'He should be here.'

'His lordship was insistent.'

'*I* could have dealt with our patron,' said Gill airily. 'Lawrence's place is in this room.'

He stared out of the window and brooded on what had happened and how it affected him. Hoode had a whispered conversation with the book holder.

'What caused the death, Nick?'

'We will not know until the surgeon arrives.'

'Did Caleb Smythe not enlighten you?'

'He is as ignorant as the rest of us.'

'But he was down there with the others.'

'His back was to Roper,' explained Nicholas. 'It is gloomy and they were in any case half-hidden from each other's gaze by the props that hold up the stage. Caleb saw nothing.'

'He must have *heard* something was amiss?'

Nicholas shook his head. 'He was deafened by the first explosion. He could not hear if Roper's powder went off or if his trap-door opened. Besides, Caleb had much to do. He had to pull his own tray of gunpowder into position, set the charge, mount the steps and make his entrance. That left him no time to look across at Roper Blundell.'

'I understand it now.'

'The first that Caleb knew of any accident was when he popped up on the stage and saw that George Dart was the only devil there. He took the action he saw fit.'

'We must be grateful that he did.'

Hoode walked across to the table and uncovered the face of the corpse. Roper Blundell still stared upwards with his mouth agape. A costume which might have provoked horror and humour on stage looked singularly out of place now. Blundell had worked on all the playwright's work for the company. Hoode spared him the tribute of a passing sigh. It grieved him that something he had written should be the scene of the man's death.

There was a faint knock on the door and it opened to reveal a wizened figure in a long robe. He introduced himself with a dark smile.

'Doctor John Mordrake!'

His reputation gained him a polite welcome. Even Barnaby Gill was temporarily cowed in the presence of so eminent a man. Mordrake saw the corpse and crossed to it in triumph.

'I knew it, sirs!' he said. 'I foretold tragedy.'

'We await the surgeon's opinion,' said Nicholas.

'But I can tell you the cause of death, my friend.'

Mordrake reached down to close the eyes of Roper Blundell then pulled the hessian back over his face. He turned to the others and spoke with devastating certainty.

'He saw the Devil himself.'

Fine wine after an excellent programme put Lord Westfield in a warm and generous mood. He showered Lawrence Firethorn with compliments that were taken up and embroidered by the circle of hangers-on. It was generally agreed that, notwithstanding the thunderstorm, the second performance of the play was better than the first. Firethorn lapped up the praise, especially when it came from the three ladies present and he managed some assiduous hand-kissing by way of gratitude. While a hired man in the company lay dead in one room, its patron celebrated in another. Westfield's Men covered a wide spectrum.

'I puzzled over one omission, Master Firethorn.'

'Yes, my lord?'

'At the Queen's Head, you gave us *three* merry devils.'

'Indeed, sir.'

'And the third was hottest from Hell.' A collective titter was heard. 'Why did we see only two of them this afternoon?'

'Three were rehearsed, my lord.'

'What prevented the third from appearing?'

'An unforeseen difficulty,' said Firethorn smoothly.

'It was a loss.'

'We accept that, my lord.'

Firethorn decided to say nothing about the death of Roper Blundell. He did not want to ruin the festive atmosphere or bother his patron with news of someone who was, in the last analysis, a disposable menial. For the sake of the nobleman's peace of mind, Blundell's fate was softened into a euphemism.

'I hope that you can overcome this—unforeseen difficulty.'

'My lord?'

'During the private performance, I mean.'

'Ah, yes. At Parkbrook House.'

'My nephew will expect a full complement of devils.'

'He will get them, my lord.'

'Francis is a very determined young man,' said Lord Westfield with avuncular affection. 'He's ambitious and industrious. He knows what he wants and makes sure that he gets it. He'll not be stinted.'

'We'll bear that in mind, my lord.'

'He writes to tell me that your visit to Parkbrook has been brought forward. It will now be in two weeks or so.'

'That is rather short notice.'

'He *is* my nephew.'

'Oh, of course, of course.'

'I trust you'll oblige him, sir.'

'Yes, yes, my lord,' said Firethorn apologetically. 'It will necessitate a few changes in our plans, that is all.'

'Work on the house was proceeding too slowly for his taste so Francis speeded it up. I can imagine him doing that. He knows the value of a firm hand.' There was a hint of a sigh. 'Unlike his elder brother, who always erred on the side of sentiment.'

'As to the performance itself, my lord...'

'It will take place in the Great Hall.'

'I only know the property by repute,' said Firethorn. 'We have played at Westfield Hall many times but never at Parkbrook.'

'Send a man to make drawings and note the dimensions.'

'Nick Bracewell is the one for such an errand.'

'I'll write to warn of his arrival.'

Lord Westfield accepted another goblet of wine when it was offered and talked about the pride he felt in his company. They wore his livery and carried his name before the London playgoing public. He chose the moment to apply a little pressure.

'I would have you give of your best at Parkbrook.'

'We will do no less, my lord.'

'Francis is very dear to me, sir,' said the other warningly.

'We have much in common, he and I. This banquet has been arranged to establish him as the new master of Parkbrook so I would not have it fall short of expectation.'

'Westfield's Men will be worthy of their patron!'

Firethorn's declaration drew gloved applause from the others.

'You shall not lose by it,' continued Lord Westfield. 'Francis will pay you handsomely for your services.'

'That thought was far from my mind,' lied Firethorn.

'He'll draw the contract up himself, if I know him. Though he enjoys his pleasures, he has never neglected his studies. Francis is no idle wastrel. He is an astute lawyer.'

'He sounds a remarkable person in every way.'

'Very remarkable.'

'And so young to occupy such a position,' observed Firethorn. 'Tell me, my lord, was not his elder brother master before him?'

'That is so, sir.'

'I am sorry to hear that the gentleman has died.'

'Alas, sir! If only he had!' The sigh gave way to an impatient note. 'But I will not brood on poor David. What's done is done and there's no changing it. Francis Jordan owns Parkbrook now. His brother, David, must fade away from our minds.'

Kirk's duties at Bedlam were far too onerous to permit him anything more than brief visits to his favourite patient. He was therefore never able to sustain any progress that had been made. David would make some small advance in the morning yet be unsure about it by the same evening. He was constantly taking two steps forward then one back. It was deeply frustrating but the keeper did not give up.

He tried to find a way to help the patient when he himself was not there. Without telling his colleagues, he smuggled some writing materials into David's room. At first, the patient reacted like a child and scrawled over the parchment. Then he began to make simple drawings of cows and sheep and horses. He would sit for hours and smile fondly at his collection of animals. The next stage came when he tried to form words. A whole morning might result in nothing more than one illegible word but Kirk was nevertheless pleased. The breakthrough would surely come.

That afternoon condemned him to the duty that he liked least. With some of the other keepers, he supervised the Bedlam patients who were on display to members of the public. Respectable men and women came to watch with ghoulish fascination as disturbed human beings enacted their private dreams. It was a gruesome event at any time but the thunderstorm made it particularly bizarre. As the thunder rolled and the lightning flashed, the lunatics kicked and bolted like horses in a stable fire. Their antics became wilder, their screams more piercing, their hysteria more frightening, their pain indescribably worse but the spectators liked the sight and urged the keepers to beat more madness out of their charges.

When it was all over, Kirk began his round of the private rooms. He glanced in through the grille in David's door and saw the latter bent over a table with a quill in his hand, writing something with great concentration. He looked serene, preoccupied, harmless. No sooner had the door been unlocked, however, than he underwent a change. David became such a mass of convulsions that he knocked over the table and fell writhing to the floor. Kirk jumped to his aid and thrust his hand into David's mouth to prevent the latter from biting off his tongue. It was a far more violent and dramatic attack than the earlier one witnessed by the keeper.

Eventually the spasms subsided and David lay there gasping. Kirk helped him on to the bed and mopped the patient's fevered brow. Beside the overturned table was the parchment on which David had been writing with such care. The keeper reached down for it and saw that ink had been thrown all over it in the accident. Whatever words had been slowly extracted from David's mind had now been obliterated.

'What did you write?' asked Kirk.

The only reply was the stertorous breathing.

'David, can you hear me? Are you listening, David?'

The patient stared up with blank incomprehension. He no longer even recognised his name. He was back once more in his twilight world. Kirk was dejected. All their hard work had been thrown away.

There was now a further problem to hold them back.

'What goes on here, sir?'

Rooksley stood in the doorway and read the scene with unfriendly eyes. He crossed to take the ink-stained parchment from Kirk's hand. The head keeper made no secret of his anger.

'Who gave him this?'

'I did, Master Rooksley, to help him recover his wits.'

'Writing materials are forbidden.'

'I thought that—'

'Thought is forbidden, Master Kirk! You are paid to obey rules and not to change them.'

'This man has the falling sickness. He needs a physician.'

'We are his physicians.'

'But he is a danger to himself.'

'Only when you interfere here. He must be left alone.'

'Master Rooksley, he was *responding* to my help.'

'You'll not visit this chamber again, sir!' said the head keeper with a snarl. 'It is closed to you from this day forward. And if you will not discharge your duties to my satisfaction, you'll leave Bedlam altogether.'

Kirk bit back his protest. There was no point in antagonising Rooksley. Only if he remained on the staff could Kirk have the slightest hope of helping the patient. The head keeper motioned him out then he locked the door behind them. Kirk glanced back in through the grille.

'Who *is* he, master?'

'A lunatic.'

'But who pays to keep him here?'

'One who would stay unknown.'

The storm which had struck London that afternoon had ravaged the Home Counties as well. Eager to ride out on his estate, Francis Jordan was confined to Parkbrook by the lashing rain. He took out his disappointment on anyone within reach and Glanville had to soothe the hurt feelings of many of the domestics. Jordan's mood altered with the weather. As soon as the sun came out to brighten up the countryside, he became happy and affable. Kind words were thrown to his staff. Compliments reached those who worked on in the Great Hall. The new master could exude charm when it suited him.

His horse had been saddled by the time he reached the stables and he was helped up by the ostler. Giving the man a cheery wave, Jordan rode off at a rising trot. Parkbrook glistened like a fairytale palace and the land all around was painted in rich hues. It gave him an immense feeling of well-being to know that he was master of it all. The wait had been a long one but it had served to sharpen his resolution and heighten his anticipation.

He now owned Parkbrook House. All that he lacked was a wife to grace it with her presence and share in its bounty. Francis Jordan let his mind play with the notion of marriage. He would choose a wife with the utmost care, some high-born lady with enough wit to keep him amused and enough beauty to sustain his desire. She would dignify his table, widen his social circle, bear his children and be so bound up with her life at Parkbrook that she would not even suspect her husband of enjoying darker pleasures on his visits to London. Jordan wanted someone whom he could love in Hertfordshire and forget in Eastcheap.

His thoughts were soon interrupted. There was a copse ahead of him and a figure stepped out from the trees as he approached. The man was short, squat and ugly. One eye was covered by a patch that matched the colour of his black beard. His rough attire was soaked from the rain and he looked bedraggled. Jordan took him for a beggar at first and was about to berate him for trespass. When he got closer, however, he recognized the man only too well.

'Good day, sir!'

Deferential to the point of obsequiousness, the man touched his cap and shrunk back a pace. But there was a calculating note in his behaviour. As he looked up at the elegant gentleman on the horse, he gave a knowing smirk. Jordan was forced to acknowledge him.

'Good day,' he said.

Then he rode on past a memory he wished to ignore.

Ralph Willoughby rolled out of the Bull and Butcher in a state of guilty inebriation. No matter how much he drank, he could not forget what had happened that afternoon at The Rose. When only two merry devils emerged from beneath the stage, he knew that tragedy had struck though it was only later that he learned what form it took. His association with the play was fatal. Willoughby believed that he had murdered Roper Blundell as surely as if he had thrust a dagger into the man's heart. There was blood on his hands.

More rain was now falling on London and turning its streets into miry runnels. Willoughby's unregarding footsteps shuffled through mud and slime and stinking refuse. Impervious to the damp that now fingered his body, he lurched around a corner and halted as if he had walked into solid rock. St. Paul's Cathedral soared up to block his vision and accuse him with its purpose. Tears of supplication joined the raindrops that splattered his face.

Lumbering across the churchyard, he eventually reached the safety of the cathedral wall. As he leaned against its dank stone, it seemed at once to welcome and repel him, to offer sanctuary to a lost soul and to rebuke him for his transgressions. He was still supporting himself against religion when he heard a wild, maniacal screech that rang inside his head like a dissonant peal of bells. His eyes went upward and a lance of terror pierced his body. High above him, dancing on the very edge of the roof, was a hideous gargoyle in the shape of a devil.

He stared up helplessly as the malign creature mocked and cackled in the darkness. Taking his huge erect penis in both hands, the devil aimed it downwards and sent a stream of hot, black, avenging urine over the playwright's head. Willoughby burned with the shame of it all and collapsed on the floor in humiliation.

Those who later found him could not understand why he lay directly beneath a foaming water spout.

Anne Hendrik took him into her bed that night and made love with that mixture of tenderness and passion that typified her. Nicholas Bracewell was both grateful and responsive. Deeply upset by the death of Roper Blundell, he came home late from the theatre and was very subdued over supper. Sensing his need, Anne led him to her bedchamber and found an answering need in herself. They were friends and casual lovers. Because their moments of intimacy only ever arose out of mutual desire, they were always special and always restorative.

They lay naked in each other's arms in the darkness.

'Thank you,' he whispered, kissing her softly on the cheek.

'Does it help?'

'Every time.' He smiled. 'Especially tonight.'

'So you will not change your lodging, sir?'

'Not unless you come with me, Anne.'

She kissed him lightly on the lips and pulled him close.

'Nicholas...'

'My love?'

'Are you in danger?' she asked with concern.

'I think not.'

'All these accidents that befall Westfield's Men are disturbing. Might not you be the victim of the next one?'

'I might, Anne, but it is unlikely.'

'Why?'

'Because I am not the target.'

'Then who is? Ralph Willoughby?'

'He is involved, certainly,' said Nicholas with a sigh. 'We cannot lightly dismiss the word of Doctor John Mordrake. On the other hand...'

'You still do not believe in devils.'

'No, Anne.'

'Then what did Roper Blundell see beneath the stage?'

'Only he knows and his lips are sealed for ever.'

'Could the surgeon throw any light?'

'He was mystified, Anne.'

'Why?'

'There were no signs upon the body.'

'What was his conclusion?'

'Death by natural causes,' said Nicholas sceptically. 'He told us that Roper died of old age and a verminous profession.'

'Poor man! Does he leave a family?'

'None.'

'Is there nobody to mourn for him?'

'We few friends.'

They fell silent for a while then she rolled over on top of him and put her head on his chest. Nicholas ran his hands through her downy hair and traced the contours of her back. Her skin was silky to the touch. When she finally spoke, her voice was a contented murmur.

'I like that.'

'Good.'

'I like you as well.'

'That pleases me even more.'

She propped herself up on her arms so that she could look down at him. A shaft of moonlight was striking the side of his face. She kissed the streak of light then nuzzled his cheek.

'Who *is* the target?' she asked.

'I do not know, Anne.'

'What does your instinct tell you?'

'Someone hates the company.'

'Someone human?'

'That's my feeling.'

'Why does the attack always come during a performance?'

'Because that is how to hurt us most,' he argued. 'There are a hundred ways to damage Westfield's Men but our enemy strikes during a play to discredit us in front of an audience. If we had abandoned a performance in the middle, it would have done enormous harm to our reputation, and reputation means everything in the theatre.'

'But you were not forced to stop, Nick.'

'Master Firethorn and Master Gill were the heroes there,' he said. 'When that creature leapt out of the trap-door at the Queen's Head, everyone turned tail except Master Firethorn. He held the play together when it might have collapsed in ruins.'

'And at The Curtain?'

'It was Master Gill who showed his experience. When the maypole broke, he made light of the accident in front of the spectators. The aim was to disrupt our performance but once again it was foiled.'

'What of this afternoon?'

'A merry devil died. That would stop most companies.'

'Yet Westfield's Men carried on and the audience was none the wiser. I saw no hindrance in the action from where I sat. And since you kept Blundell's death a secret from the company, they were able to continue their performance.'

'Yes, Anne. It brings me back to my first assumption.'

'Which is?'

'Some jealous rival seeks to undermine us.'

'Your reasoning?'

'They know best how to do it—on the stage itself.'

'But that requires a knowledge of the play.'

'That is the most puzzling aspect of it all,' admitted Nicholas. 'I guard the prompt books scrupulously yet someone knows their contents.'

'A discontented member of the company?'

'We have enough of those, I fear. Master Firethorn has never been too generous with wages or too swift in their payment. We have our share of grumblers but none of them would sink to this kind of villainy. Were it successful, it would harm their own position.'

'Then it must be some former member of Westfield's Men.'

'There you may have it, Anne.'

'Players with a grudge?'

'Two or three have left us of late,' he said. 'Embittered men who went off cursing. They might not have been able to attack us in this way but they could give help to those that could.'

'We come back to Banbury's Men.'

'I harbour doubts on that score.'

She put her head back on his chest and he stroked her hair with absent-minded affection, inhaling its fragrance. He looked at the week ahead with some misgivings.

'Tomorrow we return to the Queen's Head.'

'That will please Master Marwood,' she said with irony.

'Thank goodness that Roper did not pass away on his premises. Our landlord would not have liked a corpse beneath our stage. It would have given him fresh grounds for breaking his partnership with us.'

'How many days are you there?'

'Three, Anne.'

'Not on Saturday?'

'We perform at Newington Butts then I'm away.'

'Away where, sir?'

'Did I not tell you of my commission?'

'You hardly spoke at all when you got home tonight.'

'Master Firethorn wants me to reconnoitre.'

'Where, Nick?'

'Parkbrook House.'

'On the Westfield estate?'

'Yes,' he said, playfully turning her over on to her back. 'I'm running away from you, Anne.'

'Treachery!'

'I go to the country.'

'Not for a while, sir.'

She kissed him full on the lips and desire stirred again.

'There is no question of your visiting the country!'

'Why not, father?'

'Because you are needed here.'

'By whom?'

'By me and by your mother.'

'But you never even notice whether I am in the house or not, and mother has already given her blessing to the idea. London is stifling me. I long to breathe some country air in my lungs.'

'No!'

'Would you prevent me?'

'By force, if need be.'

Isobel Drewry expected opposition from her father but not of this strength. For all his faults, he could be talked around on occasion. This time it was different. Under normal circumstances, his daughter would have backed off and tackled him at a more auspicious moment but their old relationship had dissolved. After the incident at The Rose on the previous afternoon, she no longer accepted him as the source of authority in her life. Isobel was finding it difficult to conceal the vestigial shock of what had happened. Pushed any further, she knew that her true feelings might show through.

They were in the room that he used as his office. Drewry sat importantly behind a large oak table that was covered with business correspondence. On a court cupboard to his right stood the symbol of his trade. It was a Vivyan Salt, some sixteen inches in height. Made of silver-gilt with painted side panel, the salt cellar had a figure representing Justice on its top. Isobel caught sight of it. She wanted her share of justice now.

Henry Drewry moved from cold command to oily persuasion. He tried to convince his daughter that his decision was in her own interests.

'Come, Isobel,' he said with a chuckle, 'do but think for a moment. Nothing ever happens in the country. You will waste away from boredom within the hour. London has much more to offer.'

'Not if you deny me access to it, father.'

'Do you really wish to dwindle away in some rural seat?'

'Yes, sir,' she said firmly. 'I have an invitation.'

'Refuse it.'

'But Grace is anxious for me to accompany her.'

'Mistress Napier can flee to the country on her own,' he said with some asperity. 'It may be the best place for her.'

'What do you mean?'

'She is not a good influence on you, Isobel.'

'Grace is my closest friend.'

'It is time that friendship cooled somewhat.'

'But she has asked me to join her at their country house.'

'You are detained here.'

Isobel gritted her teeth and held back rising irritation.

Drewry felt that he had reason to dislike Grace Napier. Her father was one of the most successful mercers in London and his burgeoning prosperity was reflected in the estate he had bought himself near St Albans. Naked envy made Drewry hate the man. His own business flourished but it did not compare with that of Roland Napier. Hatred of the father led to disapproval of a daughter who was better educated and better dressed than his own. There was also a self-possession about Grace Napier that he resented. It was time to terminate the friendship.

'In future, you will not see so much of Mistress Napier.'

'Why?'

'She is not a fit companion for you.'

'Grace is sweetness itself.'

'I do not like her and there's an end to it.'

Her father's peremptory manner made her inhibitions evaporate. She would not endure his dictates any longer. It was the moment to play her trump card.

'You do not like her, you say. It has not always been so.'

'No,' he agreed. 'Most of the time I have detested her.'

'Where were you yesterday afternoon, father?' she challenged.

'Yesterday?'

'Mother says you were at a meeting of the City Fathers.'

'Yes, yes, that is true. I was at a meeting.'

'Did it take place at The Rose in Bankside?'

Drewry went crimson and jumped up from his chair.

'Why do you mention that vile place to me?' he demanded.

'Because Grace was there,' said Isobel. 'She and a friend went to see Westfield's Men play *The Merry Devils*. It was another brilliant performance, by all accounts. Grace and her friend enjoyed it.'

'What has this got to do with me?' he blustered.

'Grace believes that she may have seen you there.'

'That is utterly impossible! A slander on my good name!'

'Her friend confirms that it was you.'

'A monstrous accusation!'

'But they *saw* you, father.'

'I deny it!' he said vehemently. 'The Rose holds hundreds and hundreds of spectators—or so I am told. How could they pick one man out in such a large crowd?'

'He picked them out, sir.'

The crimson in his cheeks deepened. He swallowed hard and leaned on the table for support. Before he could even try to defend himself, she delivered the killer blow.

'Grace and her friend wore veils,' she said. 'They say that you stopped them as they left the theatre. Taking them for women of looser reputation than they were, you made suggestions of a highly improper nature. So you see, sir—you liked Grace well enough then. Rather than discover themselves, they hurried away in a state of shock.' Isobel affected tears. 'How could my own father do such a thing? And with someone young enough to be his own daughter. You forbade me to go near the playhouse yet you went there yourself. Mother will be destroyed when she hears this.'

'She must not!' he gasped. 'Besides, it is all a mistake.'

'Mother will want an explanation. The first thing she will do is find out if there *was* a meeting yesterday. If there was not, she will know who to believe.'

Henry Drewry sagged. His predicament was harrowing. He had been found out by his own child. The bombast and hypocrisy he had used to sustain their relationship over the years were now useless. She saw him for what he was and his wife might now do the same. He was a broken man. The indiscretions of one afternoon had stripped his authority from him. His daughter reviled him. His wife might do more.

'Say nothing to your mother!' he begged hoarsely.

In the silence that followed there was a decisive shift in the balance of power within the family. An agreement was reached. She would not betray him to his wife and he would no longer constrain her in any way. For the first time in her life, Isobel Drewry felt that she had some control over her own destiny. It was a heady sensation.

Her father flopped down into his chair with head bowed.

'When will you go to the country?' he asked meekly.

'Whenever *I* choose!'

Isobel was learning how to rub salt into the wound.

Chapter Eight

Glanville gave her sensible advice. He told her to make sure that the new master was busy elsewhere before she entered his bedchamber. He urged her to leave doors and windows open while she was busy at her work. In the event of any further attack, her screams would be heard and help would soon come. Jane Skinner listened to it all with solemn concentration. She did exactly what the steward told her and the problem soon vanished. There was never a chance of her being caught by Francis Jordan in his bedchamber. She was circumspect.

Her anxieties eased and her confidence slowly returned. She was less furtive in her duties. What happened before could be put down to the new master's visit to the cellars. Too much wine had put lechery in his mind and lust in his loins. It would not occur again. Jane Skinner talked herself into believing it. She was making the bed in a chamber on the top storey when that belief was fractured. The door shut behind her and she turned to see Francis Jordan resting his back against it.

'Oh!' she said. 'You startled me!'

'I came to find you, Jane.'

'How did you know I was here, master?'

'I saw you from below,' he explained. 'I was in the garden when you opened the window up here. It was an opportunity I could not miss.'

He smiled broadly and took a few steps towards her. Jane backed away and pulled up a sheet in front of her chest as if trying to ward him off. Shaking with fear, she squealed her protest.

'Do not come any closer, please!'

'If that is what you wish,' he said, stopping.

'I will scream if you touch me, sir.'

'But I came her to apologise.'

'Did you?'

'Why else? Do you take me for such a complete ogre?'

'No, master,' she said cautiously.

'Put down your sheet, Jane,' he told her. 'You are in no danger here, girl. I am sorry for what took place the other day. I was hot with wine and my behaviour was ungentlemanly. Will you accept my apology?'

'Well...yes, sir.'

'It is honestly given. As you see, I am quite sober now.'

She nodded. 'May I go, master?'

'I am not stopping you,' he said, crossing to open the door wide. 'It is not my purpose to disturb you when you have duties to perform. I know that you are a conscientious girl.'

'I try to be, master.'

'Then carry on with your work. Goodbye.'

'Oh.'

His departure was as abrupt as his arrival. He marched out of the room and left her bewildered. Instead of a second assault, she had been accorded respect and even kindness. It soothed her instantly and she went back to the bed. She was just finishing her task when Jordan sauntered up to the door again and tapped on it with his knuckles.

'May I come in, Jane?'

'If you wish, master.'

The chambermaid was surprised but not intimidated this time.

'I forgot to tell you something,' he said.

'Yes, sir?'

'It was wrong of me to jump on you like that because it was an insult to you. I see that now. You're a fine-looking girl, Jane Skinner. You deserve more than a brief tumble like that.'

'Thank you, sir,' she said, misunderstanding him.

'A young woman like you should get her full due.'

'Should I, master?'

'Come to me for a whole night.'

His casual manner reinforced the impact of his order. Jane Skinner reeled as if from a heavy blow. To be grabbed and groped by him was ordeal enough but this was far worse. Her heart constricted as she viewed the prospect ahead of her. Francis Jordan was the master of Parkbrook House. His word was law within its walls. If she did not comply, she would be dismissed from his service.

Appraising her frankly, he gave her a thin smile.

'I will send for you some time in the near future, Jane. I'll expect you to answer my summons.'

She bit her lip in distress and her mind was a furnace.

'This is a matter between the two of us,' he said. 'I would not have it discussed elsewhere. Besides, there is nobody to whom you can turn. My word is everything at Parkbrook.'

He strolled across to her and lifted her chin with his finger. Jane was petrified. His touch was like a red-hot needle. He ran his eyes over her once more then nodded his approval. Turning on his heel, he went slowly out of the room.

The chambermaid was horror-stricken. She was caught like an animal in a trap and could see no means of escape. Life at Parkbrook had held no such fears under the old master but those days had clearly gone. To defy Francis Jordan seemed impossible yet to obey him would be to surrender everything she valued in her life. It was unthinkable. As a deep panic coursed through her, she felt the need to turn to somebody. Glanville would offer her sympathy even if he could not actually save her. With a little cry of anguish, Jane ran off to find him. She felt hurt, molested and thoroughly abused.

The long journey down to the ground floor left her breathless and she had to pause for a while to gather her strength. Then she was off again, searching every room and corridor with panting urgency, asking anyone she met if they knew where Glanville was. But there was no sign of the steward. At a time when she needed him most, he was simply not there. Despair gnawed at her. It was one of the carpenters at work in the Great Hall who gave her a faint hope.

'I think he be up in his room, mistress.'

She gabbled her thanks and took to her heels again.

Joseph Glanville had apartments on the first floor in the west wing. The correct way to approach them was to go up the main staircase and along the landings. But the steward also had a private staircase, a narrow, circular affair that corkscrewed upwards at the extreme end of the west wing. It was a mark of status and nobody else was allowed to use it except Glanville but the chambermaid forgot about that rule. Needing the quickest route to a source of help, she dashed along the corridor and clambered up the oak treads of the private staircase. Her shoes echoed and her breathing became more laboured.

When she reached the door, she pounded on it with both fists. 'Master Glanville! Master Glanville!'

'Who is it?' called a stern voice from within.

'Jane Skinner, sir.'

A bolt was drawn back, a key turned in the lock and the door was flung open. Jane had no opportunity to blurt out her story. The steward glared down at her with smouldering eyes.

'Did you come up that staircase?' he demanded.

'Yes, sir. I wanted to see you about—'

'It is for my personal use! You have no right, Jane Skinner.'

'No, sir.'

'How dare you flout my privilege!'

'But I needed to—'

'It is quite inexcusable,' he said angrily. 'You have no business coming to my apartments. Nothing is so important that it cannot wait until I am available. You must never come here again, Jane. Do you understand that?'

'Yes, master.'

'And you must never use that staircase again. I forbid it!'

Glanville withdrew and closed the door in her face. She heard the key turn in the lock. Jane was totally shattered. A man who had always shown her consideration in the past was now openly hostile. The one person who might stand between her and Francis Jordan had let her down in the most signal way. Her position was worse than ever.

The hut had been built on rising ground and it nestled in a hollow. Used by shepherds in earlier days, it had fallen into decay now that the land had been put under the plough. The roof was full of holes, the door hung off its hinges and the timbers of one wall had rotted through, but it still offered a degree of comfort. Bare and inhospitable though it was, the hut was an improvement on sleeping rough along the way. He helped his wife down from the cart then carried her over to their dwelling for that night. When he had cleared a space for her in one corner, he lay her gently down on some sacking.

Jack Harsnett was consumed with bitterness and grief. His wife had a short enough time to live. The least he had hoped was that she might pass away in the comfort and dignity of her own home. But that small consolation was rudely taken from them by the new master of Parkbrook. Shelter in a dilapidated hut was the best that they could manage now. It was a warm afternoon and the place had a quaint charm in the sunlight but it would be different in the long reaches of the night. That was when they would miss their old cottage.

He went back to the cart to unhitch the horse. Removing the harness, he tethered the animal to a tree with a long rope that gave it a wide circle of operation. There was a good bite of grass on the verge and the horse whinnied as it lowered its head. Harsnett lifted a bucket out of the cart then went to check that his wife was settled. She gave him a pale smile before she started to cough again. He touched her shoulder with a distant tenderness then went out.

Harsnett set off to forage. They had no food left.

Alexander Marwood was actually pleased to see them. Fortune had smiled on him over the last couple of days. His wife had shown him affection, his daughter had obeyed him, his customers had refrained from starting any fights in the taproom and some long-outstanding accounts had been settled in cash. He had every reason to be happy and it unsettled him. The return of Westfield's Men allowed him to indulge in creative misery once more. That was where his true contentment lay.

'I hear that a member of the company died, Master Firethorn.'

'It happens, sir.'

'Is foul play suspected?'

'Roper Blundell was poisoned,' said Firethorn with a teasing glint in his eye. 'He drank too much of your venomous ale, sir.'

'I have never had a complaint before!' said Marwood defensively.

'Your victims keel over before they can make it.'

'You do me wrong, Master Firethorn.'

'That is my pleasure, sir.'

'My customers constantly praise my ale, sir.'

'A sure sign of drunkenness.'

'They speak well of its taste and potency.'

'Condemned men in love with the noose that hangs them.'

Devoid of a sense of humour himself, Marwood never saw when he was the butt of someone else's amusement. He stiffened his back and made a bungled attempt at dignity.

'The Queen's Head has a fine reputation.'

'You may put that down to Westfield's Men, sir.'

'And to our own endeavours.' He became businesslike. 'I come for my rent, Master Firethorn.'

'It will be paid at the end of the performance.'

'You still owe me money from last week, sir.'

'An unfortunate oversight.'

'It is one of your habits.'

'Do not pass remarks on my character,' warned Firethorn. 'All accounts will be paid in full.'

'I am glad to hear it.'

Marwood glanced across at the stage which had been set up in his yard. The sight always lowered his spirits deliciously. He recalled what happened at The Rose.

'I want no devilry on the boards today, sir.'

'We play *Love and Fortune*,' said Firethorn grandly. 'It is a comedy of harmless proportions but none the worse for that.'

'Good,' said Marwood. 'I want no corpses at my inn.'

'Then stop serving that dreadful ale or you'll unpeople the whole neighbourhood!'

Unable to find a rejoinder, Marwood beat a retreat with Firethorn's ripe chuckle pursuing him. Westfield's Men might venture out to the custom-built theatres in the suburbs but the Queen's Head remained their home. The place would not be the same without some domestic upset with their cantankerous landlord. It added spice to the day.

Nicholas Bracewell came across to join his employer.

'You should have let me handle him, master.'

'The only way to handle that rogue is to throttle him!'

'He needs much reassurance.'

'He needs to be put in his place which is why I spoke to him.' Firethorn inhaled deeply. 'I'll not be confined or questioned by some snivelling little innkeeper! By Heavens, sir, let him meddle with me and I'll run him through with blank verse then cut off his stones with a rhyming couplet. A rank philistine!'

'Master Marwood does not love the theatre,' said Nicholas.

'Nor does the theatre love him, sir!'

The book keeper let him sound off for a few minutes. Firethorn might enjoy his verbal feud with the landlord but the fact remained that the latter rented them his premises. Nicholas had been trying for some time to interest Marwood in the idea of converting his yard into a more permanent theatre and those negotiations were not helped by interference from the actor-manager.

'Do you know what the wretch told me, Nick?'

'What, master?'

'That he did not want a dead body at the Queen's Head. Zounds! That Marwood *is* a dead body! A walking cadaver with a licence to sell rank ale. He's a posthumous oaf!'

'Has he heard, then, of Roper Blundell?'

'No bad news escapes that merchant of doom!'

'Did you tell him the cause of death?'

'I turned it into a joke against his drink.'

'We must not let him think there was some supernatural force at work. That would only feed his anxiety.'

'Nevertheless, it is the true explanation.'

'Not in my opinion, master.'

'You heard Doctor Mordrake.'

'He was mistaken.'

'Roper Blundell was killed by the Devil.'

'If he was killed at all, it was by a human hand.'

'The two go together,' said Firethorn. 'The Devil chose to work through a human agent here and we both know his name.'

'Ralph Willoughby is innocent of the charge.'

'He's the root cause of all our misfortunes.'

'But he was sad when he learned of Roper's end.'

'That did not stop him helping to murder the man. Yes, I know you have a high regard for Willoughby but he has never been a real friend to this company. This morning I was given clear proof of that. Do you know what that priest of Hell has done?'

'What, sir?'

'Sold his corrupt talents to the highest bidder.'

'He is employed by one of our rivals?'

'Ralph Willoughby has accepted a commission from Banbury's Men.'

Nicholas was shocked. He felt profoundly betrayed.

Alchemy was an irresistible temptation for the rogue and charlatan. So little was known of the science and so much claimed for it that fake alchemists set up all over London and found a ready supply of credulous gulls. Greed and folly activated most of the people who visited the new breed of magicians. They came in search of unlimited wealth and unlimited life, hoping to turn base metal into gold and yearning to find an elixir of youth. Notwithstanding the large sums they invested in their ambition, they failed to achieve either objective. Success somehow eluded them, as did the confidence tricksters themselves when their ruses were finally exposed. In the high-sounding name of alchemy, the public was seduced daily and exploited unmercifully.

Doctor John Mordrake was one of the few scientists whose record was blameless. Dedicated to the pursuit of knowledge, he never tried to mislead or bamboozle his clients. Indeed, he often bent his extraordinary energies to unmasking fraudulent practices among his rival magicians. He never made extravagant claims for what alchemy *might* do, only for what it could do.

His furnace was kept on the ground floor of his house in Knightrider Street and its fumes were often seeking out the nostrils of any passers-by. As he stood beside it now, Mordrake watched his assistant stoke up the fire to increase the heat. The customer, an obese man in brown satin, rubbed his hands with glee.

'When will my gold be ready, Doctor Mordrake?'

'Do not be hasty, sir,' warned the other. 'There are twelve stages in the alchemical process and none of them can be rushed. The first six are devoted to the making of the White Stone.'

'And then? And then?' asked the man eagerly.

'Six more long and careful stages.'

The assistant raked the coals again and sparks filled the room. While the customer stepped back in alarm, Mordrake held his ground and let the fiery atoms of light fall around him.

'How does it work?' said the customer.

'We are not sure that it will, sir.'

'But if my metal *is* refined into gold...'

Mordrake tossed his silver locks and gave a lecture.

'All substances are composed of four elements,' he began. 'By which, I mean earth, air, fire and water. In most things, those elements are not equally balanced. It is only in gold that they may be found in their perfect proportion. That is why we prize gold above all else. It is eternal, it is indestructible.'

'It is the source of true wealth,' noted the customer.

'My friend, my friend,' said Mordrake sadly. 'Do not be moved by a sordid desire for gain. Learn from Cicero—*O fallacem hominem spem*! Oh how deceitful is the hope of man! Remember Seneca—*Magna servitus est magna fortuna*. A great fortune is a great slavery. I do not work to satisfy the greed of men. That is ignoble and not the true end of alchemical inquiry. I seek perfection.'

'Does that not involve gold?'

'Only in the initial stage of the search.' He indicated the furnace with a blue-veined hand. 'In my raging fire here, I try to bring metals to their highest state, which is gold, but I would learn the science of applying the same principle to everything in life and—yes, sir—to life itself. Do you comprehend?'

'No,' said the man dully.

'I want to clothe all creation in perfection!'

There was a long pause as the visitor assimilated the idea.

'Can we make a start with my gold?'

Mordrake patted him on the shoulder then led him to the front door. When he had shown the man out, he padded upstairs to return to his work. As the old man entered the room, an elegant figure looked up from the massive book over which he was poring.

'Have you found what you were after, sir?' asked Mordrake.

'Indeed.'

'I would not show *Malleus Maleficarum* to many eyes.'

'That is why I am so grateful to you, Doctor Mordrake.'

'We'll set a price on that gratitude later,' said the other with a scholarly grin. 'Did the book enlighten you?'

'Wonderfully, sir. It made me think.'

'*Vivere est cogitare.*'

'To live is to think. We learned that tag at Cambridge.'

'From whom?'

'Horace.'

'Cicero,' said Mordrake. 'You should have gone to Oxford.'

'Neither place could help me fulfil my destiny,' said the young man wistfully. 'I was born to serve other imperatives.'

'I am pleased that the book has been a help to you.'

'Much more than a help, sir. It has pointed out my way for me.'

Edmund Hoode was transported by delight. His performance in *Love and Fortune* had won plaudits from Grace Napier that thrilled him and congratulations from Isobel Drewry that he did not even hear. The play had been well-received by an audience who knew it for one of the staples of the company's repertoire. There had been nothing to dim the pleasure of the afternoon. Though everyone was on the alert for trouble, none came and none even threatened. Hoode's cup of joy overflowed when Grace acceded to his request.

'Yes, sir, I would like to dine with you.'

'We'll arrange a place and time to suit your convenience.'

'It will have to be after my return from the country.'

'You are leaving London?' His stomach revolved.

'At the end of the week,' she explained. 'But I will not be away for long, Master Hoode, and then we shall certainly dine together.'

'I will count the hours until that blessed time.'

'Do not wave me off so soon,' she chided with a smile. 'I do not leave for a few days yet. I will be here at the Queen's Head again tomorrow to watch *Vincentio's Revenge*.'

'And so will I,' piped Isobel.

Hoode shifted his feet. 'I am not well-cast in this tragedy.'

'It is no matter, sir,' said Grace pleasantly. 'I would watch you if you played but the meanest servant. It is Edmund Hoode that I come to see and not the part he plays.'

He kissed her hand on impulse. Isobel giggled inappropriately.

When the two of them left, he shuttled between happiness and misery. Grace Napier had agreed to dine with him but she had first to go away. Before he could be really close to her, they would have to be far apart. The thought that she might stir outside London filled him with dread. He wanted her to be in the same city as himself, if not in the same ward, the same house, the same chamber, the same bed and the same love affair. After full consideration, he dismissed the pangs of remorse and decided that he was entitled to feel triumphant. He had got his response at last. His plays, his performances and his poems had won a promise from his beloved.

It was a triumph that merited a small celebration.

'More ale, Nick?'

'I have had my fill, I think.'

'A cup of wine to see you on your way?'

'It would detain me in this chair all night.'

They were sitting together in Hoode's lodging. Desperate to tell of his good fortune, the playwright had pressed his friend to come back for an hour that had somehow matured into four. Nicholas Bracewell drank, listened, nodded at intervals and threw in words of encouragement whenever a small gap appeared in the narrative. He tried to leave more than once but was restrained by his host. Grace Napier was the centre of Hoode's world and he went round and round her with repetitious zeal.

Nicholas eventually got to his feet and contrived a farewell. Another burst of memoirs held him on the doorstep for five minutes then he broke free. Hoode went back inside to marvel at his luck and to pen another sonnet to its source. If Grace could tolerate him as a venal Duke in *Vincentio's Revenge*, she must indeed be smitten.

It was a fine night. Nicholas ambled along a street with a sense of having done an important favour to his friend. It did not hurt him to listen to the amorous outpourings of Edmund Hoode and his presence had clearly meant so much to his host. The playwright would do as much for Nicholas. Not that he would ever lend himself to such a situation. Affairs of the heart were matters of discretion to him and no man had ever heard him boast or sigh. It was one of the qualities in him that most attracted Anne Hendrik.

The incessant talk of Grace Napier turned his mind to his landlady. Most of the things that Hoode praised in his beloved were traits that she shared with Anne. In thinking about one woman, Nicholas gained some insight into his relationship with another. For that alone, it was worth keeping a babbling playwright company. Nicholas sauntered on in a mood of quiet satisfaction. Then he heard the footsteps behind him.

It was only then that he realised just how much he had drunk. His reactions were far too slow. By the time he swung round, the first blow had already caught him on the side of his head. He tightened his fists and crouched to defend himself. There were two of them, burly figures with broad shoulders and thick necks. When both of them charged him, he was knocked back against a wall and his head struck the hard stone. His assailants began to pummel him.

Nicholas fought back as best he could. Evidently, the men were not the thieves he had at first assumed them to be. If they were after his purse, they would have used a cudgel to knock him unconscious or a knife to stab his back. Though he was taking punishment, he managed to retaliate strongly. When his fist made contact with a craggy face, it came back spattered with blood. Bringing his knee up sharply, he hit one of the men in the groin then pushed him away as he bent double in agony. The second man grappled with Nicholas.

The attackers were strong but they were not skilled fighters. Had Nicholas not been slowed by drink and dazed by the blow on his head, he could have handled them with ease. They were not after his money or his life. They had another purpose and he soon learned what it was.

'There he is, officers!'

'Seize the fellow!'

'Come, sirs!'

'Stop in the name of the law!'

A young man ran along the street with two members of the watch. Before he knew what was happening, Nicholas found the two constables holding his arms. He protested his innocence and told how he had been attacked but they would not listen to him.

'This gentleman here witnessed the affray, sir.'

'Indeed, I did,' said the young man, stepping forward. 'You attacked that person with the beard and this other gentleman came to his aid.' He pointed to the man who was still doubled up in pain. 'Do you see, officers, how violent the assault must have been?'

'Leave this to us, sir,' said one of the constables.

Nicholas felt a sledgehammer inside his skull but his brain was still clear enough to work out that the three men were accomplices. With all his experience in the theatre, he could recognise stage management. They had set him up for arrest. When he tried to explain this, he was ignored. Nicholas did not cut an impressive figure with his bruised face, his torn jerkin and his slurred speech. The constables preferred to accept the word of the young man with an air of wealth about him.

Feeling drowsier by the minute, Nicholas did not hear what his two assailants were saying but they were obviously telling a prepared story. It was backed up by the young man. At one point, this individual stepped close to the lantern held by one of the constables. Nicholas had a fleeting glimpse and noticed two things. Though the book holder had never actually met the young man before, the latter's profile was somehow familiar, and on his right hand he wore a ring that gave a clue as to his identity because gold initials were embossed on black jet.

Nicholas wondered who GN could possibly be.

Having heard the statements, the constables became officious. Honest and just men, they lacked any real education and did their job as well as their meagre abilities allowed. They belonged to a profession that was much-mocked and much-maligned. London watchmen were notoriously inept and inefficient, as likely to aid a felon's escape through their stupidity as to bring him to book through their promptness. The two constables were well aware of their low reputation and they resented it strongly. Given the opportunity of such an easy apprehension of an offender, they made the most of it. One of them confronted Nicholas.

'I arrest you for assault and battery at the suit of Master Walter Grice.'

'But it was *they* who attacked me, officer,' said Nicholas.

'Come your way, sir,' said the constable.

Nicholas faced his assailants and fired a last question.

'Which one of you is Walter Grice?'

The larger of the two thrust his face in beside the lantern. There was a long cut above his right eye where Nicholas had split open his skin. Blood oozed freely down his cheek but he was not perturbed by it. Nor did he seem to bear Nicholas any ill will for the injury.

'I am Walter Grice,' he said. 'Sleep well tonight.'

The two constables took the prisoner off down the street.

It was midnight when she retired to her bed and he had not returned. When he was still absent after a further hour, Anne Hendrik became worried. Her lodger worked long and variable hours but he was usually home in time for supper. If he was going to be late, or stay away for the night, he always warned her in advance. It was most unlike him to be so late. Anne got up and went across to his bedchamber. By the light of her candle, she saw that the place was still empty. There was nothing which indicated where he might be.

She went back to her own room and climbed into bed once more, rehearsing the possibilities in her mind. Nicholas might have been asked back to the home of one of the players. That sometimes happened. Lawrence Firethorn liked to involve the book holder in any business discussions and Edmund Hoode often used him as a shoulder to cry on. Had he been to either place, he must certainly be back by now.

There were two other possibilities, neither of which was palatable to her. Nicholas had been led astray. Actors were a law unto themselves. They led strange, anarchic lives and took their pleasures along the way as and when they found them. Something of that spirit must have rubbed off on Nicholas and it was conceivable that female company had diverted him for once. Some of the company went roistering in taverns almost every night. Had Nicholas been persuaded to join them? He liked women and he was very attractive to them. What was there to stop him? Jealousy flared up and quickly turned to disgust. If he could cast her aside so easily for a casual fling, it said little for the depth of their friendship.

Anne Hendrik then remembered their blissful night together. He had been so tender and loving. No man could change so completely in such a short time. Besides, Nicholas was exceptionally honest. He was secretive but he never deceived her. If there was another woman in his life, he would be candid about it. Anne reprimanded herself for even suspecting him of infidelity. When she thought of the person she knew, with his sterling qualities and his fine values, she realised that he would not go astray easily.

That left only one option and it was fearful to contemplate. He must have met with some accident or misadventure. Violence stalked the streets of London. Even as big and powerful a man as Nicholas Bracewell could not cope with every situation which a dark night might throw up. He had been attacked, he was hurt, he was lying wounded somewhere. The more she thought about it, the more convinced she became. Nicholas was in serious trouble. She longed to be there to help him.

Where *was* he?

'Wake up, sir! Wake up! You'll have time enough for sleep inside!'

'What?'

'You've come to the Counter, sir, to take your ease.'

'How did I get here?'

'By personal invitation of our constables.'

The prison sergeant laughed harshly and showed blackened teeth. His beard was still flecked with the soup he had eaten earlier. He was a big, muscular, unprepossessing man with the reflex cruelty that went with his trade. While the constables gave their report, he scrutinised Nicholas with a cold and unforgiving stare. He had no difficulty in believing that such a man could commit such a crime.

Nicholas shook his head to focus his thoughts. His memory was playing tricks on him. He recalled the face of Walter Grice then there was a blank. Now he was standing inside the grim walls of the Counter in Wood Street, one of the many prisons in London and among the worst. He was forced to give his name and address then divulge his occupation. Mention of the playhouse brought a sneer from the sergeant.

'You'll play no scenes nor hold no book here, sir!'

'Sergeant, I have done nothing illegal.'

'That's what they all say.'

The law was slow and ridiculous but it punished those that it caught very severely. Nicholas had no illusions about what lay ahead. The privations of a long voyage had given him some knowledge of how men could degenerate. Locked away in the Counter was the detritus of society, creatures whose long voyage was made in some foul cell and who would never see the light of day again. Nicholas had no legal redress unless he could enlist the aid of friends. Only one thing mattered inside the prison.

'Where will you be lodged, sir?' asked the sergeant roughly.

'Lodged?'

'Our guests here choose their favourite chambers.' Another harsh laugh rang out. 'There's fourteen prisons in London and we're the best, sir, if you have the garnish for it.'

'Garnish?'

As soon as he spoke the word, Nicholas understood its meaning. The Counter ran on bribery. It was not the nature of his offence or the severity of his sentence which determined a prisoner's accommodation. It was his ability to pay. Those with a long purse could buy almost anything but their freedom.

'We have three grades of lodging here,' said the sergeant.

'What are they, sir?'

'First, there's the Master's Side. That's where you'll find the most comfortable quarters, sir. There'll be fresh straw in your cell and sheets that are almost clean.'

'How much will that cost?' asked Nicholas.

'I'll have to put your name in the Black Book,' said the sergeant, opening the tome in front of him. 'That will need a couple of shillings from you. And at each doorway you pass through on your way, the turnkey will expect no less.'

Nicholas made a quick calculation. His money was limited and he had to try to make it last. It was common knowledge that to be poor in prison was to be buried alive. He had to hold out until he could get help from outside.

'What is the next grade of lodging, sergeant?' he said.

'That would be the Knight's Side, sir.'

'How much is that?'

'Half as much but less than half as cosy. You'll get straw on the Knight's Side but you have to shake the rats from it first. You'll have a sheet but you'll have to fight for it with the others. There's meat and claret to wash it down, if you've the garnish, and tobacco to take away the stink of your habitation.'

'You said there were three grades, sergeant.'

The harsh laugh grated on the prisoner's ear again.

'Shall I tell you what we call it, sir?'

'What?'

'The Hole.'

'Why?'

'You'll soon find out, sir,' said the sergeant. 'There's some as likes to lie in their own soil and feed off beetles. There's some as prefers four walls with never a window in them. There's some as would rather starve to death down there than pay a penny to an honest gaoler.' He crooked his finger to beckon Nicholas forward. 'I'll tell you this much, Master Bracewell. We puts more in the Hole than ever we takes out.'

'I'll choose the Knight's Side,' said the prisoner.

'Not the Master's?'

'No, sir.'

'Very well.'

The sergeant put his name in the black prison register then charged him for the effort. He was about to motion up an officer who stood at the back of the room when Nicholas interrupted him.

'I must send a message to someone.'

'Oh, now that could be expensive, sir.'

'How much?'

'It's against the regulations for us to take messages out of here. We'd need a lot to sweeten us on that score. It would depend on how long the message was and how far it had to go.'

Nicholas haggled for a few minutes then struck a bargain. He borrowed the quill to scribble some words on the parchment then he rolled it up, flattened it out, and appended the name and address. It cost him five shillings, over half of his weekly wage. As he watched his message disappearing into the sergeant's pocket, he wondered if it would ever be delivered.

'It's late, sir. You'll be taken to the Knight's Side.'

'Thank you.'

The officer came forward to escort Nicholas through a series of locked doors. Each time they stopped, the prisoner had to pay the turnkey to be let through. It was extortion but he had to submit to it. Eventually, he reached his quarters.

'Go on in, sir,' said the officer.

'Will I be alone?'

'Oh no, sir. You've lots of company there and you'll hear lots more.' He gave a chuckle. 'The cell is next to the jakes.'

He pushed Nicholas in and walked away.

It was a bad time to arrive. It was pitch dark in the cramped cell and the other prisoners were asleep. They stirred angrily when they sensed a newcomer. All the best places had been taken and there was nowhere for Nicholas to lie down properly. As he felt his way around in the gloom, he became aware of his bedfellows. One punched him, another bit his arm, a third shrank away in fear and a fourth cried out for some affection and tried to stroke his leg.

Nicholas found a space where he could sit against the wall with his knees up in front of him. There was no straw and no covering. It was warm, unwholesome and oppressive. If this was the quality of lodging offered in Knight's Side, he wondered how much more terrible it must be to get thrown into the Hole.

The officer had been right about the proximity of the privy. Prisoners shuffled in and out all night. Nicholas was kept awake by the noise and stench of their evacuations. It was like lying in a pig sty and he wondered how long he could survive it. Certainly, his purse would not gain him many privileges. Nearly all his money had gone already and he had no means of acquiring any more at short notice. As a hand groped across for his purse, he saw that he would have a job to hold on to what he still had.

There was one tiny consolation. The squalor of his surroundings brought him fully awake and helped him to shake off the lingering effects of the bang on the head. Though he still could not remember what happened between his arrest and his arrival at the Counter, his brain was no longer swimming. Revolted by his situation, it was working madly to get him out of it.

He reconstructed his day in his mind. An early start after a nourishing breakfast at his lodgings. Rehearsal then performance of *Love and Fortune*. The removal of one load of costumes, properties and scenic items followed by the organisation of another for the morrow. An evening with Edmund Hoode and too much drink. The walk home and the unexpected attack by three men with a firm purpose.

They had succeeded in what they had set out to do. Nicholas sat up stiffly as realisation dawned. He now saw why he had been the target of the assault and what the men hoped to achieve.

It was all part of a logical pattern.

He was next.

Chapter Nine

Night was far worse than day in the hospital of St Mary of Bethlehem. It seemed longer, darker and infinitely more sinister. While the rest of London slumbered peacefully, madness was abroad in Bedlam. Strange, unreal, inhuman cries would pierce the ear and reverberate around the corridors. Someone sang hymns at the top of his voice until he was beaten then religion became a long howl of pain. Those who could not sleep woke those who could. There were fights among inmates, attacks on keepers and lacerating self-scourging. Tumescent males tried to reach the female patients. Wild-eyed maniacs tried to escape. There was such a fierce mixture of nocturnal suffering that it sounded as if the whole of Bedlam was in the process of committing suicide.

Kirk hated it. He had been put on night duty as a punishment and spent most of his time rushing to different parts of the building to cope with an emergency. The whip was even more effective than the kind word at night. He was ashamed of his skill with the former. It had long since dawned on him that he could stay at the hospital for ever. It was destroying his soul and his belief in God. All that kept him there was the hope that he might be able to rescue at least one man from the shackles of his madness.

David was now out of reach. Rooksley had taken away Kirk's key to the young man's chamber. All that the new keeper could do was to peer at his friend through the grille on the door. David was quiet that night. As pandemonium raged around him, he lay on his bed and stared up at the ceiling. Watching him from outside, Kirk wondered what thoughts were going through the man's mind and what secrets lay hidden there. If he could find the key to unlock that mind, it would unlock the doors of Bedlam for David as well.

A more immediate duty called. There was a bloodcurdling scream from the far end of the corridor that made Kirk break into a run. When he reached the cell, he looked in through the grille to see a short, grey-haired old man in the murky darkness, trying to destroy his few sticks of furniture in a paroxysm of rage. The table had been hurled against a wall, the chair had been smashed to pieces and the man was now hurling himself on his mattress in a frenzy to shred it with his bare hands.

Letting himself in, Kirk went over to restrain the patient but the latter had a strength that belied his age and he struggled hard. Only when another keeper came to his aid did Kirk subdue the man, who sank to his knees and wailed as the whip did its work. Wearing nothing but a blotched and tattered shirt, he had no protection against the sting and the bite so he curled himself up into a ball on the ground and wept piteously. Kirk stopped his companion from administering any more punishment and eased him out of the room. The old man would be no more trouble that night. A priest who toured the hospital to bring some comfort now arrived and helped the old man up. The keepers went back to their patrol.

Diverted for a time by the latest incident, Kirk's thoughts went back to David and he resolved to find out more about him. It would be risky but that would not deter him. As he walked around the corridors, he made his way towards the room near the main entrance which the head keeper used as his office. First making sure that he was not observed, Kirk reached the door and found it locked. He tried everything on his bunch of keys and found one that worked. Slipping quickly into the room, he closed the door behind him then lit the candle that was standing in a holder on the table. Stealth was essential as Rooksley himself lived and slept in the adjoining chamber.

In the centre of the room was the high desk that contained all the records of the establishment, the accumulated misery of generations of men and women who had lost their wits and been sent to Bedlam to make sure that they did not recover them again. The hospital had been dedicated to a high moral purpose but Kirk knew the reality that lay behind it. Many came to the hospital but few were released and those that *were* deemed to have been cured were turned out to beg in the streets or forage among the refuse.

The desk was scarred by age and pitted by usage. Kirk lifted the lid and took out a large, leather-bound book. He opened it to find rows of squiggles and columns of figures, both autographed with many blots. It was the account book for the hospital and not what he sought. Putting it back, he took out in its place a similar volume with covers that shone brightly from all the handling they had been given. It was the register of inmates, the endless list of unfortunates who had been coaxed, tricked or forced into Bedlam and whose whole lives were now summed up in the few lines that accompanied their names in the book.

Kirk flipped through until he came to those who had been recently committed. They were all patients he had got to know since he had been there and he found their cases heart-rending, but he could not dwell on them now. He was searching for one name that would bring clarity to his speculations and equip a dear friend with an identity.

Rooksley's hand was rough and unstylish but Kirk could manage to decipher the writing. Then he saw it and caught his breath in the thrill of discovery.

The name in the register was David Jordan.

His dream was a bruising nightmare of threatening phantoms and he came out of it with a shudder. There was no relief. A further horror beckoned. Finding that he was not alone in the bed, he looked down to see that he lay in the arms of a devil, a deformed, hideous, grotesque creature that was covered in red scales and tufted with thick, furry hair. Its touch was clammy and its odour was nauseating. As it slumbered beneath him, it snored gruffly.

Ralph Willoughby leapt out of the bed and grabbed his clothes. Not pausing for an instant, he opened the door and ran naked along the passageway, throwing himself down the staircase and racing towards the door. When he got into the narrow yard at the back of the tavern, he ducked his head in the barrel of scummed rainwater. Then he pulled on his clothes as fast as he could and lurched out into the lane.

Up in the chamber he had just left, the girl in the bed woke for an instant, wondered where he had gone, then slept again.

The cold water and the cool night air revived his brain but brought no peace of mind. Willoughby was no longer guilty about his decadent pleasures or revolted by their nature because he had come to accept himself for what he was but fear still disturbed him. They were calling him more often now and he was not yet ready to go. As a black cat came shrieking out of a doorway, he gasped in terror and hurried on with more speed.

Only when he finally reached his lodging did he feel a degree of safety. Pouring water into a bowl from a pitcher, he immersed his head again then dried it on a cloth. He felt better, more settled, more ready to address the task he had set himself. He lit a candle, sat down at his table and reached for the knife to sharpen his quill. When it was ready, he dipped it into the inkwell then wrote something in bold letters on the title page of his new play.

Ralph Willoughby regarded it with an interest that soon turned to a macabre amusement and he put back his head to let out a long, low, sardonic cackle. He wanted his play to be memorable and its title gave him a mischievous satisfaction.

The Witch of Oxford.

Day began early at the Counter. Straw began rustling at first light and gaolers came round with luke-warm porridge to sell to the prisoners for their breakfast. Having finally managed to fall asleep, Nicholas Bracewell was almost immediately roused from his slumber. One whiff of the food made him decline it but the others in his cell slurped it down eagerly. They were a motley crew that included a cutpurse, a horse thief and the master of a brothel. There was even a confidence trickster who claimed to have a tenuous connection with the theatre.

'In Bristol once, I had some handbills printed for a lavish entertainment that was never going to take place, and I raised fifteen pounds against the promise of it. By the time my audience discovered the truth, I was far away in Coventry selling the deeds of a silver mine that I invented on the journey there.'

They were cheerful rogues who had been in and out of prisons all their lives. Nicholas did not have to ask them anything. They volunteered their stories and told them with a skill that showed long practice. When the newcomer claimed that he was in prison as a result of wrongful arrest, they mocked him with their jeers.

'Arrest is arrest, sir,' said the horse thief sagely. 'If it be rightful or wrongful, there's no difference, for the prison food still tastes the same either way.'

Their attitude was not encouraging and Nicholas was dejected when he heard tales of men who had languished in prison for years for crimes that they had never committed. He wondered again if his message had been delivered. Unless he could make contact with the outside world, nobody would know that he was locked away and his dwindling funds would eventually oblige him to shift to the Hole, which was a prospect too gruesome to contemplate. The cutpurse described what might be expected in the third grade of lodging at the Counter.

'Here, we are but next to the jakes, sir,' he said, wrinkling his nose in disgust. 'There, you are in it!'

Nicholas was appalled. He had to escape somehow.

While most of his companions were frankly garrulous, there was one who never uttered a word. A huge, bearded giant of a man who seemed about to burst out of his clothes, he sat quietly in a corner with a wistful expression on his beefy face. Nicholas saw that the man did not fit in with the others. They were habitual criminals for whom a prison was second home while he was weighted down by the ignominy of his situation. Nicholas moved across to sit beside him and talked to him kindly. He gradually drew the man's tale out of him.

'My name is Leonard, sir. I am a brewer's drayman.'

'What's your offence?' asked Nicholas.

'Too much drink at Hoxton Fair.'

'They arrested you for that?'

'No, sir,' explained the other. 'The ale led to something else that I am ashamed to talk of and yet, God knows, I must for a sin must be admitted before it can be pardoned.'

There was a gentle sadness about the man that touched Nicholas. Here was no son of the underworld who lived on his wits. Leonard was an honest workman who had been led astray by friends when he was in his cups and who was now paying a dreadful price for it.

'Have you heard of the Great Mario, sir?' asked the drayman.

'The wrestler who travels the fairs?'

'He'll wrestle no more, sir,' said the other with sombre guilt. 'Mario came from Italy to try his skill in England. He fought for six years and was never bested until he came to Hoxton.'

'You took up his challenge?'

'Oh no, sir. I'm no brawler. I want a quiet life.' He sighed. 'But God made me strong and my fellows at the brewery know how I can toss the heavy barrels around so they put me up to it. The Great Mario was at Hoxton Fair all week. Younger men and bigger men tried to lower his reputation but he was master of them all. Then I and my fellows went to the fair on Saturday last and took some ale along the way.'

'They talked you into it,' guessed Nicholas.

'I saw no harm in it, sir, so I did it in fun to please them. There was no thought of winning the bout.'

'What happened?'

'He hurt me,' said Leonard simply. 'We wrestled but Mario could not throw me because I was too strong for him, so he uses tricks on me that were no part of a fair fight. He pokes and punches, puts a finger in my eye and another down my throat, stamps on my foot and bites me on the chest as if he would eat me. I still bear the mark.'

'You lost your temper.'

'It was the ale, sir, and the shouting of the crowd and the Great Mario cheating his way to victory. Yes, I lost my temper. When we grappled once more, I was angrier than I've ever been in my life. And there were my fellows urging me on and telling me to break his neck.' He gave a shrug. 'And so I did. I snapped him in two. He died within the hour.'

'Is that why they brought you here?' said Nicholas.

'The Counter is but a place for me to rest, sir. They mean to hang me when they can find a rope strong enough for the task.'

The vast frame shivered involuntarily then lay back against the wall. Nicholas was sufficiently moved by his predicament to forget his own for a moment. It was a cautionary tale. Leonard was the victim of his own body. Had he been a smaller or a weaker man, he would not have been forced into the contest by his friends.

He had led a blameless life yet would go to his death with a shadow across his heart.

As Nicholas reflected on it all, he was halted by a sudden thought.

'Was Hoxton Fair a large one this year?'

'Bigger than ever, sir,' said Leonard with a sad grin. 'They had fools and fire-eaters, ballad singers, a sword-swallower, hobby horses, gingerbread, roasted pig, games for children, a play for those of wiser sort, drums, rattles, trumpets and old Kindheart, the tooth-drawer. They had everything you care to mention at Hoxton, sir.'

'Acrobats?'

'Oh yes! The strangest creatures you ever did see, sir.'

Nicholas listened with total fascination.

Vincentio's Revenge was not just a play which gave Lawrence Firethorn unlimited opportunity to display his art, it was a highly complex drama that required enormous technical expertise. Spectacular effects were used all the way through it. A large cast swirled about a stage that gradually became more and more littered with dead bodies as the ruthless Vincentio began to depopulate the city of Venice. Since actors became properties once they were killed, they had to be lugged away somehow and this called for careful organisation. The vital but unobtrusive work of Nicholas Bracewell was everywhere in the production. He devised the effects and orchestrated the action. Important to every play performed by Westfield's Men, the book holder was absolutely crucial to this one. To stage it without him was inconceivable.

'Where is Nick?' demanded Firethorn.

'Master Bracewell is not here, sir,' said George Dart.

'Of course, he is here, you ruinous pixie! He is *always* here. Rather tell me that the Thames is not here or that St Paul's has tip-toed away in the night. Nicholas is here somewhere.'

'I have searched for him in vain.'

'Then search again with your eyes open.'

'No fellow has seen him today, master.'

'You will be the first. Away, sir!' He watched the other trudge slowly away. 'Be more speedy, George. Your legs are made of lead.'

'And my heart, sir.'

'What's that?'

'I miss Roper.'

'So do we all, so do we all.'

Firethorn saw the tears in his eyes and crossed to put a hand of commiseration on his bowed shoulder. For all his bravado, the actor-manager had been shaken by the incident at The Rose.

'Roper died that we may live,' he said softly. 'Cherish his memory and serve the company as honestly as he did.'

George Dart nodded and went off more briskly.

Almost everyone had arrived by now and it was time for the rehearsal to begin. The musicians, the tiremen, the stagekeepers all needed advice from Nicholas Bracewell. The carpenters could not stir without him. The players grew restless at his absence. Barnaby Gill caused another scene and demanded a public reprimand for the book holder. He and Firethorn were still arguing when George Dart returned. He had been diligent in his search. Nicholas was nowhere at the Queen's Head.

'Then run to his lodgings and fetch him from his bed!'

'Me, sir?' asked Dart. 'It is a long way to Bankside.'

'I will kick you every inch of it if you do not move, sir!'

'What am I to say to Master Bracewell?'

'Remind him of the name of Lawrence Firethorn.'

'Anything else, sir?'

'That will be sufficient.'

'I fly.'

But George Dart's journey was over before it had even begun. As he turned to leave, the figure of a handsome woman swept in through the main gates and crossed the inn yard towards them. Anne Hendrik moved with a natural grace but there was no mistaking her concern. Firethorn gave her an extravagant welcome and bent to kiss her hand.

'Is Nicholas here?' she said.

'We hoped that he would be with you, dear lady.'

'He did not return last night.'

'This is murky news.'

'I have no idea where he went.'

'I can answer that,' said Edmund Hoode, stepping forward. 'Nick came with me to my lodging to share some ale and discuss some private business. It was late when he left for Bankside.'

'He never arrived,' said Anne with increased anxiety.

Firethorn pondered. He knew the dangers that lurked in the streets of London and trusted his book holder to cope with most of them. Only something of a serious nature could have detained Nicholas.

'George Dart!' he called.

'Here, master.'

'Scour the route that he would have taken. Retrace his steps from Master Hoode's lodging to his own. Enquire of the watch if they saw anything untoward in that vicinity. Nicholas is a big man in every way. He could not vanish into thin air.'

'Roper Blundell did,' murmured the other.

'Think on hope and do your duty.'

George Dart went willingly off on his errand and several others volunteered to join in the search. Nicholas was a popular member of the company and everyone was keen to find out what had befallen him.

'Let me go, too,' said Hoode.

'No, sir.'

'But I am implicated, Lawrence.'

'You are needed here.'

'Nothing is as important as this.'

'It is—our art. We must serve it like professional men.' Firethorn raised his voice for all to hear. 'The rehearsal will go on.'

'Without Nick?' said Hoode.

'It is exactly what he would have wished, Edmund.'

'Yes,' agreed Anne. 'It is. Nick always put the theatre first.'

'To your places!'

Firethorn's command sent everyone scurrying off into the tiring-house. A difficult couple of hours lay ahead of them. They all knew just how much the book holder contributed to the performance.

Anne Hendrik searched for a crumb of reassurance.

'Where do you think he can be, Master Firethorn?'

'Safe and sound, dear lady. Safe and sound.'

'Is there no more we can do, sir?'

'Watch and pray.'

Anne took his advice and headed for the Church of St Benet.

Francis Jordan gave her a couple of days to muse upon her fate then issued his summons. He wanted Jane Skinner to come to his bedchamber that night. Implicit in his order was the threat of reprisal if she failed to appear, but he had no doubt on that score. The girl had been meek and submissive when he spoke to her and all resistance had gone. He would enjoy pressing home his advantage.

Glanville reacted quickly to orders. He had drafted in some extra craftsmen and work on the Great Hall was now advancing at a much more satisfying pace. Jordan gave instructions for the banquet and the invitations were sent out. He began to relax. The steward ran the household efficiently and gave him no real cause for complaint so the new master could enjoy the fruits of his position. Jane Skinner was one of them. Riding around his estate was another.

'Good morning, sir.'

'What do you want?'

'A word, sir.'

'We've said all we need to say to each other.'

'No, sir.'

'Get out of my path.'

'Listen.'

The unkempt man with the patch over one eye was lurking around the stables as Jordan rode out. There was the same obsequiousness and the same knowing smirk as before. He bent and twisted as he put his request to the master of Parkbrook House.

'They tell me Jack Harsnett's gone, sir.'

'I dismissed him for insolence.'

'So his cottage is empty?'

'Until I find a new forester.'

'Let me live there, sir.'

'You're not fit for the work.'

'I've always liked that cottage, sir,' said the man, sawing the air with his hands and trying an ingratiating grin. 'I'd be warm in winter there. It's a quiet place and I'd be out of the way.'

'No.'

'I ask it as a favour, sir.'

'No!'

The reply was unequivocal but it did not dismay him. The smirk came back to haunt and nudge Jordan who fought against the distant pull of obligation. The man revolted him and reminded him.

'You weren't always master here, sir.'

'I am now,' said Jordan.

'Thanks to a friend, sir.'

'You were well-paid and told to leave the country.'

'The money ran out, sir.'

His single eye fixed itself on Jordan and there was nothing humble in the stare now. It contained a demand and hinted at a warning. Jordan was made to feel distinctly uncomfortable. He thrust his hand into his pocket and brought out a few silver coins, hurling them to the ground in front of the man. The latter fell on them with a cry of pleasure and secreted them at once.

'Now get off my land for ever,' ordered Jordan.

'But that cottage is—'

'I don't want you within thirty miles of Parkbrook ever again. If you're caught trespassing here, I'll have you hanged! If I hear that you're spreading stories about me, I'll have your foul tongue cut out!'

Francis Jordan raised his crop and lashed the man hard across the cheek to reinforce his message. He did not stop to see the blood begin to flow or to hear the curses that came.

The rehearsal was a shambles. Deprived of their book holder, Westfield's Men were in disarray before *Vincentio's Revenge*. Scene changes were bungled, entrances missed, two dead bodies left accidentally on stage and special effects completely mismanaged. Prompting was continuous. Lawrence Firethorn stamped a measure of respectability on the performance when he was on stage but chaos ruled when he was off it. The whole thing ended in farce when the standard that was borne on in the final scene slipped out of the hand of Caleb Smythe and fell across the corpse of Vincentio himself who was heard to growl in protest. As the body was carried out in dignified procession, it was the turn of the musicians to add their contribution by playing out of tune.

Lawrence Firethorn blazed. He called the whole company together and flogged them unmercifully with his verbal cat o' nine tails. By the time they trooped disconsolately away, he had destroyed what little morale had been left.

Edmund Hoode and Barnaby Gill adjourned to the tap room with him.

'It was a disgraceful performance!' said Firethorn.

'You have been better,' noted Gill, scoring the first point.

'Everybody was atrocious!'

'The play needs Nick Bracewell,' said Hoode.

'We do not *have* Nick Bracewell, sir.'

'I am bound to say that *I* did not miss him,' observed Gill.

Firethorn bristled. 'What you missed was your entrance in Act Four, sir, because the book holder was not there to wake you up.'

'I never sleep in the tiring-house, Lawrence!'

'Only on stage.'

'I regard that as gross slur!'

'You take my meaning perfectly.'

'This will not be forgotten, sir.'

'Try to remember your lines as well, Barnaby.'

Hoode let them fight away and consulted his own worries. Concern for his friend etched deep lines in his forehead. It hurt him to think that he might be indirectly responsible for any misadventure into which Nicholas stumbled after leaving the playwright's lodging. If anything serious had happened, Hoode would not be able to forgive himself. Meanwhile, there was another fear. Grace Napier would be in the audience that afternoon. He trembled at the thought of her seeing a calamitous performance by the company because it was bound to affect her view of him. It was some years since he had had anything more than abuse thrown at him from the pit. *Vincentio's Revenge* could change that. Hoode did not relish the idea of being pelted by rotten food while his beloved looked on from the balcony.

'Here's George Dart!' said Firethorn.

'Alone!' observed Hoode.

'That does not trouble me,' added Gill.

Dart came to a halt in front of them and gabbled his story. He had found nothing. When he approached the watch, he was told that the operation of the law was none of his business and sent away with a flea in his ear. The one piece of information he did glean was that a man was killed in a brawl on the north embankment around midnight.

His three listeners immediately elected their book holder as the corpse. Dart was interrogated again then dismissed. Firethorn slumped back in his chair and brooded.

'I see Willoughby's hand in this!'

'You see Willoughby's hand in everything but in your wife's placket, sir,' said Gill waspishly.

'We must look into this at once,' decided Hoode.

'*After* the performance,' said Firethorn.

'*Instead* of it, Lawrence.'

'Ha! Sacrilege!'

They returned to the tiring-house to find it a morgue. Everyone had now heard George Dart's tale about the murder on the embankment and they were convinced that Nicholas Bracewell was the victim. Nor was it an isolated incident. In their febrile minds, they saw it as the latest in a sequence that began with the appearance of a real devil in the middle of their performance. Devil, maypole, Roper Blundell—and now this. The cumulative effect of it all was overwhelming. They mourned in silence and wondered where the next blow would fall. Not even a stirring speech from Firethorn could reach them. Westfield's Men had one foot in the grave.

The irony was that *Vincentio's Revenge* had attracted a sizeable audience. They came to see blood flow at the Queen's Head and that put them into good humour. Grace Napier and Isobel Drewry were there to decorate the gallery and act as cynosures for wandering eyes. They knew the play by repute and longed to while away a couple of hours in a more tragic vein. Grace was a little uneasy but Isobel was brimming with self-confidence, discarding her mask and coming to the theatre for the first time as an independent young woman with a mind of her own. As the glances shot across at her, she returned them with discrimination.

Seats filled, noise grew, tension increased. The genial spectators had no notion of the accelerating misery backstage. They did not realise that they might be called upon to witness the low point of the company's achievement. Blood and thunder were their priorities. With a bare five minutes to go before the start, the latecomers wedged themselves into their seats and insinuated their bodies into the pit.

Panic gave way to total immobility in the tiring-house. They were turned to stone. Firethorn chipped manfully away at it with the chisel of his tongue but he could not shape it into anything resembling a theatrical company. He tried abuse, inspiration, reason, humour, bare-faced lying and even supplication but all failed. They had given up and approached the coming performance with the hopeless resignation of condemned men about to lay their heads on the block of their own reputation.

With execution two minutes away, they were saved.

Nicholas Bracewell entered with Margery Firethorn.

The whole place came back to life at once. Everyone crowded around the newcomers with excited relief. Firethorn pushed his way through to embrace the book holder.

'A miracle!' he said.

'Do you have no welcome for me, Lawrence?' chided his wife. 'You have me to thank for his release.'

'Then I take you to my bosom with joy,' said her husband, pulling her close for a kiss of gratitude. 'What is this talk of release?'

'From prison.'

'Mon Dieu!'

'I was locked in the Counter,' said Nicholas, 'but there is no time for explanation now, sir. The spectators have paid their money and they want their play.'

He took charge at once and the effect was incredible. With their book holder back at the helm, it might yet be possible to salvage the play. The only disturbing factor was the presence of Margery.

'You cannot stay here, my love,' said Firethorn.

'Why not, Lawrence?'

'Because it is not seemly.'

'Do you think I have not seen men undressed before? It will not fright me, I warrant you.' She pointed at the half-naked John Tallis who was being helped into a skirt. 'I will look on the pizzle of the Duchess of Venice and not be moved.'

'I share your disappointment!' said Gill wickedly.

'Stand by!' called Nicholas.

They were actually straining to get on stage now.

The axe bit hungrily into the wood before it was thrown aside. Jack Harsnett took the piece of ash and used his knife to hack it into shape. He then reached for the other piece of wood and bound the two together with a stout twine that would withstand bad weather. Having tested the result by banging it on the ground, he got his knife out again and gouged a name on the timber. It took him a long time but he kept at it with surly patience, sustained by the memory of an occasion when he had carved the same name alongside his own.

His work done, he walked over to the pile of stones that marked the grave and looked down with a wave of grief washing over him. Then he lifted the cross high and brought its sharpened end down hard into the hole that he had dug for it, kicking the earth into place around it and stiffening its hold with some small boulders. His spade patted everything firmly down.

Burial in an anonymous field was the best that he could manage for his wife and only his crude handiwork indicated the place. After one last glance at the grave, he walked quickly back to the cart. There was no point in driving any further now.

Harsnett headed back towards Parkbrook.

Lawrence Firethorn displayed his flowering genius yet again. His portrayal of Vincentio sent shivers down the spines of all who saw it. He was exactly the kind of villain that they liked—dark, handsome, ruthless, confiding, duplicitous and steeped in a black humour that could raise a macabre laugh during a murder. He stalked the stage like a prowling tiger, he sank his speeches like a spear into the topmost gallery and he used a range of gestures so expressive and so finely judged that he would have been understood had he been dumb.

Seeing him as an unscrupulous Italian nobleman, it was hard to believe that he was only the son of a village blacksmith. His voice, his face, his bearing and his movement were those of a true aristocrat but his origins were not entirely expunged. With exquisite refinement, he laid each part that he played on the anvil of his talent and struck a magnificent shower of sparks from it with the hammer of the actor. The theatre was his forge. His art was the wondrous clang of metal.

Absorbed in his role on stage, he could shed it in an instant when he entered the tiring-house. When he got his first real break from the action, he sidled across to Nicholas for elucidation.

'Well?'

'I was falsely imprisoned for assault and battery.'

'How?'

'Two men attacked me. A third brought constables and swore that I was the malefactor. My word did not hold against theirs.'

'Rakehells! Who were they?'

'I mean to find out.'

'But how did you obtain release?'

'I bribed an officer to take a message to Mistress Firethorn.'

'Why to my wife and not to me?' said the other peevishly.

'You had enough to do here, sir,' said Nicholas tactfully. 'Besides, I knew that your good lady would move with purpose.'

'Oh yes!' groaned Firethorn. 'Margery does that, sir!'

'Did I hear my name, Lawrence?' she asked, coming over.

'I was singing your praises, sweeting.'

'And so you should, sir,' she said bluntly. 'The message reached me in Shoreditch well after noon. That left me little time and much to do within it. My first thought was to repair to the Counter in Wood Street and demand that Nicholas be handed over to me, but I reasoned that not even my writ would run there.'

Firethorn made a mental note of a possible future refuge.

'The message urged me to contact your patron,' she continued, 'so I flew hither and was told he was too busy to see me. That was no obstacle to me, sir. My business was imperative and so I forced my way into Lord Westfield's presence. When he recognised who I was, he praised my appearance and asked why I did not visit the theatre more often.'

'Keep to the point, woman!' said her husband.

Nicholas interrupted to wave four soldiers on to the stage and then to cue in a canon that had to be rolled out from the tiring-house.

Margery returned to her tale with undiminished zest.

'I had caught him just in time for Lord Westfield was about to depart for the country. Hearing of our problem and rightly judging its serious effect on the company, he wrote a letter in his own hand there and then. With a man of his for company, I was driven to the Counter in his coach and that could not but impress the prison sergeant. When he read the letter, he did not hesitate to obey its command. Nicholas was delivered within a matter of minutes. We hastened here and you know the rest.' She broke off to watch some actors stripping off their costumes. 'I had not thought that Master Smythe had such comical haunches.'

She drifted off to view the spectacle from a better angle.

'We have been fortunate, Nick,' said Firethorn.

'I know it well.'

'But why were you imprisoned in the first place?'

'To keep me from holding the book here, master.'

'A vile conspiracy!'

'Which landed me in a vile lodging.'

'It has the stink of Banbury's Men about it.'

'No, master, I'm convinced of that.'

'But someone wants to damage the company.'

'Not the company,' said Nicholas. 'Lord Westfield himself.'

Before Firethorn could react to the news, the book holder cued him and the actor tore on to the stage to challenge one of his intended victims to a duel. After he had dispatched the man with the poisoned tip of his sword, he shared his thoughts with the audience before he withdrew again. Nicholas sent on actors for the next scene and resumed his conversation.

'I see it plain now, master.'

'Our patron is the target?'

'Without question.'

'But it was *we* who suffered the attacks, Nick.'

'Only when Lord Westfield was present,' said the other. 'He was here when we first performed *The Merry Devils*. He was at The Curtain for *Cupid's Folly* and he joined us at The Rose. On each occasion, someone tried to discredit us in order to hurt him.'

'I begin to see your point, sir.'

'There was no trouble during *The Knights of Malta* or *Love and Fortune*. Our patron was not here in person to be embarrassed. That is why his enemies stayed their hand.'

'But he is not here today either.'

'It does not matter,' argued Nicholas. 'The attack is not through the play itself. We'll have no devil or falling maypole or unexpected death. Lord Westfield's enemies had failed three times already and were angry at their failure. They sought a new approach.'

'To disable the book holder.'

'That would not stop the performance—which was the intention in the other three cases—but it might impair the quality and that would reflect badly on our patron.'

Firethorn was impressed and punched him softly.

'You did some thinking in that prison, sir.'

'I'd choose more fragrant places for my contemplation.'

'You'll be in one tonight unless I'm mistaken,' said the other with a roguish grin. 'Mistress Hendrik came looking for you. When she sees that bruise on your face, I'm sure she'll make you lie down so that she can tend it properly.' He cocked an ear to listen to the action on stage. 'Why did such a beautiful Englishwoman marry such a boring Dutchman?'

'That has never come up in conversation.'

Firethorn stifled his mirth so that it would not distract.

'The Counter was a grim experience,' said Nicholas, 'but it gave me one valuable piece of information.'

Firethorn made another entry to stab a rival in the back and deliver a soliloquy of thirty lines while straddling the corpse. He sauntered off to applause then shook the Venetian court away to turn once more to his book holder.

'Valuable information, you say?'

'I know where to find our merry devil.'

Francis Jordan lay on the bed with a glass of fine wine beside him. It was a warm evening and the casements were open to let in the cooling air and the curious moon. He was naked beneath a gown of blue and white silk that shimmered in the light from the candelabra on the bedside table. Everything was in order for his tryst with Jane Skinner. The room had been filled with vases of flowers and a second goblet stood beside the wine bottle. He felt languid and sensual.

The clock struck ten then there was a timid knock on the door. She was a punctual lover and that suggested enthusiasm. Jordan was pleased. He rolled over on his side.

'Come in!' he called.

Jane entered quickly, closed the door behind her and locked it. He did not see that she withdrew the key to hold it behind her back.

'Welcome!' he said and toasted her with his goblet.

'Thank you, sir.'

'I want you to enjoy this, Jane.'

He appraised her with satisfaction. She wore a long white robe over a plain white shift and had a mob cap on her head. Her feet were bare. Even with its worried frown, the face had warmth to it and there was a country succulence about her body which roused him at once.

'Did my brother ever bring you to his bedchamber?'

'No, sir,' she said. 'The master respected me.'

'Virgins among the chambermaids! I never heard the like.'

'We were treated well before, sir.'

'You'll be treated well tonight, Jane.' He waved an arm. 'These flowers are for your benefit. Come, share some wine with me and we'll be friends. Take up that goblet.'

'I will not drink, sir.'

'Not even at my request?' Her silence annoyed him slightly. 'I see that I am too considerate, Jane Skinner. You give me no thanks for my pains. So let us forget the flowers and the wine. Step over here.'

She began to tremble but did not move at all.

'Come,' he said, putting his goblet aside. '*Now*, Jane!'

'No, sir,' she murmured.

'What did you say?'

'No, sir.'

'Do you know who I am and what I am?' he shouted.

'Yes, sir.'

'Then do as you're told girl, and come over here.'

Jane Skinner took a deep breath and stayed where she was. Her hands tightened on the large brass key in her hands. Prickly heat troubled her body. Her mouth was quite dry.

'I'll give you one more chance,' he said with menace.

'No, sir,' she replied with her chin up. 'I will not.'

'Then I will have to teach you.'

He hauled himself off the bed but he was far too slow. Caught between disgrace and dismissal, Jane wanted neither and chose a third, more desperate course. As Francis Jordan tried to come for her, she tripped across the room, jumped up on to the window sill then leapt out into the darkness. There was a scream of pain as she landed with a thud on the gravel below.

Jordan rushed to the window and looked down. She was squirming in agony. Doors opened and lighted candles were taken out. Two bodies bent over her in concern. Jordan was both furious and alarmed. Lying beside her was the key to his bedchamber. Before he could pull back from the window, one of the figures looked up to catch his eye.

It was Joseph Glanville.

It was good to be back in the saddle again. Nicholas Bracewell was a fine horseman who knew how to get the best out of his mount. He was proceeding at a steady canter along the rough surface of the road. It was early on Saturday evening and Westfield's Men had not long given a performance of *Mirth and Madness* to a small but willing audience at Newington Butts. Instead of staying to supervise their departure, Nicholas was allowed to ride off on important business. The fair which had been at Hoxton the previous week had now moved south of the river. It was at the village of Dulwich.

He heard the revelry a mile off. When he reached the village green, he first saw to his horse then went to explore. The fair was in full swing and it was not difficult to understand why Leonard had enjoyed it so much. Booths and stalls had been set up in a wide circle to bring a blaze of garish colour to the neighbourhood. People from all the surrounding districts had converged in numbers to see the sights, eat the food, drink the ale, buy the toys, watch the short plays, enjoy the entertainments and generally have fun.

Visitors could see a cow with three legs or a sheep with two tails, a venomous snake that wound itself around its female keeper and hissed to order, a dancing bear or a dog that did tricks, a cat that purported to sing in French, a strong man who bent horseshoes and the self-styled Heaviest Woman in the World. The wrestling booth struggled on without the Great Mario and Nicholas spared a thought for Leonard.

Vendors wandered everywhere. They sold fans, baskets, bonnets, aprons, fish, flowers, meat, even a powder that was supposed to catch flies. Kindheart was pulling out teeth with his pincers and the ratcatcher was selling traps. One of the most popular vendors had a tray of cosmetics and a melodic voice.

> Where are you fair maids,
> That have need of our trades?
> I'll sell you a rare confection.
> Will you have your faces spread
> Either with white or with red?
> Will you buy any fair complexion?

The village girls giggled with high excitement.

Nicholas eventually saw them. They were three in number, tiny men in blue shirts and hose, demonstrating their agility to the knot of spectators who gathered around their booth. They were midgets, neat, perfectly-formed and seemingly ageless, doing somersaults and cartwheels for the delight of the crowd. They came to the climax of their routine. One braced his legs as his partner climbed up on to his shoulders. The third then climbed even higher to form a human tower. Applause broke out but changed to a moan of fear as the tower appeared to fall forward. Timing their landing, they did a forward roll in unison and stood up to acknowledge even louder clapping. A woman in a green dress, smaller than any of them, came out from the booth with a box and solicited coins. The villagers gave freely.

He could hear them talking as he went around to the rear of their booth. The woman entered and discussed the takings. Nicholas called out and asked if he could come in.

'What do you want, sir?' said a high voice.

'To discuss a business proposition.'

The flap of the booth opened and a midget studied him. At length, he held the flap back so that Nicholas could enter. The other two men and the woman were resting on benches. Now that he could see them closer, Nicholas could discern that there were age differences. The man who had let him in was older than the others.

'I am Dickon, sir,' said the man, then indicated the others with his doll-like hand. 'This is my wife and these are our two sons.'

'You mentioned a business proposition,' said the woman.

'It's one that concerned Westfield's Men,' he said.

The two sons started guiltily but the father calmed them by showing the palms of his hands. He confronted Nicholas without fear.

'What are you talking about, sir?'

'Merry devils.'

'We do not understand.'

'I think your sons do.'

They tried not to fidget so much and averted their eyes.

'Leave us alone!' said Dickon with spirit.

'You caused a great deal of trouble, sir.'

'We are poor entertainers.'

'I saw your entertainment at the Queen's Head in Gracechurch Street,' said Nicholas. 'The Curtain in Shoreditch. The Rose in Bankside. I was not amused.'

'Get out of our booth, sir!'

Dickon had the ebullience of a man twice his height and weight. He was going to admit nothing unless he had to do so. His sons, however, were less skilled in deception. Nicholas decided to play on their fears with a useful fiction.

'Lord Westfield is a very influential man,' he said.

'So?' replied Dickon.

'He could close this whole fair down if he chose. He could get your licence revoked, then your booths would not be able to stand anywhere. That is what he threatened to do but I tried to talk him out of it.'

Dickon had a brief but wordless conversation with the others. Alarm had finally touched him and he was not sure what to do about it. Nicholas quickly exploited his advantage.

'Unless I go back with some answers, Lord Westfield will pursue this fair through the courts. He wants revenge.'

Another silent exchange between the midgets then one of the sons cracked, jumping up and running across to the visitor.

'We did not mean to do any harm, sir.'

'Who put you up to it?'

'It was all in jest, sir. We are clowns at a fair.'

'There's nothing clownish in the sight of a dead man.'

'That was my doing, sir!' wailed the son. 'I still have nightmares about it. I did not mean to fright him so.'

The mother now burst into tears, both sons talked at once and Dickon tried to mediate. Nicholas calmed them all down and asked the father to give a full account of what happened. Dickon cleared his throat, glanced at the others, then launched into his narrative.

The fair was at Finchley when a young man approached them and asked if they would like to earn some money. All that they had to do was to play a jest on a friend of his. Dickon undertook the task himself. A costume was provided and details of when and how to make his sudden appearance. The young man was evidently familiar with the details of the performance.

'How did you get into the Queen's Head?' said Nicholas.

'In the back of a cart, sir.'

'Then you hid beneath the stage?'

'When you are as small as us, concealment is not difficult.'

'You were told to cause an uproar then disappear.'

'That is so.'

'What about The Curtain?'

'I did not even have to dress up for that,' said Dickon. 'When you all withdrew after the rehearsal, I came out from behind the costume basket where I lay hidden. It was the work of five minutes or so to saw through that maypole.'

'Did you not think of the damage it could cause?'

'The young man assured us nobody would be hurt.'

'What of The Rose?'

'My sons were both employed there.'

Dickon's account was straightforward. Instructed in what they had to do, the two boys had visited the theatre in costume on the eve of performance to search for places of concealment and to rehearse their antics. Hearing footsteps up on the stage, they could not resist shooting up through the trap-doors to startle whoever it was. Nicholas admitted that he had been duly startled.

The boys had slipped under the stage after the performance had started and lay hidden under sheets in a corner. When Roper Blundell came down to prepare for his own ascent from Hell, he tripped over one of the sheets and lifted it. The mere sight of a crouching devil had been enough to frighten him to death. Terrified themselves, the two brothers fled as soon as they could and did not make the double entry on stage that had been planned.

Nicholas felt that he was hearing the truth. The midgets were not responsible for what they did. They were only pawns in the game. Paid for their services, they were told that everything was a practical joke on friends. That joke turned sour at The Rose and they refused to work for the young man again. Nicholas saw no virtue in proceeding against this peculiar family. It was the person behind them who was the real villain. He sought help.

'Was he a well-favoured young man with a ring on his right hand?'

'Yes, sir,' said Dickon. 'It bore his initials.'

'Do you know what they stand for?'

'No, sir. Except that...well, there was one time when his coachman called him Master Gregory.'

G.N. Master Gregory. It was enough for Nicholas.

He now knew who their enemies really were.

Chapter Ten

Sunday was truly a day of rest for Henry Drewry. It was the end of the worst week of his life and he was exhausted from his labours. He could not even stir to take himself off to matins. Having tried to prevent his daughter from going to the country with Grace Napier, he felt an immense relief when she actually left the house. Her presence now diminished him in every way. Terrified to offend her lest she speak to her mother about a Bankside theatre, he crept around quietly and kept out of her way. All hope of marrying the girl off could now be abandoned. He had too much compassion to wish such a creature on any other man.

As he reclined in his chair in the parlour with a restorative pint of sherry, he saw how much he had squandered by one foolish action. He was an opinionated Alderman of the city of London, yet he dared not assert himself any longer in his own home.

There was a tap on the door and a manservant entered.

'Master Pollard is without, sir.'

'Tell him that I am not here.'

'But he says he has called on a most important matter.'

'Get rid of the fellow!'

The servant went off to implement the order but Isaac Pollard would not be sent way. Knocking on the door of the parlour, he surged in like a monstrous black bat and fluttered over Drewry.

'Why do you send me lies, sir?'

'You must be mistaken,' said the other with a gulp.

'I am told you are not at home and you sit here drinking sherry.'

The Puritan glared disapprovingly at the liquid.

'I take it on medical advice,' said Drewry quickly. 'I am unwell.'

'You must be if you tell untruths on the Sabbath.'

'What brings you here, Isaac?'

'Profanity, sir!'

'Again?' muttered the other wearily.

'Wickedness is abroad.'

'I have not yet been out to see.'

'*The Merry Devils* is to be performed again.'

'Do not mention that play to me!' howled Drewry.

'But I hear that it will be given at Parkbrook House on the estate of Lord Westfield. It must be stopped.'

'If it is a private performance, we can do nothing. Besides, we have no power in the county of Hertfordshire.'

'We have the power of God Himself,' said Pollard impressively, 'and that covers every shire in the land. There is a way to halt this performance if we but move swift enough.'

'And what is that, sir?'

'Get the play declared a blasphemous document and have its authors incarcerated for their sins. There must be legislation that favours us. We must attack with a statute book in our hand.'

Henry Drewry preferred to relax with a pint of sherry in his.

'I grow tired of all this, Isaac,' he said.

'Tired of God? Tired of our Christian duty? Tired of the paths of righteousness?' Pollard rippled the eyebrow at him. 'We must fight harder than ever against the Devil.'

'He has a strong voice at our meetings.'

'What say you?'

'My fellow Aldermen do not share your opinion of the theatre.'

'It is a market-place of bestiality!'

'Haply, that is what draws them thither,' said Drewry under his breath. 'I put the case against the Queen's Head and they would not hear me.'

'Speak louder, Henry.'

'Alderman Ashway has more powerful lungs.'

'Shout him down.'

'Nothing is so vociferous as a brewer whose inn is under threat.'

'Strong drink is the potion of Hell.'

'Yes,' agreed the other, downing some sherry. 'But it can bring a man more comfort than a pinch of salt.' Disillusion set in. 'I chose the wrong trade, I see it now.'

'What's this, sir? Are you slipping?'

'I tried, Isaac, but they will not enforce the law against the Queen's Head. It will still be used as a playhouse.'

'We must fight on regardless!'

'I'll lay down my weapon and take my ease.'

'Do I hear you aright, Henry?' said Pollard with horror. 'You cannot stand aside from the fray, sir. That is to condone what goes on at that vile place. Have you so soon forgot what we said on our journey back from The Rose? You saw the depravity there with your own eyes.'

'Ah, yes,' recalled the other with nostalgia.

'Would you let your daughter visit such a place?'

Fatigued by being browbeaten, the salter hit back with the truth. 'I would, sir.'

'Expose the child to corruption?'

'It is her own choice and she is old enough to make it. Isobel went to the Queen's Head on Wednesday, on Thursday and again on Friday. She saw three plays and came home smiling each time. I would not vote to close an entertainment so dear to her.' He took a long, defiant sip of his sherry. 'Changes have occurred, Isaac, and you must bear the blame. It was you that got to The Rose. It has cost me more than I can say. Wave your puritanical fist at the theatre alone, sir. I withdraw!'

Isaac Pollard could not believe that he had heard such words on a Sunday. He had put on the whole armour of God and now found that it was full of chinks. His eyebrow writhed across his forehead like a snake impaled on a spike as he tried to cope with a new experience.

He was rendered speechless for the first time ever.

Nicholas made an early start to his long journey. It was the best part of twenty miles to Lord Westfield's estate which lay to the north of St Albans. He needed to nurse his horse carefully over such a distance. Since there was no performance on the next day, he was to stay the night at Parkbrook and ride back at his leisure on the Monday. Anne Hendrik was sad to be parted from him. She had spent two long nights comforting him after his ordeal at the Counter and had hoped to spend a third in like fashion but his visit was important and she had to accept it.

He made frequent stops at hostelries along the way to rest his mount, refresh himself and garner what information he could. One coaching inn had an observant landlord. He saw Lord Westfield's crest driven past on Thursday evening and remembered two fine young ladies who stopped their carriage there on Saturday and talked of reaching St Albans before nightfall.

It was late afternoon when Nicholas reached his own destination. Westfield Hall was a familiar landmark to him now but he had never been to Parkbrook House before. As he viewed it from the crest of the hill, he was struck by its severity and sense of proportion. If the Hall was the visual embodiment of its master, Parkbrook could claim to be the like. Francis Jordan was echoed in his architecture. The place was cold, unyielding, ungenerous behind a striking façade.

Nicholas Bracewell soon met the new master.

'Welcome to Parkbrook, sir!'

'Thank you, Master Jordan.'

'Your journey was a long but necessary one. An event like this needs careful forethought and preparation.'

'We are honoured to be invited to such a fine house,' said Nicholas politely. 'Master Firethorn sends his regards and assures you that we will strive to please you in every particular.'

'Good. I must have *The Merry Devils* played here. It will be a rousing start to my time here at Parkbrook and I feel that it will somehow bring me luck.'

It had not done that for Westfield's Men.

Francis Jordan conducted him across to the Great Hall. Progress had been marked. Plasterers and carpenters had now completed their work and only the masons and the painters remained, the former providing a musical clink as they chiselled away at the bay window and the latter adding an astringent smell with their paint. Nicholas noted that none of the men dared to stop working and he could sense their resentment of their employer.

The new master pointed to the far end of the room.

'I think that the stage should be set up there to catch the light on two sides. Tables will be arranged in a horseshoe so that our guests may eat and drink while they view the entertainment. There is a door in the corner, as you see, sir, and the room beyond can be your tiring-house.' He smiled complacently. 'I believe I have thought of everything.'

'Not quite, Master Jordan,' said Nicholas, looking around with interest. 'It would far better suit our purposes if we played at *this* end of the hall.' He used his hands to indicate. 'There is a minstrels' gallery above that is ideal for our musicians. If we hang curtains down from that, it forms a tiring-house beneath the balcony. The stage will thrust out in this direction and your tables can be set the other way around. Your guests may still dine while we act.'

'But you throw away the best of the light.'

'That is the intention, sir. We would in any case draw the curtains on all the windows to darken the interior. You have seen *The Merry Devils* and know its supernatural elements. They will flourish more by candlelight. We have to take advantage of our playing conditions, sir. We are open to the sky in London and may not control the light at all. Here we may manipulate it to our own ends and to the greater pleasure of our spectators.'

The argument was convincing but Jordan was nevertheless peeved that his suggestions had been ruled out so effortlessly. He threw up another objection out of churlishness.

'If you play at this end of the hall, sir, you block the main entrance. How are my guests to come into the place?'

'Through that door you commended to me but now,' said Nicholas. 'I notice that the room looks out upon that broad lawn. If the weather is as fine as we have a right to expect, you would receive your guests in the garden, conduct them into that room for drinks then usher them through into here for the banquet and the performance.'

'Leave the arrangements to me, please, sir!' snapped Jordan.

'I was only replying to your question, master.'

The book holder was right and the other finally conceded it. A practical man of the theatre knew how to pick his ground and his view had to be respected.

'You'll need to take measurements and make drawings,' said Jordan curtly. 'I'll send my steward in to attend to your needs.'

'Thank you, sir.'

'I still feel that *my* idea was the most sensible.'

He flounced out and left Nicholas in the hall. The book holder did not waste his time. In the two minutes that it took Glanville to appear, Nicholas chatted to one of the painters and learned why the new master was so disliked, how the forester had been dismissed and what happened to one of the chambermaids. Parkbrook House was not a happy place. The coldness of its exterior was reflected inside as well.

A tall, stately figure glided in through the entrance.

'Master Bracewell?'

'Yes, sir.'

'I am Joseph Glanville, steward of the household.'

'Well met!'

'How may I best help you?'

'I have a number of enquiries...'

There was something about the steward that alerted Nicholas. Accustomed to working among actors, he could usually discern when someone was masking his true self. Glanville was altogether too plausible and controlled for his liking. The man answered all his questions very courteously but he was holding something back all the time, and Nicholas was keen to know what it was.

'What about your stage, sir?' asked the steward.

'We shall bring our own and set it up on trestles.'

'Master Jordan is anxious to spare you that trouble. We have enough carpenters at our command and they can build to order. You will have plenty to bring from London as it is.'

Nicholas closed with the offer. Transporting the stage was a problematic business as they found when they were obliged to go on tour in the provinces. Besides, the one used at the Queen's Head was far too high for their needs at Parkbrook House. Glanville was surprised when told this.

'Will you not need trap-doors for your devils, sir?'

'They will enter by some other means.'

'Not from below, as Master Jordan described to me?'

'No, sir,' said the other. 'A height of eighteen inches will content us. Two feet at most. There will be no crawling beneath the stage on this occasion.' He thought of George Dart and Caleb Smythe. 'That will gladden the hearts of our devils, I can tell you.'

They talked further then Glanville escorted him up to show him the bedchamber that had been assigned to him. It was on the first floor in the west wing and as they walked down the long corridor towards it, Nicholas probed.

'I hear that one of your chambermaids had an accident.'

'That is so, sir.'

'A broken leg, they say.'

'The girl is recovering in the servants' quarters.'

'I may find time to visit her,' volunteered Nicholas. 'I know the misery of a leg in splints.'

'Oh, I could not permit that, sir,' said Glanville firmly. 'Jane Skinner is in a state of shock. The physician has advised against stray callers. They tire the girl.'

Nicholas did not believe the explanation and wondered why he was being kept from the invalid. They stopped outside a door. Nothing the circular staircase at the far end of the corridor, the guest asked if it led down to the Great Hall.

'It is not for general use,' said Glanville smoothly. 'I am the only person allowed to use it, Master Bracewell, and it is a privilege that I jealously guard.'

'Is it not a quicker way down for me?' said Nicholas.

'That is immaterial. You may not use it.'

'What is the punishment for offenders, sir?'

There was a note of ironic amusement in the question but the steward did not hear it. His response was deadly serious. Behind the unruffled calm was a surge of hostility.

Nicholas saw that he had made an enemy.

He sold the horse and cart in the first village. All that he kept or needed was his axe and it was always by his side. Jack Harsnett went to the nearest inn and drank himself to distraction. It was a few days before he was ready to move on. A morning's trudge brought him to a wayside tavern and he slumped down on to the settle that stood out in the sun. Food and drink was brought out to him and he began to recover his breath. He was far too old to tramp the roads for long.

Laughter from inside the tavern made him prick his ears and a few snatches of conversation drifted out. Though he could not hear what was being said, he recognised the principal voice in the group. It made him sit tight and wait. One by one, the customers tumbled out and went back to their work or their homes. The man for whom Harsnett was waiting was the last to leave. Drink had blurred the sight of his one eye and he walked past the forester without paying any heed.

Harsnett followed and cornered him against a wall.

The single eye blinked until it managed to focus.

'Jack!' said the man with the patch. 'How are you?'

'What do you care?'

'I heard you'd left Parkbrook.'

'Thrown out.'

'Master Jordan is a hard man, sir.'

'I heard you use his name in the tavern.'

'Did I?' An evasive smile came. 'I doubt it.'

'What did you say?' grunted the forester.

'Who knows?'

'Tell me.'

'About Master Jordan?' He gave a drunken laugh then became rueful. 'There's things I could say about that one! He's bad, Jack, bad as they come. He gave me this here on my face.' He exhibited the long scar that had been caused by the riding crop. 'Keep out of his way.'

'Why?'

'No matter. I must go.'

'Answer me,' said Harsnett, holding him by his hair.

'More than my life's worth, Jack, and that's the truth.'

'Tell me about Master Jordan,' insisted the forester.

The man with the black patch twitched and whined.

'He'll kill me if I do that.'

Harsnett thrust the blade of his axe against the other's throat.

'*I'll* kill you if you don't.'

It was a pleasant ride across the estate. Nicholas borrowed a horse from the stables so that his own could recover against its journey on the morrow. Having got directions from the ostler, he headed in the direction of the adjoining property and reached it after a couple of miles. It was less of a mansion than an overgrown cottage but its half-timbering was well-maintained and the thatch was recent. Stables and outbuildings spread out behind it and it was towards these that Nicholas now spurred his horse.

The man was cleaning the carriage with a rag that he dipped into a bucket of water. Though his back was to the visitor, Nicholas knew him at once. The thick bandage that was wound around his head and down over the top of one eye was further confirmation.

Hearing the approach of hooves, the man turned around with easy curiosity. His smile froze when he saw who it was and he dropped his rag back in the water. Nicholas dismounted, tethered his horse then came across for a confrontation. From his garb and his bearing, it was clear that the man was a coachman.

'I was arrested at your suit, Master Grice.'

'Yes, sir.'

'I did not like my lodging at the Counter.'

'Nor I the cut over my eye,' said Grice warily. 'Besides, you would have been released after a couple of days. The case would have been dropped long before it came to court.'

'That does not salve my wounds.'

He took a step towards Grice who put up his large fists.

'Stay where you are, sir, or you'll feel the weight of my punches again.' He turned to the house to raise the alarm. 'Master!'

Reaching for the driving seat of the carriage, he then grabbed his long whip and drew back his arm but he was given no chance to demonstrate his skill. As he tried to lash Nicholas, the latter stepped smartly out of the way then dived at Grice, twisting the whip from his hand within seconds. Grice was powerful but he had none of the other's experience in a brawl. Nicholas punched his body hard and ducked the savage blows that came in return. A punch on Grice's chin made the coachman reel. Recovering after a few moments, he flung himself at Nicholas with such force that he would have knocked him flying had the charge succeeded.

But the book holder used the man's lunge against himself. As he came in, Nicholas dodged him, caught hold of his shoulders and pushed him hard against the side of the carriage where Grice's head took the main impact. He buckled at the knees and cursed violently.

'Hold still, Walt! I will take him.'

The other nocturnal assailant came running out of the house, followed by the young man with the signet ring. Nicholas squared up to the newcomer then flashed out a straight left which drew blood from the other's nose. Enraged by the pain, the man flailed and kicked but he was unable to make contact. Another straight left darkened his cheek and a sequence of punches to the body slowed him right down. Mustering his strength for a last effort, the man dashed to the stable, caught hold of a hay rake, then brandished it above his head as he stormed back. Nicholas ducked just in time as the rake scythed through the air. He closed with the man and wrested the implement from him. Grice was now getting up to rejoin the fray and that could not be allowed. Holding his opponent by one arm, Nicholas suddenly swung him around with great force and let go. The hurtling body collided with Grice and both went down groaning.

'That will be enough from you, sir,' said the young man.

Nicholas was now threatened by the point of a rapier.

'Why have you come here?' continued the swordsman.

'To settle a score.'

'Leave us while you still may.'

'No, Master Napier,' said Nicholas. 'That *is* your name, I believe? You had a familiar look and I remember where I had seen it before. It was upon your sister, Grace. You are her brother, Gregory.'

The young man held him at bay with the sword but it was a very temporary advantage. With dazzling speed, Nicholas stooped to take hold of the bucket and hurl its contents all over the young man. Before the latter could resist, he had the rapier plucked from him and was pressed backwards against the carriage. Nicholas kept the point of the sword against Gregory Napier's heart to discourage either of his servants from coming to his aid. The young man paled.

'Do not kill me, sir! We meant you no harm.'

'You have a peculiar way of showing it.'

'We bore no grudge against you.'

'I know,' said Nicholas. 'Lord Westfield was your target. You sought to hurt him through me just as you tried to damage the company with your merry devils. You wanted revenge, Master Napier. Why?'

'I cannot tell you.'

'Then I will have to loosen your tongue, sir.'

He let the sword-point gently explore the other's doublet.

'Have a care, Master Bracewell!'

'You had no care of me when I was thrown into the Counter.'

'Please, sir. Be gentle with that sword.'

Nicholas let the rapier slice through the satin doublet.

'Why did you attack Lord Westfield?'

'Do not ask me.'

'I'll have an answer if I have to cut it out of you,' said Nicholas dangerously. 'We have suffered much at your hands, sir. A whole company was terrified because of you. One of our sharers narrowly escaped injury. A stagekeeper lost his life. So do not wave me away.' He split the doublet open again. '*Why* did you do all this to Lord Westfield?'

The voice behind him was clear and unashamed.

'Because *I* made him, Master Bracewell.'

Grace Napier stood in the doorway of the house.

It was not an entirely new play. Ralph Willoughby had devised the plot some time earlier and constructed scenes in his mind. When he got the commission from Banbury's Men, therefore, he was not starting from scratch. Rather was he developing and refining a drama which he had carried around inside his head for months. Now that he came to write it, the words flowed freely and he remained at his table for long hours each day, sustained by an inner fire and by the firmness of his purpose. There was no drinking during the period of composition and no debauchery. It obsessed him totally. Appropriately, it was finished on a Sunday.

Willoughby had never before worked so quickly or felt so happy with the result of his creative endeavours. As he blotted the last line, he knew that the play was exactly as he envisaged it. With the crucial help of Doctor John Mordrake, he had given it a texture of authenticity that would beguile spectators. Banbury's Men would appreciate the play's wit and wisdom, its topicality at a time when there was growing witch-mania, and its sheer entertainment value. They would also enjoy his many clever allusions to the part of Oxford-shire from which their noble patron hailed.

What they would not at first see was the peril that lay at the heart of the work. Willoughby had disguised it very carefully. He turned back to the first page and began to read. His dark laughter soon filled the room. He was truly delighted with the play.

The Witch of Oxford would be a fitting epitaph.

Nicholas Bracewell was candidly surprised. As he sat in the parlour of the house and listened to Grace Napier, he saw that his major assumption had been wrong.

'I thought that you used Edmund Hoode to get information at the request of your brother,' he said. 'You needed an inside knowledge of our work and friendship with our playwright was a way to obtain it.'

'Yes,' she agreed. 'I am sorry to have taken advantage of Master Hoode in this way. It must seem to you that I toyed cruelly with his affections but I took no pleasure in it, sir, and it caused me much heartache. But my hand was forced. The end justified the means.'

'What was that end?' he asked.

'Revenge.'

If Nicholas was surprised then Isobel Drewry was openly amazed. She sat alongside Gregory Napier and heard the truth emerge for the first time. It showed her just how little she really knew her friend.

'You *are* a deep one, Grace!' she said.

'I was not able to confide in you, Isobel.'

'It is just as well,' added the other with a giggle. 'I could never keep a secret. As it was, I had no notion that any of this was going on and can now understand why you were always a little disappointed at the performances.'

'Yes,' said Grace. 'My plans did not quite work out. I wanted to humiliate Westfield's Men in public but we failed each time. I own that I needed your company at the theatre to hide my purposes. I hope that you will not feel too abused, Isobel.'

'Not at all,' said the other chirpily. 'I had some wonderful afternoons that have helped to change my whole life.'

'Let us come back to the revenge,' suggested Nicholas. 'What reason could you have for hating Lord Westfield so?'

'His callous treatment of his nephew.'

'Master Francis Jordan?'

'Do not mention that foul name to me, sir,' she said with asperity. 'It is not to stand alongside that of his brother. I am speaking of David Jordan.' A mixture of pride, anger and intense passion made her features glow. 'David is the cause of all that has happened.'

'How?'

'I will tell you, sir.'

Grace Napier was calm, poised and highly articulate. Her story was a revelation. Instead of being simply a mercer's daughter who liked to visit the theatre, she was a young woman so deeply and desperately in love that she would stop at nothing to avenge what she saw as the terrible wrong done to her inamorato. She had met David Jordan over a year earlier when she was out riding near the boundary of his land. He was in a severely depressed state. His wife had died recently and the baby daughter who survived her lingered for only four days before she went off to join her mother. David was distraught. The double blow shattered him completely.

Friendship with Grace Napier slowly helped to restore him. It was a gentle, unforced courtship that lasted many months. Drawn more and more together, they reached the point where they could think of nothing but sharing their whole lives together.

Tears sparkled in Grace's eyes as she recalled it.

'David proposed to me in the wood nearby. The sky was blue and the sun was slanting down through the branches of the trees. Birds were singing. Everything was so beautiful and tranquil.'

'The romance of it!' said Isobel, carried away.

'Naturally,' continued Grace with a soft smile, 'I accepted the proposal. It was arranged that I would go to Parkbrook next day and the engagement would be formally announced.'

'What happened?' said Nicholas.

'I never saw David again.'

'Why?'

'He was thrown from his horse and badly injured.'

'Did you not rush to his bedside?' said Isobel.

'Immediately, but they would not admit me.'

'But you were his fiancée.'

'They would not accept that,' said Grace. 'Our courtship had been conducted in secret for obvious reasons. Father is wealthy but he is still only a tradesman. David comes from a family with noble blood. He wanted to announce our engagement when it was too late for anyone to stop the marriage from going ahead.' She winced as a memory haunted her. 'I was turned away from Parkbrook.'

'Did you not speak with Master Jordan's physician?' said Nicholas.

'That was forbidden as well.'

'By whom?'

'Master Francis Jordan. He was staying at Parkbrook when the accident occurred and he took charge. Nobody was allowed in. I called, I wrote, I even tried to bribe the servants for information but it was to no avail. David was kept from me.'

'You must have been in despair!' said Isobel.

'I was. In the end, I turned to Lord Westfield for help but he would not see me. I was told that his lordship could not spare the time. He was always too busy at court or spending time with his company. His nephew was in a parlous condition and Lord Westfield was watching plays! You can see I came to hate the company. Westfield's Men became a symbol of all the things I detested.'

'Lord Westfield has his faults,' conceded Nicholas, 'but I cannot believe there was anything calculated in his behaviour. He was not to know that you had been on the point of joining the family.'

'That was not the only reason I despised him, sir,' she said. 'It was he who allowed Parkbrook to be taken from David. It was Lord Westfield who helped his other nephew to become the new master.'

'How was that done?' wondered Nicholas.

'Yes,' said Isobel in bewilderment. 'I know little of such things but how could one man inherit when his elder brother was still alive and well?'

'David was alive—but far from well.'

'That does not alter the situation, Grace.'

'It does, Isobel. I puzzled over that very point because it had such significance for me. After all, I was to have been the new mistress of Parkbrook. I felt that both David *and* I had been robbed.'

'So what did you do?' said Nicholas.

'I consulted a lawyer in the Inns of Court. He explained that there *was* a way that David could lose his inheritance. If he failed to pass an inquiry *De idiota inquirendo* then he could be dispossessed. It is unusual but not unknown. The lawyer told me of a case in which he was involved some years ago. It concerned a large house in Petersfield. I cannot remember all the details but it was to do with the conveyance of the fee simple and involved a breach of the entail. Anxious to get the house for himself, the offended party challenged the conveyance on the grounds of the vendor's incompetence by reason of idiocy to conduct affairs. The Queen's Escheator in Sussex was charged with an inquiry to establish the vendor's sanity, with a view to placing the estate under the Court of Wards and Liveries.'

'Stop, stop!' cried Isobel. 'This is far too complicated for me, Grace. What are you trying to tell us?'

'If it can be proved that someone is too insane to manage his own affairs, he can legally be relieved of ownership. David's brother would be well aware of this because he has been a student of the law.'

'Are you certain that this is what happened?' said Nicholas.

'There can be no other explanation, sir.'

'What do you mean?'

'How else could they keep me away from him? I was within six weeks of becoming his wife. No two people could have been closer. No matter how bad his injuries, David would have sent for me.'

'Then why did he not do so?' said Isobel.

'It was not just his body that was damaged,' said Grace. 'It was his mind.'

The cottage was exactly the same and yet there were some radical changes. All sign of habitation had gone. The rough cosiness had been replaced by an atmosphere of neglect. His wife was no longer there to clean and tend and fill the place with her chatter. It was no longer a home.

Jack Harsnett threw down his axe and walked to the window. He looked in the direction of Parkbrook House. All his misfortunes could be placed at the door of the new master and he wanted recompense. After his talk with the one-eyed man, it was not only on his own behalf that he sought redress. Others had been wronged, too.

There was no hurry. He was safely hidden away in his woodland clearing and nobody would bother him there for a while. He would bide his time until his moment came.

Then he would pay a call on Master Francis Jordan.

The ride back gave Nicholas time to reflect on the extraordinary development in the situation. He had been so moved by Grace's story and by the poignancy with which she told it that he could almost forgive her what she had done in the name of revenge. Convinced that Lord Westfield was most to blame, she launched her attack at something that was very dear to him. She became involved with Edmund Hoode so that he could, unwittingly, feed her the information she required, even down to precise details of text, staging and costume.

Another point struck Nicholas. The theatre was the only place where Grace Napier could get anywhere near Lord Westfield. To cause him maximum embarrassment, she seized on the opportunity provided by *The Merry Devils*, a play discussed freely in advance by its co-author. Had the performance ended in the fiasco she hoped, it would have taken Westfield's Men a long time to regain their credibility.

Grace Napier had caused untold upset. Having learned how vital the book holder was to the staging of *Vincentio's Revenge*, she was even ready to contrive the arrest of Nicholas Bracewell to keep him out of the way. He still felt jangled by the experience but now took a more philosophical view about his night in the Counter. If nothing else, it had introduced him to Leonard who had pointed him in the direction of the fair. There was thus a gain as well as a loss involved.

It was dark when Nicholas reached Parkbrook. He stabled his horse and strolled towards the west wing, intending to go right around to the main entrance of the house. Something alerted him. There was a clump of rhododendron bushes ahead of him and he thought he caught a glimpse of movement behind them. Preparing himself for trouble, he continued his walk as if he had seen nothing. When he reached the bushes, he jumped into them to confront whoever lurked in wait.

The horse whinnied and tried to nuzzle his shoulder.

He could not understand why it was tethered in such a secluded place then he noticed the small door at the rear of the west wing. He tried it, found it open and went in. To his right was the corridor that ran towards the main building but directly ahead of him was something of much more interest. It was the steward's private staircase and he could hear muffled voices at the top of it.

Nicholas withdrew into the shadows as feet descended with an echoing clatter. Joseph Glanville led a middle-aged man in dark attire to the door and showed him respectfully out. The horse was heard trotting off with the visitor then the steward returned.

He was startled when Nicholas came over to him.

'What are you doing here?' he demanded angrily.

'I lost my way.'

'The main staircase is *that* way.'

'Can I not get up to my room here?'

'No, sir,' said Glanville sharply. 'I have told you before that this is my private mode of access. You may not use it.'

Nicholas watched him shrewdly then put a question.

'You do not like plays, do you?'

'No, sir.'

'If it was left to you, Westfield's Men would not come here.'

'Most certainly not.'

'What do you have against us?'

'I do not care for strangers in my house.'

Glanville went off up the staircase with dignity.

Nicholas returned to his own room by the recommended means and slept well. After breakfast early next morning, he completed his work in the Great Hall then got ready to leave. He managed to spare a few minutes to call on Jane Skinner. Lying in bed with splints on her leg, she was flattered by his interest and told him how the accident had occurred. He also pumped her about Glanville and heard how she had revised her former good opinion of the man.

The book holder wished her a speedy recovery and went off to begin the long ride home. Francis Jordan detained him at the stables.

'We look forward to your next visit, sir.'

'Thank you, Master Jordan.'

'The cream of the county will be your audience.'

'It is a pity that your brother will not be among them, sir.'

'My brother?' Jordan shot him a hostile glance.

'I hear that he was very fond of plays.'

'Who told you that?'

'Jane Skinner.'

Francis Jordan squirmed. The incident with the chambermaid was still a grave embarrassment to him. He had warned his staff not to speak about it to anyone. If the guest had actually talked with the girl herself, he might know the story and be in a position to carry it to Lord Westfield. Jordan's manner became openly antagonistic.

'Goodbye, sir!' he said dismissively.

'May I ask you one question?' said Nicholas casually. 'Where *is* your brother now?'

'Don't be so damned impertinent, man!'

'Nobody seems to know, sir, and he must be somewhere.'

Jordan treated him to a glare of fierce hatred.

'He is in the best place he could be.'

Nell was pleased to see him again. Of all her regular clients, Ralph Willoughby was the most generous and the most likeable. His departures were sometimes abrupt but they usually enjoyed themselves together. When Nell came into the taproom of the Bull and Butcher that night, she saw Willoughby through the thick fog. Drink in hand and dressed with his customary extravagance, he was singing a bawdy ballad to his companions. Seeing her amble over to him, he put an arm around her and welcomed her with a warm kiss.

'Nell, my heart's delight!' he said effusively.

'Away with that talk, you traitor,' she teased. 'I have been lying in a cold bed since you left me, sir. I have not seen hide nor hair of you for five or six nights.'

'That is all changed, Nell.'

'I think you have another sweetheart.'

'Oh, I do! She is called *The Witch of Oxford* and she has kept me groaning with pleasure at night. I have been bent over her until now but her hold on me is at an end. She went off to Banbury today so I am a free man again. That is why I came post haste to you, Nell.'

'Will you stay the night?' she coaxed.

'No.'

'You scurvy rogue! Am I not good enough for you any longer?'

'Shall I tell you why I will not stay the night?'

'Go back to your witch of Oxford!'

'But you may like my reason,' he said. 'I will not stay the night because I intend to stay the whole week.'

Nell let out a roar of approval and flung herself at him.

Bedlam was vibrating with noise. The public came to see the lunatics at play and egged them on to wilder antics. There was trouble in a private cell from an old man who tried to hang himself. Another patient attempted to escape and had to be restrained. It was a day when Rooksley was under immense pressure and he did not welcome casual visitors.

'I am sorry but I may not speak with you now,' he told them.

'Stay awhile, sir,' said the younger of the two men.

'Bedlam has gone mad and I must doctor its madness.'

'That is my interest,' said the older man.

Nicholas Bracewell had brought Grace Napier and Doctor John Mordrake with him to the hospital. Her love for David Jordan had been proved beyond a doubt. No matter how sad or wretched his condition, she wished to dedicate herself to his care. While she was excited at the prospect of a reunion, therefore, she was also fearful. To be locked away in Bedlam would turn a sane man into a lunatic. She wondered what state her beloved would now be in.

'We have come to see Master David Jordan,' said Nicholas.

'Who, sir?' Rooksley was uncooperative.

'You heard the name.'

'I hear it but I do not recognise it,' said the keeper. 'We have nobody of that name here, sir, and I am acquainted with them all. I can tell you their date of birth, the colour of their hair and eyes, what food they eat each day and at what time of the morning they are like to pass water. I know everything in Bedlam, sir, but I do know a Master Jordan.'

Grace Napier looked crushed but Nicholas did not give up.

'He must be here,' he insisted. 'Lord Westfield would not let a nephew of his rot away in a county asylum. This is the only place to which he would commit the young man.' He indicated the others. 'You do not know what distinguished company you are in, sir. This is Mistress Napier, who is affianced to Master Jordan, and beside her is Doctor John Mordrake, sometime astrologer to Her Majesty, Queen Elizabeth.'

Rooksley was impressed. Mordrake's name was known to everyone.

'Come, sir,' said Nicholas briskly. 'You are busy, we can see. Do but have someone conduct us to Master Jordan and we will trouble you no longer. Do I have to go back to Lord Westfield himself to get a written permission from him?'

The head keeper pondered. The clamour of madness intensified. Nicholas helped him to reach a decision by slipping some coins into his hand. Rooksley pocketed them and nodded.

'That will buy you five minutes with him.'

He went off for a moment and Grace turned to thank Nicholas.

'You are wonderful, sir. I thought of Bedlam and sent my brother here to enquire but he did not get past the door. They told him the lies that we have just heard.'

'Nobody should be in this place,' said Mordrake, looking around with scholarly disgust. 'The insane need special care.'

Rooksley returned with Kirk and handed the keeper a bunch of keys. Kirk led the visitors down a long corridor then swung right. Grace Napier was increasingly tense and Nicholas understood how difficult this moment might be for her. The man whom she loved had parted from her in prime health. What she would now see would be a grotesque shell of that same person.

Kirk was interested that his friend had visitors.

'Have you come from Parkbrook House?' he asked.

'Indirectly, sir.'

'David is a good young man. We have no trouble from him.'

'What state is he in, sir?' asked Mordrake.

'His brain is addled and he has the sleeping sickness.'

'Ah yes,' sighed the old man. 'That often follows if a violent blow damages the mind. Memory will go and the patient will lapse back into childhood.'

'Who committed him, sir?' asked Nicholas. 'Do you know that?'

'His physician, master. I have seen the records. One Francis Jordan pays the charges to keep him here but he was delivered to Bedlam by another hand.'

'What was the name?'

'Joseph Glanville.'

Nicholas reacted with interest but his companions did not even hear the keeper. They were peering eagerly through the grille of the door outside which Kirk stopped. Inside the chamber, sitting motionless with his back to them, was the young man in the now ragged white shirt and dark breeches. He was staring up at the window and humming quietly to himself.'

As the door was unlocked, Grace Napier could hardly contain her emotions. A long and painful journey had at last come to an end. She had found the man she loved.

Kirk had to hold her back as she tried to lunge in.

'Do not touch him,' he warned. 'Stay by me.'

He let them step into the room then spoke to the patient.

'Hello, my friend.'

The young man stirred as if waking from a deep sleep.

'You have visitors.'

He looked at the wall ahead of him in search of them.

The tension was now agonising. Grace was biting her lip and shaking so much that she seemed to be on the verge of collapse. Nicholas supported her with one hand but kept his attention on the young man, anxious to meet the person who had indirectly caused such trouble for Westfield's Men. Mordrake was there in his professional capacity as a physician to see if the patient was beyond hope or if there was some way that he could recover his wits.

'Come, sir,' said Kirk. 'Welcome your friends.'

'David,' whispered Grace. 'It's me.'

Mention of his name made the young man turn round. His face became a childlike beam when he saw Grace Napier but her expression changed at once. Pain and disappointment overwhelmed her.

'What ails you?' asked Nicholas. 'Is this not David Jordan?'

'No,' she said. 'I have never seen this man before.'

Jack Harsnett was back on his own territory. He knew where to forage and how to hide. Nobody else on the estate was aware of his return or of the grim purpose which prompted it. He kept Parkbrook under surveillance. It was early on a Tuesday morning when he heard the rumble of carts and the trot of horses. Having broken their journey with a night at a nearby inn, Westfield's Men now headed for their next venue with alacrity. While the rest of the company travelled in the carts with the scenery, costumes and properties, Lawrence Firethorn led the procession on a chestnut mare. Spotting the house, he waved a commanding arm.

'Onward!'

The forester hid behind some bushes and watched. Evidently, there was to be an entertainment of some sort at Parkbrook and that would mean that the whole household would be preoccupied. It could be just the chance for which Harsnett was waiting. As the last of the carts wended its way down the slope, he left the bushes and padded off through the wood until he reached his cottage. He picked up his axe and took from his pocket the stone which he kept to sharpen it.

With patient care, he began to hone the blade.

Westfield's Men arrived at Parkbrook House to find a stage set up in the Great Hall. Curtains hung from the minstrels' gallery to create a tiring-house beneath the balcony. Everything was exactly as requested. Glanville gave them a polite but muted welcome, then left them alone. Adapting at once to their new performing conditions, they set up and rehearsed. It was a surprisingly refreshing experience. A play which had always been so problematical before now unfolded smoothly and without error. The amended version of *The Merry Devils* worked uncannily well.

It was as if a curse had been lifted from it.

When the company adjourned for a meal at noon, they were in a happy, almost optimistic, mood. They now had three hours before they were due to give their command performance before a select audience. It gave them time to relax.

Nicholas Bracewell did not join them. Ever since his visit to Bedlam, he puzzled over something that might now be resolved. While his colleagues enjoyed their food and their banter, he slipped off to the west wing of the building and ascended the private staircase, slapping his feet down hard so that there was an echoing clack on the oak treads. It achieved the desired result.

Joseph Glanville appeared at the top of the stairs.

'What does this mean, sir?' he said with subdued anger.

'I have come to see you, Master Glanville.'

'This staircase is closed to all but me.'

'Then why does the physician use it?'

'Physician?'

'I believe I saw him with you the other night,' said Nicholas. 'You descended together in earnest conference. He came down the steps like a man well-used to their peculiarities.'

Glanville was as enigmatic as ever. His face betrayed nothing.

'Return to your company, Master Bracewell,' he said. 'They have need of you. There is no reason for you to be here.'

'There is, sir.'

'What?'

'David Jordan.'

The steward blinked but his voice was still calm.

'I have nothing to say to you on that subject,' he returned easily. 'Your concern is solely with the staging of your play and I suggest that you go back to it now. I myself have urgent duties.'

Nicholas caught at his sleeve as Glanville moved away.

'Who is that young man in Bedlam?' he asked.

'Bedlam?' There was more than a blink this time.

'You delivered the wrong David Jordan. *Why*?'

The steward glared at him then tried to push him away but Nicholas would not be shifted. Grabbing the man by the shoulders, he pinned him against the door of his own room.

'I have come for some answers, Master Glanville,' he said with emphasis, 'and I will not leave until I have them. It is not on my own account. I am here on behalf of Mistress Grace Napier who was contracted to marry Master Jordan. She is in grave distress and I would ease that distress with the truth.' He tightened his hold. 'Speak, sir. Tell me what happened to the gentleman.'

Glanville was wrestling with his thoughts, quite unsure what to do. He made an attempt to fight his way free but he was overpowered by the book holder. The steward fell back on an excuse.

'It was the physician who called the other night,' he said. 'He came to see Jane Skinner.'

'At such a late hour?'

'The girl was in some pain.'

'Physicians do not come at the beck and call of a chambermaid,' said Nicholas. 'Besides, I called on Mistress Skinner the next morning. She told me she had not seen her physician for days.' He exerted even more pressure on the other. 'Tell me the truth, Master Glanville.'

It was the only option left to the steward. His composure fell away to be replaced by candid apprehension. The calm voice now took on a note of apprehension.

'Help us, sir. We are almost there.'

'We?'

'Do not undo our good work.'

'Explain, Master Glanville.'

'Step into my room.'

Nicholas released him then followed him into the room. The steward closed the door, turned the key in the lock and slid home the heavy bolt. The book holder glanced around. It was a small but neat apartment. The oak floor and the panelled walls gleamed. Clearly, the occupant had a passion for order and tidiness. Nicholas turned on him.

'Who is that patient at Bedlam?'

'A miller's son from the next county, sir.'

'How came he there?'

'He fell from a loft and injured his head badly. Doctor Renwick, the physician whom you saw, heard of the case. The symptoms were almost identical. The boy's mother had died and there was nobody to tend him. Putting him into Bedlam was Doctor Renwick's idea.'

'So that Master David Jordan could be spared that ordeal.'

'Yes, sir.'

'Where is he now?'

'Where he can be looked after properly,' said Glanville with obvious sincerity. 'I could never desert my old master, sir, nor see him consigned to a place like that. Though it cost my life, I would rescue him from such a fate. It has been difficult, Master Bracewell. It has been the Devil's own work but we have stuck to our task and our caring has been rewarded. The old master is steadily recovering.'

Nicholas studied him and realised how mistaken he had been in the man. Instead of being an enemy, Joseph Glanville was the most loyal friend. To protect David Jordan, he had risked everything. If the new master had learned what he had done, dismissal was the least that the steward would have faced. Glanville was brave as well as constant.

Wrong about him, Nicholas was right about one thing.

'I believe that he is here, sir.'

'In the next room, Master Bracewell.'

'I should like to meet him.'

Glanville thought it over then crossed to the door.

Distinguished guests began to arrive in their carriages from all over the county. Luxuriating in his role as the new master of Parkbrook House, Francis Jordan welcomed them on his lawn then guided them into the ante-room for a cup of wine. Word of the play had leaked out and provoked much excitement. The reputation of Westfield's Men extended well outside the city. Last to appear, the company's esteemed patron was the first to take his seat in the Great Hall where the sumptuous banquet had been laid out in the shape of a horseshoe. Francis Jordan sat beside his uncle at the very heart of the horseshoe, diametrically opposite the stage.

Both men were resplendent in their finery and they competed for attention with their poses and their brittle laughter. Lord Westfield was, for once, outshone by his nephew who favoured doublet and hose of such a deep blood-red silk that it gave him a decidedly satanic look. Sleeves and breeches were slashed through with black and the high ruff was pink. Francis Jordan wanted to be his own merry devil.

The banquet was lavish to the point of excess. Beef and mutton were followed by veal, lamb, kid, pork, coney, capon and venison besides a variety of fish and wild fowl. Wine and sherry were served in silver bowls, goblets and fine Venetian glasses. A wide range of desserts was supplemented by huge dishes covered with fresh fruit. No sooner had one course finished than another was brought in from the kitchens by liveried servants on loan from Westfield Hall. The entire assembly was soon lulled into a feeling of well-being. There were toasts and speeches and sustained over-indulgence.

Then it was time for the play.

The curtains were closed to throw the hall into semidarkness. Flickering candelabra had been cunningly placed by Nicholas Bracewell to throw their light upon the stage. Up in the gallery, the musicians played in the gloom like so many ghosts. The effect was carefully judged so that the audience could only see what they were allowed to see. Francis Jordan was beside himself with glee, convinced that his guests would have an experience without compare.

The third and last performance of *The Merry Devils* began.

It exerted total control over its spectators. Lawrence Firethorn was as astonishing as ever in the role of Justice Wildboare. He even included an affectionate parody of Lord Westfield at one point and set off an explosion of mirth that lasted for several minutes. Richard Honeydew was enchanting as Lucy Hembrow and the other agencies supported him well in the female roles. Droopwell amused everyone with his whining impotence. Doctor Castrato was an instant success.

The major change came with Youngthrust. Still played with verve by Edmund Hoode, the part had been changed considerably in the very hour before performance. At the request of the book holder, the playwright had done a lot of last-minute alteration. Instead of being a young lover who pined for his mistress, Youngthrust now had a sinister streak to him. He still sighed for Lucy Hembrow but with an air of calculation. Here was a patent fortune-hunter masquerading as a passionate swain.

Both Youngthrust and the actor who played him were changed men. Nicholas had taken on the delicate job of telling his friend the truth about Grace Napier. Devastated at first, Hoode eventually rallied by persuading himself that he was involved in a major romance after all. It was not between him and Grace but between her and David Jordan. To help her and to be somehow instrumental in reuniting her with her true love was a task that he took on with enthusiasm.

Act Three stoked up fresh anticipation in the audience. The devils were due to appear. Lord Westfield and Francis Jordan had seen the play before when the creatures had popped up from below the stage, but that was impossible here. From where would they come? Both men leaned forward with gluttonous interest.

Doctor Castrato extinguished several candles so that the stage was almost in darkness, save for a central barrage of light. It was now so dim in the hall, and everyone's attention was so firmly fixed on the stage, that nobody saw the two figures flit in through the door at the back to watch from the shadows. Each had a special reason to be there.

Grace Napier stood beside Joseph Glanville.

Barnaby Gill savoured his best scene and summoned the devils in his high and ridiculous voice. There was a huge explosion from behind the curtains then they parted for Hell's Mouth to be wheeled out with real flames shooting out of it so realistically that screams of fear went up from the ladies. The effect had been devised by the book holder who had taken Firethorn's professional advice. Having been brought up in a forge, the actor-manager knew how to heat up a brazier and use bellows to produce dazzling flame.

The spectators were spellbound as three merry devils came dancing out of the inferno, for all the world as if they had been spewed up from the mouth of Hell. George Dart, Caleb Smythe and Ned Rankin pranced about comically in their devil costumes then submitted themselves to their new master. Some additional material had been supplied by Hoode and mocking laughter was raised by some obvious allusions to the new master of Parkbrook.

As the play brought new delights in each scene, an unexpected guest arrived. Lurking outside in the trees, he ran stealthily to a window and peered in through a chink in the curtain. Jack Harsnett could see little but hear everything. He crept along the wall with his axe over his shoulder and made his way furtively towards the kitchens.

In the Great Hall, meanwhile, *The Merry Devils* approached its crowning moment. Justice Wildboare and Droopwell were discarded and the marriage of Lucy and Youngthrust was announced, a less than satisfying ending as the latter was such an arrant

Machiavel. At the wedding ceremony itself, the priest brought the couple together at the altar and asked if anyone had any reason why they should not be joined together.

A voice rang out from the gallery.

'Yes!'

It was David Jordan.

He stood in a circle of light created by three candelabra and was surrounded by musicians who played soft, sacred music. There was a close resemblance to his younger brother but David was altogether more poised and dignified. Grace Napier, who had not been let in on the secret, gasped as she looked up at the man she loved. He was safe and well.

The spectators were astounded. Everyone knew about the sad case of David Jordan and yet here he was—apparently fit and healthy—standing up before them. He even went on to deliver a short speech at Youngthrust, accusing him of stealing his greatest treasure. The newcomer was no actor and declaimed the lines dully as if he had learned them by rote, but their effect could not have been greater if they had been spoken by Firethorn himself. Through the medium of the play, David Jordan put his brother on trial at the banquet.

Lord Westfield's mind was blurred by drink but he could still catch the gist of what was going on. He turned angrily to his nephew.

'Is this true, Francis?'

'No, uncle!'

The elder brother pointed a finger from on high and challenged the new master to step forward so that he could be judged by his peers.

'Be quiet!' yelled Francis Jordan, leaping up on to the table. 'All of you—be quiet! None of this is true! David should be locked away in a madhouse! He's insane!'

But it was the younger brother who was now closer to insanity. Jumping off the table, he ran to the stage and looked up at David to hurl abuse at him. The audience was captivated as a play turned into a real-life drama of surging intensity.

'I am the master here!' shouted Francis Jordan. 'Nothing changes that! Parkbrook is mine!'

Jack Harsnett crept into the hall and kept in the shadows as he worked his way towards the stage. Francis Jordan had dominated his mind for weeks. When he looked at the new master, he saw his wife buried in a mean grave, he saw the cottage they had shared for so many years, he saw the horse and cart they had owned. He also heard the voice of a one-eyed man who had been paid to frighten the mount of David Jordan as the latter rode at full gallop along a ride. The accident had not brought about the death that Francis Jordan had intended for his brother but it nevertheless made him into the new squire.

'Parkbrook is *mine*!' he repeated. 'I defy anyone to take it from me.'

Harsnett accepted the challenge willingly.

He struck with terrifying force. Charging on to the stage with his axe held high, he needed only one vicious downward sweep of the blade to split the skull wide open. Blood spurted everywhere. In the general panic that ensued, Nicholas Bracewell darted forward to grapple with the forester and relieve him of his weapon. Burly servants came to his aid and they dragged Harsnett out.

The new master of Parkbrook lay dead on stage. With a gesture that was at once theatrical and tactful, Lawrence Firethorn removed his cloak and spread it over the corpse. Lord Westfield was stunned by it all and all the guests were dumbfounded. They were transfixed by the sight of the dead body of Francis Jordan.

Nicholas spared a thought for the elder brother and looked up at the gallery in time to see a breathless Grace Napier arrive. She walked towards David with her arms outstretched. He took time to recall who she was then he took her into a warm embrace. As one brother had met with grim justice, another was given a new lease of life. David Jordan was far from well but he would continue to recover now that he had Grace to nurse him.

The drama was not yet over. While everyone was still dazed by the spectacular murder on stage, a massive explosion went off and the Mouth of Hell was wheeled forward yet again. The flames were much bigger this time because they were consuming the prompt book of *The Merry Devils*, and because they were being intensified by sterner action on the bellows. As the fire blazed away in front of them, the audience saw the most extraordinary sight yet. A tall, elegant man, clad in red and black, stepped out of the Mouth of Hell in such a way that he seemed to be on fire. When they looked again, they saw that the flames were real.

Ralph Willoughby was burning to death before their eyes.

He was not afraid and seemed to be in no pain. He was even able to execute a short comic dance. Willoughby had planned it all with meticulous care. As he took his own life, he was also destroying the play which had caused so much disaster. There was a poetic justice to it all. Arms aloft in a gesture of farewell, he became a solid ball of flame and collapsed in the centre of the stage. When buckets of water finally arrived, they were years too late.

Willoughby had gone back to his Maker.

Problems during performance were not confined to Westfield's Men. Ten days later, at The Theatre in Shoreditch, Banbury's Men presented their new play, *The Witch of Oxford*. It was well played and equally well received until the moment when the witch cast her first spell. As she tried to summon up a black dog to act as her familiar, it appeared out of the air with gnashing savagery and chased everyone within reach. The play was abandoned and the company spent the night in prayer.

Ralph Willoughby had tricked them from beyond the grave.

'You must take most of the credit, Nick.'

'Oh, I do not think so,' said the book holder modestly.

'But you tracked down those acrobats and forced Grace to confess the truth. Yes, and you also suffered much for our sakes at the Counter.'

'That is behind me now, Edmund.'

The two friends were walking up Gracechurch Street on their way to the Queen's Head. Their voices were raised above the babble all around them. Parkbrook still bulked large in their minds.

'The house is to have a new guest,' noted Hoode.

'The miller's son from Bedlam.'

'Thanks to Doctor John Mordrake.'

'Yes,' said Nicholas. 'That is something else we owe to Ralph. He introduced us to that remarkable man. It was Mordrake's belief that the patient would slowly improve if taken away from Bedlam. The young man will get plenty of care at Parkbrook.'

'Master Jordan feels indebted to the fellow.'

'He is indebted to his steward as well.'

'And to Grace!' said Hoode fondly. 'I worshipped her, Nick, and part of me always will, but I can see that he is better for her than me. Sonnets to beauty are all very well but who reads verses when they have been married a fortnight? No, she and David Jordan have earned each other. We endured much to bring them together but our afflictions are now easy to bear. He needs the loving attention that only she can provide. That is true devotion.'

They turned in through the main gates of the Queen's Head and strolled into the yard. The stage was set for another play and they stopped to gaze at it for a few seconds.

Hoode heaved a long sigh of regret.

'I will miss Ralph,' he said.

'Yes, he brought something rare to Westfield's Men.'

'Lawrence thought he betrayed us when he wrote that play for Banbury's Men but he was only setting a trap for them.' Hoode turned to his friend. 'Where is he now, do you think?'

'I am not sure.'

'Ralph wanted to go to Hell.'

Nicholas considered the matter then smiled affectionately.

'He was far too merry for Heaven.'

To receive a free catalog of other Poisoned Pen Press titles, please contact us in one of the following ways:

Phone: 1-800-421-3976
Facsimile: 1-480-949-1707
Email: info@poisonedpenpress.com
Website: www.poisonedpenpress.com

Poisoned Pen Press
6962 E. First Ave. Ste 103
Scottsdale, AZ 85251